PRAISE FOR THE GODWICKS SERIES

"Provocative." — *O Magazine* on *The Red*

"Deliciously deviant... Akin to Anne Rice's 'Beauty' series." — *Library Journal* (Starred Review) on *The Red*

"A delightful, wicked fairytale." — Smart Bitches, Trashy Books on *The Red*

"This is erotica done right." — *Publishers Weekly* (Starred Review) on *The Pearl*

"...beautifully blends high art and absorbing prose with the sensual rendezvous of famed pairs in Greek legend... An otherworldly, titillating endeavor." — *Library Journal* (Starred Review) on *The Rose*

"Will entrance readers..." — BookPage on *The Rose*

"[A] best romance of the month." — Goodreads on *The Red*

"Smart and intriguing." — NPR on *The Red*

READ THE GODWICKS SERIES

Standalone Novels
THE PEARL
THE RED
THE ROSE

Standalone Short Stories
THE BEGUILING OF MERLIN*

---

*published in *Best Bondage Erotica of the Year, Volume 1,* edited by Rachel Kramer Bussel, and also in a special paperback edition available at TiffanyReisz.com

Trade Paperback ISBN: 9781949769166

Audiobook available from Tantor Audio

Cover design by Tiffany Reisz and Andrew Shaffer. Elements used under license from Arcangel.

The Pearl Hotel logo designed by Andrew Shaffer

Interior paintings are reproduced from public domain images. Credits: *The Pearl* by Lilla Cabot Perry (1913), *The Umbrella* by Marie Bashkirtseff (1883), *Woman With Pearl Necklace in a Loge* by Mary Cassatt (1879), and *Phosphorus and Hesperus (Morning Star and Evening Star)* by Evelyn de Morgan (1881).

www.8thcircle.com

First Edition

THE PEARL

TIFFANY REISZ

CONTENTS

Dedicated to

Frida Kahlo
Remedios Varo
Leonora Carrington
Evelyn de Morgan
Bridget Bate Tichenor
Baya Mahieddine
Alma Thomas
Georgia O'Keeffe
Artemisia Gentileschi
Bridget Riley
Tamara de Lempicka

and to all the women who picked up paintbrushes and made
themselves immortal

I paint flowers so they will not die.

FRIDA KAHLO

PART I

THE UMBRELLA

The day progressed as days usually did for young Lord Arthur Godwick, but it took a turn for the strange when a young woman in a red raincoat and red Wellington boots knocked on the door of the Godwick townhouse in Piccadilly. When he opened the door, his first thought was "red alert."

She was a pretty young woman, bow lips that spread into a mischievous smile like he was in trouble and just didn't know it yet.

"Can I help you?" Arthur asked the girl in red.

"You Lord Arthur Godwick?" Her accent was decidedly East End, making the "Lord" sound like a joke.

"Guilty."

She held out a small envelope to him, cream-colored and on heavy paper like a wedding invitation.

"What is this?" he asked, taking it. His name was written on the envelope, but he got no answer. When he looked up, the girl in the red raincoat was already at the iron gate, then through it, then at the sidewalk and then...gone.

Bizarre. Arthur had never had a note hand-delivered to him before.

Slowly he removed the notecard. Hotel stationery from The Pearl. He knew the place well. His sister had gotten married there not too long ago. The hotel's name was in all black on the outer flap, with a white pearl nestled into the middle of the A.

We need to discuss your brother, it read inside. *The Pearl, penthouse at five.*

The note was signed only with a looping R.

Who was "R," and what the hell had Charlie done this time? Could be anything knowing him these days. Gambling? Girl in trouble? Punched the prime minister?

Fuming, Arthur trudged up the stairs to his room on the second storey of the townhouse. It was already past four. He had on jeans and a t-shirt but needed socks, shoes, and a jacket. He pulled them all on, grabbed his keys, his mobile phone. Into his wallet, he stuffed as much cash as he could fit. Good chance Arthur would be paying damages on something tonight. A broken vase. A broken nose. A broken heart.

Although it was November, grey with rain threatening, Arthur decided to walk across the park to Mayfair. He needed to clear his mind before the inevitable confrontation with Charlie. If it had been any other hotel, he might not have been so worried, but this was The Pearl.

In Queen Victoria's day, it had served as the elaborate London townhouse of a dissipated lord who spent all his money on whores and gaming until he had nothing left but the townhouse and then he didn't have that anymore. It was sold, turned into a seven-storey hotel. A respectable-enough looking place these days. White and gleaming, black awnings, fine dining. Not a tourist trap. A haven for the wealthy, the titled. Usually both. The interior was dark with heavy oak paneling, the furniture Edwardian, the lights murky and dim. The fallen paradise of aging lords.

It was also a brothel, hence the family connection. Hence Arthur's fear for his brother.

He'd learned from his older sister Lia about the hotel's past. She'd told him about how their great-grandfather Lord Malcolm was a fixture at The Pearl in its heyday, living there as a bachelor gentleman about town and playing there practically every night of his wicked life. That's why Lia had gotten married there. She was a Godwick, after all.

Arthur arrived just before five o'clock. As he looked up at the black iron sign reading THE PEARL over a set of double doors, the first raindrops began to fall. Hurrying inside, he strode across the lobby as if he belonged there. He had a title, and he had money. That's all one needed for entrée into The Pearl. If pressed, he had the note as well, an invitation to a party he did not want to attend.

As he crossed the lobby to the gleaming golden lifts, he imagined he could still smell the cigars of the thousands of lords and industrialists who'd met here, slept here, supped here, and fucked here. The fucking, of course, being the main attraction. Arthur guessed he had been summoned here to scrape his baby brother off the floor of someone's bedroom or bathroom.

And he'd do it. Someone had to, with their parents away in New York City until Christmas. Even if they'd been in London right now, they'd mostly washed their hands of Charlie. He was eighteen, they liked to remind Arthur. Time for their youngest to stand on his own two feet.

But what if Charlie falls while trying to stand? Arthur

would demand. Well, in that case he'd have to learn how to pick himself up.

Easy for them to say. Charlie didn't call them at four in the morning when he was too drunk to find a way home. They weren't the ones who answered the phone when Charlie was detained by the police for starting a fight in a pub. No, it was Arthur. Always Arthur. "King Arthur," his brother would drunkenly proclaim. "King Arthur saves the day again."

The lift deposited Arthur on the top floor. He found a set of grand double doors at the end of the corridor with a brass plaque that read PENTHOUSE.

He took a deep breath to calm his nerves, then knocked.

The blonde who'd given him the note opened the door. "She's on the terrace," the girl said. "With your brother."

She pointed to a set of French doors along the far wall that opened to the outside. Before Arthur could thank her, she exited the penthouse, leaving him standing by himself in the entryway.

Arthur's first thought upon seeing the interior of the suite was that his brother was flying in very high circles these days. He'd never seen a grander, more decadent hotel room, and he'd stayed in some of the finest hotels in the world when on holiday with his parents. The walls were gold damask wallpaper with black trim. An enormous gas fireplace with a black china marble mantel dominated the sitting room. To the right of it was a curving staircase that led to a second level, where he imagined he'd find a luxurious bedroom. Black leather club chairs framed the fireplace, and above the mantel hung an oil painting of a pretty young woman wearing a black raincoat and holding an umbrella. As the son of art lovers who owned dozens of galleries, Arthur reflexively glanced at the plaque on the frame as he passed it on the way to the terrace. *The Umbrella* by Marie Bashkirtseff, a Ukrainian-French painter. Not your typical bland mass-produced hotel art.

Arthur was nearly at the terrace when he stopped next to a golden velvet chaise lounge. Another painting was propped up in the seat, another original he recognized at once.

The subject was a handsome gentleman wearing a three-piece suit, with black hair and dark eyes, the subtlest smile on his lips...Lord Malcolm Godwick, thirteenth Earl of Godwick. The portrait he'd last seen hanging in the hallowed halls of Wingthorn, the Godwick ancestral estate. It should have been there now, so what was it doing here?

Arthur went quickly to the French doors and peered through one of the panes. For a split second, the sight was so uncanny, he thought the painting over the fireplace had come to life. A woman stood on the terrace in the rain, black trench coat belted tightly at her narrow waist and black umbrella overhead.

Not a painting come to life. Just a coincidence. Her umbrella was being held by someone, a young man facing the city. He needn't turn around. Arthur would have known that rust-colored hair anywhere.

He pushed open the door and stepped onto the spacious garden terrace. It was filled with so many green plants and small trees, it was like walking into a miniature forest. He went straight to the iron railing to find his brother wearing an expression of pure defeat. Charlie was clutching the umbrella and staring down at his own shoes.

"What the hell are you doing?" Arthur hissed, shielding his face from the rain with his hand. Before Charlie had a chance to answer, Arthur turned to the woman. "Who are you, and why are you forcing my brother to hold your umbrella in the freezing rain?"

Arthur had expected a much older woman for some reason—maybe because of the commanding tone of her note—but no, she was young. Thirty, if that. She had chestnut-brown hair that hung in a long French plait over her left shoulder. Her face was lovely and her eyes wide, intelligent, and grey as the rain. Pale olive skin. Peach lips, full and soft. She wore a white-collared shirt under her coat, a pearl choker draped around her graceful neck.

And what was she doing while Charlie held the umbrella over her head? Feeding raw meat to a raven perched on a brass ring on the railing.

"Things aren't what they seem," she told Arthur. "Your brother offered to hold it for me. Didn't you, Charlie?"

Charlie nodded without emotion. Something about the woman, the way she looked at Arthur, so cool and superior, convinced him he was dealing with some kind of ice queen. Who else would make an eighteen-year-old stand in the cold autumn rain holding her umbrella?

"Charlie, go inside," Arthur said.

His brother didn't budge. He stood there in his stupid skinny jeans and leather jacket that he'd probably bought with a credit card "borrowed" from their mother.

"Go inside and warm up," Arthur said, this time more forceful. "I'm handling this."

"He may go, but someone has to hold my umbrella while I'm feeding the baby," the woman said, smiling at the raven.

Arthur rolled his eyes. He held out an open palm and accepted the umbrella from Charlie, who'd been holding it with a white-knuckle grip.

As Arthur took over umbrella duty, Charlie bent his head and whispered a miserable "Sorry."

Arthur put his arm around his brother's neck. He couldn't help it. Charlie didn't return the embrace, but accepted it without protest.

Charlie disappeared into the penthouse. Arthur watched as the woman fed another morsel of meat to the raven. It took the red flesh right out of her fingers, so well-trained it ignored the hunk of bleeding meat in the butcher paper in her other hand.

"All right. What did he do this time?" Arthur asked.

She smiled. "Whatever happened to, 'Hello, how do you do?'"

"Hello," he said. "How do you do? And what did Charlie do this time, and why do you have one of our paintings inside? Better?"

"Much better."

"Hello."

That came from the raven. Arthur stared at it, wide-eyed. "Did that bird just speak?"

The woman laughed softly. "He did." She sounded surprised. "He's never done that in front of anyone besides me, though. Not that he says much besides 'hello' and 'baby.' This is Gloom. Gloom, this is Lord Arthur Godwick. Say 'Hello, my lord.'"

"Hello, baby."

Arthur smiled despite himself—he'd never been flirted with by a bird before—and replied, "Hello, Gloom."

The evening had taken on a strange, dreamlike quality.

The girl in the red raincoat with her summons. Silver-grey clouds, fat as circus tents hovering overhead. The elegant ice queen feeding a talkative raven.

"You can pet him if you like," she said. "He's in a good mood when he's eating. Just watch your fingers. He's not too picky about the sort of meat he eats."

Arthur couldn't resist. He raised the back of his hand and stroked the silky black breast feathers of the bird. "The longer you wait to tell me what Charlie's done, the more scared I get."

"I know."

"Please?"

"Ah, well, since you said please. Your brother has graced us with his presence the last ten nights and managed to rack up quite a bill."

Arthur sighed. "How much?"

"A hundred grand."

The raven gulped another bite from her fingers.

Arthur stared. "A hundred grand? You must be joking. What room costs ten grand a night?"

"It's not merely the room. He ordered...room service."

Arthur quietly groaned. Room service. She didn't mean coffee, tea, and the soup *du jour*. She meant a girl who'd serviced him in his room. As his father had jokingly called it once, *room cervix*.

"And you let him rack up a hundred grand bill?" Arthur said. "Why?"

"He's the son of an earl. Why wouldn't I?" She gave a shrug, careless and elegant. "We give our special guests a great deal of leeway, but when the tab hits six figures, we call it in. Hotel policy."

Arthur stared up at the cloud-wild sky. It was strange, having this conversation while huddled under a black umbrella. They stood very close to each other, barely a foot apart. He could smell her scent, like evening fog. Or was it just the rain on her skin?

"A hundred grand is above my pay grade," he said. "I'll have to call my parents."

"No need. He's paid the bill. I accepted a painting in lieu of cash. This little meeting is simply an act of courtesy. And so that I have a witness it was not stolen but given in payment for his debt. Would you like to see the itemized receipt?"

"No. No. Absolutely not. That painting of Lord Malcolm is—"

"Mine," she said. "You can go home now. Please. I've had enough of the Godwicks for the day."

She wiped the blood from her fingers and plucked the umbrella from his hand.

But Arthur refused to be dismissed. "Enough of the Godwicks? What are you—"

"Rich, spoiled, entitled brats, the whole lot of you. Handed everything on a silver platter and still not happy. Do you people ever take no for an answer?"

He couldn't argue with anything she'd said, so simply ignored it. "What did we ever do to you?"

"You exist. Bad enough."

He scoffed. "Sorry, but I don't have time for an 'eat the rich' debate, especially not with a woman feeding filet mignon to her pet raven on the terrace of a five-star hotel penthouse. Whatever you think of us, it doesn't matter. Charlie stole that painting from my parents. Keeping it would be accepting stolen goods."

And incredibly foolish, he didn't add. To his family, that painting might as well have been a holy icon, though he didn't want to explain why. She'd think he was mad as a hatter.

"Call the police then," she said. "You can tell them who you are, and I'll tell them who I am, and we'll see whose surname scares them more."

Gloom flapped his dark wings and flew off as if sensing things were about to get ugly on the terrace.

"Who are you anyway?" Arthur demanded.

"Regan. Regan Ferry. Lady Regan Ferry. As in the late Sir Jack Ferry. My late husband, to be clear, not my late father. People sometimes make that mistake. And yes, he did leave The Pearl Hotel to me."

Brilliant. Just brilliant. Could Charlie have chosen a worse person to cross? This wasn't some sleazy pimp he could call the cops on. Sir Jack Ferry had been a billionaire in life, a hotelier extraordinaire with connections in high places.

The Godwicks were rich and titled.

Sir Jack Ferry had been rich, titled, *and* powerful.

Lady Bloody Ferry.

She continued, "I don't usually take a personal interest in the boys who try to skip out on their bills, but the Godwick surname got my attention. Lord Malcolm Godwick was The Pearl's best customer in his day. It's nice to have him back."

"Do I have to tell you again? You can't keep that painting. It wasn't Charlie's to give."

"Oh, isn't it, though? That painting, according to Charlie, belongs to the Godwick trust which—also according to Charlie—is composed of all members of the Godwick family who are over the age of eighteen. Therefore, the painting is at least partially Charlie's. Would you like me to show you where the door is?"

She was technically right. This was a legal battle they probably couldn't win.

"Fine," he said. "We'll give you a painting if that's what you want, but it can't be that one."

"Why not?"

"That painting is my parents' most prized possession. It's the reason they met. It's the reason they're married. It's sacred in our family."

"Sacred? Lord Malcolm? The biggest rake and whore-monger in the history of England, and I'm including the second Earl of Rochester."

"He's sacred to us. I know it doesn't make any sense, but please...would you consider taking another painting? Or money? I don't have a hundred grand, but I'm sure if you give me a couple weeks—"

"No. I have what I want, and I want nothing else."

"The portrait of Lord Malcolm isn't worth a fraction of what our least valuable Degas is worth. And that painting means everything to my parents."

"Means *everything* to your parents? In that case, I wonder what the Earl and Countess of Godwick would pay to get it back..."

Arthur nodded. "Oh, of course. You asked Charlie for the one painting my parents would sell their souls to buy back."

"Or suffer the most for losing."

Finally, she deigned to meet his eyes. She had bright eyes, bright and gleaming. Her beauty stunned him. It shocked him with every fresh look at her. She stirred something in him, some half-buried longing trying to claw its way to the surface.

"I think I'll hang his portrait over the fireplace in my bedroom. Or maybe over the bed..." She rested the umbrella on her shoulder and twirled it. Rain misted Arthur's face. "Oh, you're still here. Why is that?"

"Lady Ferry, please—"

"Regan."

"Regan...when my parents find out Charlie gave you that painting, they will cut him off. He's on his last warning."

"So?"

"So? He's only eighteen. He'll have nothing. No job. No money. Nowhere to live."

"I'll give him a job at the hotel. He can wash dishes in The Oyster," she said, speaking of the hotel's five-star restaurant. "That's where I was working when I met Sir Jack."

"He won't survive being cut off. He's barely surviving now. He's...he's not doing well. He's got a load of problems he's dealing with. My fault mostly. Entirely."

"Really? He blamed his troubles on a girl who broke his heart. Someone named Wendy? Ring a bell?"

"My ex-girlfriend," Arthur said. "And I don't want to—"

"I see." Regan nodded. "You both liked her, and she picked the heir over the spare. Now he's suffering from a terminal case of inadequacy. It all makes sense now."

That wasn't what happened, not really, but Arthur was happy to let Regan believe that.

"Please, I'm begging you," he said. "Is there anything I can do to make this go away for him?"

She crossed her arms over her chest and tilted her head to the side, the umbrella caught on her wrist so that it stayed put on her shoulder.

"I never thought I'd live to see the day a Godwick went begging," she said. "The Queen will be at my front door selling magazine subscriptions to pay for Prince Philip's heart pills next."

Arthur's stomach clenched. Charlie did nothing these days but make bad decisions in bad company. A wealthy earl's son was an easy target for all sorts of predators— social climbers, criminals, con artists. Anything could happen to Charlie if he was left on his own, which is why Arthur would do anything to help him. That, and a little guilt, too. If things hadn't blown up with Wendy...

"Anything, Regan. I will do anything. Please."

"Anything?"

"Anything," he said. *"Anything."*

He would get on his knees right now and kiss her boots if she'd show a little mercy. He'd scrub her kitchen floor with his toothbrush. As long as it wasn't murder, rape, or kicking a dog, he'd do it.

She smiled again and shook her head. "Anything," she repeated. "Well, that *is* a tempting offer."

Arthur almost sank to his knees in relief. Whatever she asked of him, he told himself, no matter how degrading or humiliating, he would do it.

"If you need a dishwasher, I'll wash your dishes. I'll wash the hotel's dishes. I'll hold your umbrella in a hurricane. I'll—"

"Sleep with me?"

He stared at her. "Now you *are* joking."

"I'm a widow. It's been lonely since Sir Jack died. Busy with the hotel. Too busy to date. How old are you?"

"Twenty-one."

"Perfect age," she said. "Old enough not to put me in prison, young enough you can still be taught."

Taught.

Every nerve in Arthur's body rang like a bell at that

word. The implications of it, the insinuations...the images it brought to mind. His breathing quickened. His body warmed. Even in the cool November air, he burned.

"I can't sleep with you," he said. "We don't even know each other."

"Oh, Charlie's told me loads about you. Accepted into both Oxford and Cambridge. Instead you picked Sandhurst, where you excelled, of course, because you apparently excel at everything you do. I hear you're joining the army in January. Congratulations, Lieutenant Godwick. You're considered something of the black sheep of the Godwick family simply because you've never gotten into any trouble. Must be the milkman's boy."

"We don't have a milkman."

"Charlie seems to think you're a regular Mary Poppins —practically perfect in every way. No wonder he hates you."

"My brother doesn't hate me."

"You're right. He hates himself because of you. Even worse. Personally, I don't think you are practically perfect in every way. If you were, you would have already said no to my offer."

"You're an attractive rich widow. There's absolutely no reason you'd need to buy someone to have sex with you."

"No, no, no. I don't *need* to. I *want* to."

He let that sink into his soul and settle down there. "Just sex?"

"Of course not. It'll be much more interesting than that," she said. "Shall we say ten nights? That's how many nights Charlie spent here. Ten for ten. And then you can skip home to glorious Wingthorn Manor with Lord Malcolm under your arm, Mummy and Daddy Godwick none the wiser."

She checked her watch. "Offer expires in sixty seconds. You know, I haven't been with anyone since my husband died. Don't you feel sorry for me?"

"No."

"I wouldn't either if I were you. My husband was a controlling old prick, and I'm in heaven now that he's dead and gone. But I'm only thirty, and I haven't been fucked in months. Just this morning, I was thinking how pleasant it would be to tie a nice young man to my bedposts."

"Tie me to your bedposts." He had to be sure he'd heard her correctly.

"I tend to be a bit domineering in the bedroom."

"Shocking."

She glared at him, then smiled as if she hadn't heard the sarcasm. "It's why it's so hard to find someone to keep me company." She sighed melodramatically. "I'm too demanding for most men. But something tells me you aren't like most men."

She leaned back against the terrace railing and crossed her booted legs at the ankles. Once again she checked her watch. "Thirty seconds."

"What does your tattoo say?" Arthur asked. Her face showed her surprise. "You have a tattoo under your watch. Words. What does it say?"

It wasn't under her watch so much as hidden by her watch, as if she were embarrassed by it. That's the only reason he asked. A tattoo is a scar. A scar is a wound. She'd poked at his wounds. Time to poke hers.

She pursed her lips, obviously annoyed. "It's an old tattoo. Got it ages ago."

"What does it say?" He was going to keep asking until she told him or gave up.

"It's a quote from the painter Evelyn de Morgan, from

her journals when she was a teenager. It says, '*Art is eternal, but life is short. I have not a moment to lose.*' There you go. My husband hated tattoos, so I've gotten in the habit of wearing my watch band over it. And now you have fifteen seconds."

Was he actually considering this? He hadn't said no yet, which meant he was thinking about it. He had said he would do anything for Charlie. Being tied to Sir Jack Ferry's widow's bed did qualify as "anything."

"You know," she said, "my great-grandmother was one of the whores here in Lord Malcolm's day. He cut quite a swath through The Pearl's girls. There's something rather poetic about this, isn't there? The great-grandson of The Pearl's most infamous customer becoming a whore for the great-granddaughter of one of The Pearl's best whores? How the mighty have fallen. And the meek do inherit. Not the Earth, maybe, but five-star hotels sometimes."

She laughed softly, the least meek woman he'd ever met. He liked her laugh. He didn't want to like her laugh, but it was low and throaty, and it caused his body to be very aware of itself.

"That painting has to be hanging on the walls of Wingthorn by the time my parents come home from the States for Christmas. If it's not, Charlie's life is in your hands."

"Then we best stop wasting time. Art is eternal, remember, but life is short."

"Fine. I'll do whatever you want," he said. "Let me take Charlie home first."

He started for the terrace door, but she stopped him by putting her umbrella in front of him to block his way. She held it there. He waited and knew he was getting a glimpse of his future, a slave to her whims.

She smiled. "You agreed to that far too easily. You must be the sort of man who likes being tied to beds. Yes?"

He didn't answer. He wouldn't answer.

"Move your umbrella," he said. She didn't. "Please."

Lifting her umbrella, she smiled and put it on her shoulder and twirled it again. It glinted against the London skyline like a black halo.

2

THE GILDED CAGE

Arthur called for a taxi. When he started to give the driver the address of their townhouse in Piccadilly, Charlie cut in with a different address in Vauxhall.

"We're going home, Charlie," Arthur said.

"I'm staying with friends," Charlie said. "You can go home after you drop me off."

Unbelievable. Arthur wanted to argue but knew Charlie would just hop out of the car at the next light and disappear again. Fine. He knew to pick his battles.

The entire trip, Arthur kept waiting for his brother to say something, explain himself, at least apologize. Charlie simply stared out the rain-splashed window at the dark city streets, sunk deep into the backseat, his face half-hidden by his coat collar.

They reached Vauxhall. Not a word had been spoken between them on the twenty-minute car ride.

Arthur asked the driver to wait for him, and escorted his brother to the front door of the building.

"Are you going to say anything?" Arthur asked, stopping to huddle with his brother under the awning.

Charlie stared at his boots. "I said I was sorry."

"I know. You're always sorry. Never sorry enough not to do it again though."

Silence.

"Why Lord Malcolm's painting? Of all the paintings, you just had to give her—"

"It's the only one she'd take."

"Why?"

Charlie shrugged. Arthur could only assume she knew the story behind the painting, that it meant the world to his parents. Or was there another reason?

"You're not going out again tonight, are you?" Arthur asked. "You're going to stay in, right? No pubs. No parties. No hotels."

"Yeah. Course."

"All right. Go on. Get some rest. I'll call when I can."

"You're really getting the painting back from her?"

"Yes. I hope."

"How?"

"Doesn't matter. Nothing you need to worry about. Go on. Take a shower. You smell like a brothel. Wonder why."

"Do you hate me?" Charlie asked.

Arthur sighed. "I don't hate you. I just wish you'd grow up."

"Stop treating me like a child then, and maybe I would."

"Stop acting like a child, and I'll stop—"

"Yes, King Arthur. Anything you say, King Arthur." Charlie shoved open the door and disappeared into the building.

"Love you, too," Arthur muttered.

When Arthur returned to Piccadilly, he took a long hot shower, standing under the water until his skin turned red. He dressed in dark jeans, a grey t-shirt, a navy jacket, and his most comfortable boots.

He could still hear Regan's voice taunting him. *You agreed to that far too easily. You must be the sort of man who likes being tied to beds...*

No. Of course he wasn't that sort of man. But he was the sort of man who would do anything he had to do to help his brother. That's all. Even if it meant sex with a veritable stranger who clearly loathed him.

Regan, he decided, must be one of those women who got off on hurting their partners or humiliating them. This was her darkest dream come true, then—a man selling himself to her to save his brother. The son of a peer on his hands and knees in front of her. His cock stiffened at the thought, but he ignored his erection, telling himself his body was confusing excitement with dread.

It was nighttime proper when he returned to The Pearl and parked in their underground garage. As he made his way to the lobby, he did a quick online search for anything he could find about Regan. Rule number one in *The Art of War:* Know thy enemy.

He didn't get much right away except her husband's obituary. Jack Ferry had been a hotelier and a good thirty-five years older than Regan. He'd left her very wealthy, with sole ownership of the hotel.

An image search returned photos of Regan and Sir Jonathan "Jack" Ferry at various parties in Milan, Paris, and Rome, Regan on Jack's arm, looking like his doting daughter. A few photos showed the Ferrys with various political figures, including the prime minister at Royal Ascot. She was connected and protected. If Arthur didn't "earn" Lord Malcolm's portrait back from her, then he knew there was a very good chance they would never get it back.

So he was fucked, literally and figuratively.

The lift opened onto the seventh storey and Arthur walked slowly to the door. It couldn't be that bad, could it? She was beautiful—truly, easily the most attractive woman he'd ever met. Not even that much older than him. Only nine years. All right, so she'd probably tie him up and flog him or whatever women like that did. He'd survived the Royal Military Academy, he could survive her. Nothing to do but soldier on.

And maybe, just maybe, Charlie would feel so terrible about his brother cleaning up his mess, he'd clean himself up finally.

If only.

He knocked lightly on the door. This time Regan opened. She waved her hand and let him inside, shut the door behind him, then engaged the brass hotel lock.

"There he is," she said. "I wasn't sure you'd really come."

"I said I would. Here I am."

He stood behind the gold velvet chaise longue in front of the fireplace, as if to put a wall between himself and Regan.

"Did we see Charlie home safely?" she asked as she sauntered over to the large walnut drinks cabinet and took out two highball glasses, added ice, then whisky.

"He's staying with friends. I use the word 'friends' loosely."

"Eighteen. Hard age," she said. "It's a...vulnerable age. Isn't it? Suddenly seen as an adult, and yet you have no idea how to go about it. Possibly why I married Sir Jack so

young, barely twenty. Fear of being on my own, unprotected... I thought I was being smart and savvy. Instead I
was being very reckless."

She was reckless, all right. Marrying an older man when
she was twenty. And him. This...whatever this was they
were doing. Her rash offer. *Ten for ten*. His foolish,
desperate acceptance.

"Did he really make you call him Sir Jack?" Arthur
asked.

"Not in private, but in public. With the staff, too.
'Wife' was basically a staff position for him anyway."

"He sounds like a quite a catch."

She laughed. "Ah, well, my mother died when I was
very young, and my father was gone all the time for work.
I wanted safety, security. Whatever faults Sir Jack had, I
will always be grateful he left me quite secure."

"Prisons are secure," Arthur said.

"Yes, well...I know that now." She lifted her glass in a
mock toast and took a long drink.

Arthur glanced around, trying to get his bearings since
he'd be spending a lot of time here in the next few weeks.

"Welcome to the penthouse of The Pearl Hotel,"
Regan said. "Like it?"

"It's impressive," Arthur said. This was more than
luxury. He'd grown up in luxury. This place was pure
decadence.

"When the hotel opened in 1909, this suite was
reserved for the most special clients with the most
exacting needs."

"So...rich men who needed pretty girls."

"Or boys. If they could pay, they were provided whatever they wanted. Your great-grandfather even lived here
in his day."

"Looks like the sort of a place a rake like my great-grandfather would live."

"I suppose that makes me a rake then. And the penthouse is once more being used for its intended purpose—to debauch young lords, my Lord Arthur."

Arthur ignored that comment and her smile. Something had caught his eye. She'd changed the painting.

Over the fireplace, so enormous he could have burned a whole coven of witches inside it, hung a painting of a pretty young woman and her ugly old husband. Arthur could tell the young wife wanted out because she was practically banging on the window with her hands while a parade passed outside the house. The old man's face wore an expression of *Well, go on, why don't you? Nobody's stopping you,* so it was clear they'd had this argument before.

"*The Gilded Cage,*" Regan said, pointing with her highball glass, "by Evelyn de Morgan. What do you think?"

"I think...if that painting is what you hang in your sitting room, I'm not sure I want to know what you hang in your bedroom."

She laughed. "It's a lovely painting."

"It's not very happy," he said.

"Marriage isn't very happy," she said. "Trust me. I speak from nearly ten years' experience. You know why I changed the painting?"

"Needed to cover a hole in the wall?"

"I was married to Sir Jack for over nine years, and I wasn't allowed to move so much as one book to another shelf. Everything always had to be in its place, and 'its' place was where Sir Jack wanted it and nowhere else. Now I change my paintings as often as I change my outfits."

She had changed her outfit, too. Gone was the black trench coat and black boots. Now she wore a black silk kimono with a red sash. No more tasteful pearl choker around her neck. Now she wore pearls dangling from her earlobes. They glinted in the firelight as she crossed the rug to bring him his drink. He took it but didn't taste it.

"Evelyn de Morgan," Arthur said. "Wasn't she a Pre-Raphaelite painter? Something like that?"

She applauded by lightly slapping her free hand against the wrist that held her highball glass. "You do know a little something about art, don't you?"

"Yes, well, the Godwicks own over a dozen art galleries. I grew up in a house with a billion pounds of art hanging on the walls, and my name is literally Art."

"Such a brat," she said. "I think that's what I'll call you. My Brat."

She laughed that low throaty laugh that had affected him so profoundly earlier. The laugh of a woman playing a game who already knew the outcome, but he couldn't quite tell if she knew she'd already won or already lost.

"Some trophy wives buy clothes, handbags, shoes. I bought artwork. Great art always goes up in value and you can sell a painting for quick cash if you ever have to make a dash for it. Luckily, Sir Jack died on me before I had to do that."

"Why did you marry him if he was so awful?"

"You sold yourself to me to protect your brother. I sold myself to protect *me*. Everyone has their price, yes?"

That morning Arthur would have sworn on a stack of Bibles that he couldn't be forced, strong-armed, coerced, or blackmailed into doing anything that went against his own will, his own conscience. Example: having sex with a total stranger. Apparently, she was right. Everyone did have their price and she'd found his. He consoled himself that he could be bought for love while she'd sold herself for Jack Ferry's money.

"I suppose so," Arthur admitted. "Maybe you got a bad deal."

"I got what I wanted, to never be caught short. Whenever it got bad, I'd repeat these three words to myself—*I chose this.*" She looked at him. "And so did you."

She pointed at the decadent luxury that surrounded them and then finally at herself. He could have left Charlie here. He could have let her have the painting and let his parents sort it out with lawyers. But no...he signed up for this. No one to blame but himself.

She touched his glass with her own. He still didn't drink.

"It's not poisoned," she said. "Or do you not drink?"

"I don't know what you're planning to do with me or to me. Thought I'd stay sober to be on the safe side."

"Scared?"

"Who wouldn't be?" He wasn't too proud to admit to being afraid. "I don't know you. I don't make a habit of sleeping with women I don't know."

"Then have a seat. Get comfortable. Let's get to know each other."

With easy grace, she draped herself on the golden chaise. Arthur started to sit in a leather tufted club chair to the right, but she shook her head and pointed at the floor.

It took a great deal of self-control to not roll his eyes. He took off his jacket and laid it over the arm of the chair he wasn't allowed to sit in, then lowered himself on the floor, his back to Regan, his face to the fireplace.

He set his untouched drink on the hardwood by the mantel. "Why did you say—"

"Turn around, Brat. I know you're sitting that way to spite me."

He was. He turned to face her, feeling annoyingly young and vulnerable sitting on the floor at her feet.

"So," he said. "Why did you—"

"Oh no, I'm asking the questions." She took another drink. "Question one. Why don't you use your titles? You're a Viscount, yes? What did Charlie say? Viscount Mansfield?"

"Have you ever been to Mansfield?"

"Never."

"Neither have I. It's just a courtesy title. Doesn't mean anything."

"Means the difference between getting the best table in a restaurant and one by the kitchen door."

"I don't mind sitting by the kitchen door as long as the food is edible."

"And Sandhurst?" she said. "Really?"

"Every Godwick heir has served in the British Army. Even my father in his early twenties."

"Charlie said your father tried to talk you out of it."

"Obviously he didn't succeed."

"Your father's much more a lover than a fighter, if the rumors are true."

"They are, but I'm not much of a fighter either. I'm planning to be a medical support officer, not a warlord."

"Intriguing choice."

"I love my parents but they're...frivolous. They buy art, they sell art, they throw parties—"

"And orgies."

"Yes, thank you for reminding me. Even my older sister is frivolous. All she cares about is Greek mythology and swanning around the Mediterranean with her husband.

None of us are good for anything, really. I mean, art is lovely and all that, but no one with cancer was ever cured by a trip to a gallery. No drowning victim was ever resuscitated by a hand job—"

"Perhaps if it were a vigorous-enough hand job," she said.

"Anyway, I want to do some good for the world. That's all."

She gave him a strange look, as if she saw someone or something else than she'd expected to see when she looked at him. It was there, he'd seen it, then it was gone again just as fast. Now she was looking at him as if he were a disappointment, which seemed to be her default facial expression.

"You're a very unusual young man," she said. "Not still a virgin, I hope?"

"No."

"What age?"

"Eighteen."

"Late bloomer. For a Godwick."

"I take after my mother's side."

"Oh, hardly. You're the spitting image of Lord Malcolm. Black hair. Dark eyes. Impossibly handsome. I heard he was quite well-endowed. Just how much do you take after him?"

"I would prefer not to talk about or think about the genitals of my great-grandparents, if you don't mind." Bad enough he had to know about his living relatives' perversions. Did he have to think about the dead ones, too?

She sipped her whisky again. "So, how many conquests have you made? Tell me when to stop." She held up one finger. Then two. Then—

"Stop."

"Only two? Who was number one?"

"Wendy, my first girlfriend."

"And the other?"

"Naledi, my mother's PA. Former PA. Not because of me. Mum liked us dating, but she moved home to Botswana to be closer to her family."

"How long has it been?"

He hated talking about this. Couldn't she just push him down, get on top, and get it over with?

"Before Sandhurst," he said. "A year? Or more?"

"Long time. You must be about to explode. I'll be sure to put some newspapers down on the floor in case of a mess."

"Now may I ask a question?" he said. "Please?"

"The Brat is learning some manners. Yes, I'll let you ask one question."

"Why me? Why did you...you know, want me?"

"I told you how handsome you are. Do you really need to hear it again?"

He didn't need to hear it again. Not that it would hurt his feelings, but they both knew that wasn't what he was asking. "You said you thought I was different from other men. What did you mean by that?"

She lifted her chin, gave him a half-smile. "That bothered you, didn't it? That I said you were different. Don't like being different?"

"I'm only asking what you meant."

"Come here, Brat," she said. She crooked her finger, beckoning him to move closer to the chaise. He sat up and moved closer, between her knees. She rested her arms lightly over his shoulders and around his back, as if she was going to kiss him. She stroked his hair lightly.

"What?" he asked.

She cupped his chin, forcing him to meet her eyes. "That's what I meant," she said. "You're sitting on my floor at my feet and answering to the name 'Brat.' You can tell me you don't like it, and *you* might even believe you, but *I* don't believe you."

"I'm doing this for Charlie."

"Right. Yes. Of course. For Charlie." She tugged his earlobe. He found it weirdly sensual, which he didn't like. Or he did like it, but he didn't like that he liked it. What adult man would enjoy being treated like the spoiled pet of a pampered princess?

He moved his head aside, trying to escape the touch he found so unnerving. Surprisingly, she let him.

"Did you know when Lord Malcolm used to frequent The Pearl, one of his favorite games was to reenact erotic paintings?"

"I hadn't heard, but I'm not surprised."

"Ever played that game?"

"No."

"Wrong. You are right now." Pointedly, she glanced toward the painting on the mantel. "You're my bird now— my bird in my gilded cage. How does it feel, getting treated like your great-grandfather used to treat his whores?"

"Knees hurt. Bit peckish. Otherwise...no complaints."

"Peckish? Sore knees? Let's fix that then." She left him on the floor and fetched a small cushion off the chaise by the wall. With a sardonic bowing of her head she presented it to him. Then she turned and disappeared through another door and came out a few minutes later carrying a linen napkin and a silver bowl.

She sat on the chaise again and motioned him to move between her open knees. Arthur did as she commanded, cushion on the floor, knees on cushion, eyes lowered, not wanting her to see how much he wanted to see her. If the room were colder, steam would rise off his skin. He settled in between her naked thighs, the robe opening enough he could see all the way to her lace-edged black knickers. Casually, Regan wrapped her legs around him and locked him against her, with her ankles crossed behind his thighs.

"For my poor hungry Brat." She lifted the linen off the bowl revealing grapes, cut pineapple, round fresh strawberries.

His mouth watered.

She lifted one strawberry by the stem. "Open up."

He stared.

"I said, open up."

"You're going to feed me?"

"I feed my pet raven. Why shouldn't I feed my raven-haired pet?"

There were no words to describe the incredible awkwardness of being fed. He was twenty-one, a grown man who could feed himself. Just opening his mouth enough to let her press the sweet gritty edge of the strawberry to his lips took a Herculean and humiliating act of self-abasement. He did it though, opened his mouth and took a bite from the tender red flesh.

The juices burst against his tongue and he swallowed. It went down like a chunk of pavement.

"There," she said. "That wasn't so bad, was it?" She wasn't being sarcastic or mocking now. She spoke to him with the same tenderness in her voice she'd spoken to her raven. "More?"

The craving for that tenderness was stronger than the urge to stand and bolt for the door.

He let her feed him a bite of pineapple. The juices ran

down his chin. Instead of using the linen napkin, she caught them with her fingers and licked them off her hand.

As she brought a plump black grape to his mouth, he realized he wanted it. He wanted the grape, and he wanted her to feed it to him. If only for the pleasure that seemed to fill her grey eyes as he ate from her hands.

Another bite of pineapple. When the juices dripped this time, she caught them with her tongue. Arthur's eyes closed and his breath caught as her gentle tongue lapped them off his chin and the corner of his mouth. Before he'd planned to do it, he turned his head one inch to let his lips come to hers. She smiled into the kiss but didn't return it, merely allowed it.

Another fat black grape. She popped it into his mouth and flicked his lips with her fingertips. Lightly, but it shocked him into laughing the grape out into his hand.

"That wasn't sexy," he said, palming the grape and setting it back into the bowl.

"I beg to differ." She took a sip of whisky on the rocks. "I love to watch you react to me. No matter how hard you try to hide, I see you."

"I'm not hiding. I'm right here."

"Yes, I see you. I see a spoiled, entitled brat, but so, so lovely…"

He warmed at her words. He wasn't used to being talked to like this, being treated like this, being touched like this. When she picked up the grape again he found he was starving for it. She brought it to his lips and he almost bit into it, but she said, "No, not until I say so."

Its smooth dark skin was cool on his mouth. He waited, waited, then she put it in her palm and said, "Now you may have it."

He dipped his head and took it into his mouth, chewed

and swallowed. This time it went down like honey. Bitter honey. How long had he been here with her? An hour, if that? And here he was...already on his knees, already eating out of her hand.

She ran her fingers through his hair again. He shivered as she found the sensitive skin at the nape of his neck and caressed him there. His body screamed at him to wrap his arms around her and pull her close. But he fought the urge and let his hands lay flat on the golden velvet of the chaise. He was hard, painfully hard in his jeans. He told himself it was because her legs were wrapped around him and her knickers were black and lacy and because she had eyes the color of rain clouds. That's all. He didn't like being treated like this—like a pet—but he'd suffer through it if he had to. For Charlie.

And for Charlie, he let his head fall back when she tugged roughly on his hair. For Charlie, he didn't fight when she pressed her mouth to the side of his neck and bit it lightly, didn't ask her to stop when she licked the hollow of his throat, didn't complain when she raised her head and brought her mouth to his mouth. All for Charlie.

The kiss was hot but quick, only the lightest brushing of her lips over his but it caused his cock to stiffen even more. It throbbed, pressing against his zipper. It wanted out, wanted touching. He couldn't help but push his hips forward, to rub against the inside of her thigh, seeking some kind of relief.

She tightened her legs around his hips, bringing him closer to her, tightening her grip on his neck, fingernails pricking his skin deliciously. Why couldn't he hate this as much as he wanted to?

"This is going to be interesting tonight," she said. "I haven't been with anyone since my husband died. You haven't been with anyone since before Sandhurst. I'm a grieving widow—supposedly. What's your excuse?"

"No excuse. It's impossible to date when you're at Sandhurst. And why bother getting into a serious relationship when I don't plan to get married for years anyway? It would only cause unnecessary pain all around."

"And you don't like unnecessary pain."

"Who does?"

"Me." She reached behind him and slapped his arse, hard.

He rolled his eyes. "Were you trying to swat a fly?" he asked. He'd barely felt a thing, other than surprise at the fact a woman so cold was capable of being playful.

She shook her hand like it had stung. "I think I swatted your wallet." She patted him down. "No wallet. You just have a very tight arse."

"You wouldn't be the first to tell me that."

"Let's do this properly." She slid her hands under the back of his shirt, caressed the small of his back and then into his pants, and down. Her hands were cool and soft on his skin.

He closed his eyes, said nothing.

"Very nice," she said into his ear. "Very, very nice. But what else would you expect from a hundred-grand whore besides perfection? And you know what they say...when you buy quality, you only cry once."

She gave that low throaty laugh again that made his toes curl. She was rubbing his bottom now, kneading him, and his hips were moving with her hands. He was going to come in his pants like a teenage boy if she didn't stop.

A soft sigh escaped his mouth, soft and involuntary.

"Poor Brat. This is terrible, isn't it?" She slid her hands underneath his t-shirt and up his back. Up and up they went until they could go no further, and she had him lift his arms overhead so she could strip the shirt off of him. She ran her hands over his naked shoulders and torso.

"Broad chest," she said, resting a small hand over his heart. "Broad chest and a strong heart. It's beating so fast against my palm I think it might burst out and run away if I moved my hand. But I think I'll move it anyway."

He watched her slide her hand down his stomach to his jeans. She found the button of his trousers, then the zipper came down, slowly, too slowly. His chest panted as, inch by inch, she freed his cock. It came out into her hands like it had been waiting all its life for her. She took it and held it, stroked it. Arthur dug his fingers into the golden velvet, enduring it more than enjoying it. He could not let himself come. He bit his tongue and the pain calmed him.

"Beautiful cock," she said, staring at it with admiring eyes. "Big and beautiful and very thick. I can't even wrap my fingers all the way around it."

She couldn't. He hated how good that made him feel, but it did.

"Do you want to put your cock inside of me?"

He lowered his head, his eyes shut tight. "Yes," he breathed.

"What was that? A little louder." She touched his chin, lifted it, forced him to meet her eyes. "Yes?"

A little louder, as requested, he said, "Yes."

"Good," she said. "I want it, too. I want your cock so deep inside my cunt I can feel it in my throat, and I want your cock so deep inside my throat I can feel it in my cunt."

Arthur's chest heaved and she laughed her mocking laugh that made him aware of every nerve in his body.

"But not here," she said. "In the bedroom. Come with me."

With long-legged grace she slid away from him and stood, then patted her thigh and waved for him to get up and follow her.

He didn't. The last vestiges of his pride kept him there on the floor. Her words rang in his ear.

You're my bird now—my bird in my gilded cage. How does it feel, getting treated like your great-grandfather used to treat his whores?

What else would you expect from a hundred-grand whore besides perfection?

When you buy quality, you only cry once...

If he did this, had sex with her right now, on her terms, these terms, he really was her whore. Selling himself to earn back his great-grandfather's portrait. Selling himself to keep Charlie in his parents' good graces. Selling himself because his body was the only currency she would accept.

Regan came back to him, stood next to him so close he could have rested his forehead on her stomach. Her cunt was inches from his face, hidden by lace and the silk of her robe. He thought he could feel the heat emanating from inside her.

She dug her hand into his hair and brought his head to rest on her hips.

"It's all right," she said, running her fingers through his hair again. "The first time you sell yourself is always the hardest. Don't worry, it gets easier. So much easier you'll wonder why you were ever fool enough to give it away for free. I sold myself and look what I got." She raised her hands to indicate the penthouse, the art, the hotel, the world. "Come on now, Brat. As the Americans say, you're on my dime."

As cold as her words were, they worked. He rose off the floor. Though she was tall, he was taller. He was still in jeans, she was in her flimsy kimono. He was male, she was female. But as he stood there silently awaiting her next command, it was clear to both of them who was in charge here.

If he hadn't been grateful for his military training before, he was now. At the very least, he knew how to follow orders.

"Three things," she said. "One. When I want you here, you will be here. When I don't want you here, you will not be here. Otherwise, you are free to go about your life. Two. I can't have children, and I haven't been with anyone but my elderly husband in years, so you don't have to worry about catching anything, including a baby, from me. So let's not bother with condoms unless you insist. And three, when you are here, you will do everything I tell you to do, give me everything I want given to me. Is that understood?"

"Yes, ma'am."

"Four. Don't call me ma'am. Oh, and five," she said, "remember—no one forced you to do this. You could have walked away and let your parents deal with it, but you chose this." She pointed at herself. "What did you choose?"

Arthur took a long breath before answering.

"This," he said.

HE FOLLOWED her up the staircase and through a red door into the bedroom, which was splendid red and gold from top to bottom. The damask curtains on the floor-to-ceiling windows, the wallpaper, the canopy on the enormous four-poster bed—all red and gold. Brass lamps with matching shades cast shadows all around.

He took in every detail, cataloging the room like he was doing inventory. It was all he could do to avoid thinking about what he was doing here, what was about to happen in this room.

Arthur didn't want to think, didn't want to feel. Because if he thought anything, he might have thought about how drawn to Regan he was. If he felt anything, he might have felt something like excitement. Anticipation. Even, terrifyingly...relief.

"Stand there," Regan said, pointing at the floor in front of the fireplace. He waited on the soft plush carpet while she switched one of the bedside lamps off, this one in the shape of a woman holding the moon. The room grew dimmer.

Outside the rain had picked up again and the wind blew hard against the windows. Regan drew the heavy drapes, but he could still hear the rain, only softer now.

"Are you warm enough?" asked Regan as she shut the bedroom door.

"Fine," he said.

"Comfortable?"

"I'm fine," he said, his voice heavy with sarcasm. "And how are you?"

"Better," she said, ignoring his derisive tone. "I'm surprised to find I like having you here, even if you are a brat."

"I'd hope you would. It was your idea."

"It was, wasn't it? One of my better ones. Take your clothes off."

He took off his shoes and socks, set them on the floor. Then came his trousers and boxer briefs in one push, like ripping off a bandage. And there she stood, watching him do it, staring at him like he was nothing more than a statue in a gallery.

"You have a perfect body," she said.

"If you say so."

"I'm never letting an old man touch me again. Nothing but younger men for the rest of my life. Lay down on the bed. In the center."

He stared at the golden sheets and red pillows piled high, at the reality of it—undeniable now.

"Your great-grandfather used to fuck his whores in this bed," she said, leaning against the post at the foot.

"Hope you've changed the sheets since then."

"You're making jokes because you're nervous. You don't have to be. You can put your clothes on and leave. Anytime. All you have to do is say the word."

"What word?"

"*No*, of course. Lay down on your back in the center of the bed."

The shame came rushing back again. If she would just kiss him or drop the ice-queen act for a few seconds... But no. This was what she liked, being in command, in control.

He might have been doing this for Charlie, but there were worse jobs in the world than letting an incredibly attractive woman use his body.

He didn't say no. He didn't say anything as he stepped from his shed clothes and onto the bed.

He lay on his back in the center, small pillow under his head. The counterpane was a rich thick brocade and the raised pattern of gold threading pricked against the back of his body. The silk tickled. The fabric was cool, though growing warm quickly. Regan's eyes were on him, and he felt ridiculous, embarrassed by his erection, his penis hard and dripping, resting on his stomach for all the world to see. What was worse—being hard when you didn't want to be or not being hard when you needed to be?

Regan untied a golden cord from the curtains at the foot of the bed. "I wasn't joking about putting you in a golden cage," she said, "and tying you to my bedposts."

She climbed onto the bed and sat beside him. She beckoned for him to give her his arm, which he did without reluctance. His willpower had been worn down. She wrapped the cord around his wrist with quiet efficiency. Never in his life had he felt more like an object.

He stared up at the canopy, pretending to care about the intricate red paisley pattern, impossible to see them as anything other than enormous sperm swimming in a sea of gold.

"Tell me if it ever gets too tight," she said, threading the cord around a bar in the headboard and wrapping it around his other wrist. "I've never actually done this before."

"Tied someone to your bed?"

"Never. Fantasized about it, yes, but first time ever doing it. Not Sir Jack's cup of tea."

He felt an unexpected pang at her confession. That he was her first. He couldn't say he felt honored, but he did feel...chosen. He'd chosen this, but she'd chosen *him*.

As soon as she was finished—as soon as he was trapped and tied down—something changed. Suddenly he was blameless, without agency. He could do nothing wrong because he could do nothing at all. A sweet and easy surrender came over him. Strangely, he felt safe. Though he didn't understand why he felt this way, he also didn't feel any urgency to understand. Later, yes. Not now.

"Comfortable?" she asked.

He answered honestly this time. "I think so."

She sat beside him, stroking his chest, his stomach. She wrapped her hand around his cock again.

It felt too good. He wished he didn't enjoy it so much, but how could he not? Soft hand, firm grip. It had been a long time since he'd had any hand on him but his own.

She was looking down at him, at her hand stroking him. She smiled as she touched the wetness dripping from the head. "Do you know why they named this place The Pearl?"

"No idea," he said. "Was Pearl some famous prostitute back in the day?"

"Rumor has it they called it The Pearl because of this..." With her fingertip she gathered a drop of his come and held up her hand, displaying the proof of his desire, the pearl of his semen. "Now tell me again why you're doing this? For you or for Charlie?"

"For Charlie. I wouldn't be here if it weren't for him."

"We met because of him, but tell me the truth. If I'd handed the painting right over...you'd still be here, wouldn't you?"

"I'd be home in my own bed."

"Why won't you admit you like this? Every inch of your body tells me you want this, every part of you but your lying tongue."

With a flick of her tongue, she licked the come off the tip of her finger. Arthur grew even harder.

She smiled at him. "Poor Brat. We'll get there. Until then, I suppose you'll simply have to suffer through it."

She slipped off the bed and untied her kimono, tossing it over a red wingback chair. He stared at her as she worked her black knickers down her legs. Long shapely legs and smooth firm thighs and at the apex of them, a patch of lustrous brown hair.

The bed moved as she climbed back onto it and that small vibration was like a shock wave through his body. His heart was pounding hard again, almost through his ribs. She straddled his stomach, her small hands on his chest for balance.

He wanted to touch her but was glad he couldn't. If he did touch her, wouldn't that prove her right, that he wanted this? Not just the sex, but this...submission, this obedience. This eating out of her hand like a pet.

She bent low and her face came to his, only inches away. She ran her hand through his hair, and he met her eyes. He didn't mean to, but once their eyes locked there was no unlocking them.

Her fingers came to his face and caressed his cheek, his chin, his lips. "Do you want to kiss me?"

"Yes."

"Maybe next time I'll let you."

His cock was straining toward her. She was so close he could feel her soft pubic hair tickling his lower stomach. She was warm between her legs. He felt her heat, craved it. She pushed back, her cunt against the tip of his penis and he felt the wetness along the seam of her body. He groaned softly. This made her smile, and it was like he'd won a prize. He knew now that he wanted her to come tonight more than he wanted anything else in the world.

She moved lightly on top of him, brushing her warm mound against his stiff organ. He wanted to sink inside her, bury himself in her, but other than lifting his hips to seek out more of her, he couldn't do a thing but wait for her to use him.

God, he wanted her to use him.

As if she heard his silent plea, she took him in her hand again, and guided him through her slick folds until the tip of his cock kissed the entrance of her vagina. She was tight. The end was thick, and he didn't want to hurt her. Apparently she didn't care about that very much. She pushed down and onto him, forcing the head into her. Arthur watched her closely, her chin lifting and her breasts rising and falling with her breaths, and the little wince around her mouth and her eyes but then came a sound...a murmur of pleasure as she slid herself down onto him. Her body opened to receive him though it was a slow process of sliding up and down the length of him, working it into her.

Yes, she was wet, wet, and scalding hot inside but narrow. Her inner muscles squeezed around him as her passage enveloped him inch by inch.

With her hands on his chest for balance, she moved her hips, rising and falling on her knees. Every undulation sent waves of pleasure through him. The heat of her around him, engulfing him...he couldn't help but move under her, pumping his hips into her. Then they were fucking, really and truly and thoroughly fucking. She wasn't just fucking him. Even with his hands tied, he was fucking her. He pushed his heels into the bed and lifted his hips, thrusting his cock up and into her from below. Her head fell back, exposing her bare throat. He wanted to lick her from the center of her chest to the tip of her chin until he met her mouth in the hottest kiss in history. That she denied him the kiss made it even hotter. This was pure unadulterated fucking they were doing, without tenderness or emotion. Just the thick inches of his cock spearing her as she rode him.

Her fingernails dug lightly into his chest as she pumped, slowly at first and then faster. The pressure built in his hips, in his stomach, down the back of his thighs. He strained against the cords on his wrists as she leaned back and grabbed his thigh. Thank God she hadn't blindfolded him, he thought as he watched his own cock splitting her, disappearing through the soft curls and into that hot little cavern that captured him and held him inside her.

Two fingers found her own clitoris and she stroked it. Arthur envied those fingers. He wanted to touch her clitoris and her cunt, put his fingers into her and open her up, explore inside of her. But for now he had to be content to lay there and let her ride his cock for her own pleasure. And he was happy to do it as long as her face was flushed like that, a blazing rose, and she kept making those pained sounds of pleasure, those pleased sounds of pain.

The bedroom was an oven. They were both sweating and slick and their bodies were soon so tightly joined together, sealed like hot wax, that there was no telling where he ended and she began. She ground herself into him, moving her pelvis in tight ovals that let his cock move even deeper into her.

She opened up completely for him and he felt the tip press against the entrance of her womb. Her head fell back again, and she worked herself hard and fast, rubbing her clitoris, pumping her hips. Her breaths were fast and labored and small cries escaped her mouth, cries of pleasure that would ring in his ears for days.

Arthur watched her. She was there, almost there...and then she came with quick tight contractions all around his length. She clutched him so hard, his shoulders came off the bed and he came inside her without warning. It was sudden—the muscles in her squeezing him, like the tug of a hand. Shocked by the sudden pleasure, he released into the core of her, filling her with spurt after spurt of his semen.

His orgasm was blinding. He felt a completion like he'd never experienced before. As Regan came to rest on top of him, his cock still inside her, he took huge deep breaths, swallowing air. Her hands were on the bed, her head hung down, the tip of her plait fell over her shoulder and brushed his stomach.

Slowly she lifted her head. He felt her vagina giving its final little flutters and gasps around him.

"Remind me, Brat...who was that for—you or Charlie?"

He was too spent to lie.

"For you," he said.

Her eyes widened suddenly—suddenly and subtly, but he saw he'd gotten to her. She wore the look of a woman who'd just had a glass of water thrown on her face without warning. Or been kissed by a stranger. Or slapped by a friend.

She rose up and his softening penis slipped out of her and dripped onto his stomach. She wrapped her kimono quickly, carelessly around her, then reached over his head and untied his wrists.

"Are we...are we done?" he asked, surprised and a little wounded to be set free so fast.

"Get dressed," she said, and stood with her back to the fireplace mantel, her arms crossed over her chest. "When I want you again, I'll contact you. Fly away home now."

She waved her hand to dismiss him, and then waited by the mantel as he dressed in front of her, awash with embarrassment, hurt. They'd been so close only a few minutes ago that they couldn't have been any closer, and now she was so far away she might as well have been in another world.

He held his shoes to his stomach. He'd put them on when he was downstairs. "Did I do something wrong?"

She wouldn't look at him. She looked at the bed where they'd just fucked.

"I haven't had good sex in years and I'm not going to be..." She paused as if reaching for words. "I won't be young forever. I bought you to fuck you, not to fall in love. So get used to it."

"Did you ever get used to it? Your gilded cage?"

Now she looked at him—a quick glance that revealed a wound as deep or deeper than his own.

"No."

He didn't know what else to say. Arthur slipped out of the golden bedroom and went down the stairs, put on his shirt, jacket, and shoes. He left The Pearl.

In a daze, he drove to the Piccadilly townhouse and parked in the drive. Almost midnight. He stepped out of his car and into the cold night. The street was dark and quiet, the ancient elms covered the moon, the soaring townhouses of the rich and the powerful blocked out the faraway lights of the city. A cold wind blew through him. Dry autumn leaves scratched and skittered across the brick walk to the backdoor. The air smelled damp and cloying, the corpse of summer rotting underfoot, a scent he usually loved—the scent of autumn. Tonight, however, it troubled him. Everything troubled him—how it had happened, why it had happened, how it had ended...and how much he'd liked it.

God, he'd liked it.

Arthur found his way to his bed in the dark. Although he knew he really ought to take a shower—he was covered with the fluids of sex, his and hers—he simply stripped naked and slid under the covers, the cotton sheets cool against his burning body.

The question Regan asked him echoed in his mind.

Who was that for—you or Charlie?

That was the question, wasn't it?

That was the hundred-thousand pound question.

3

THE PSYCHE MIRROR

Thursday. Three days later. Arthur lay in his bedroom on the big oak bed at his parents' Piccadilly townhouse. His old childhood bedroom unchanged since his school days at Harrow. An enormous Union Jack hung on the opposite wall. Over his bed hung posters for a Blur concert his sister had dragged him to, and another poster for the Arctic Monkeys when he'd returned the favor. Polo gear, unused for years, lay piled in the closet along with his rugby kit and all the other flotsam and jetsam of his teenage years, long abandoned, long forgotten. He only noted it now because it felt so incongruous to be lying there, surrounded by artifacts of his childhood while dreaming about the thirty-year-old widow he was suddenly sleeping with...

Arthur had never wanted to be a child. Even as young as nine or ten, if given the chance, he would have happily skipped right over childhood and all its embarrassments and indignities to become an adult immediately. An old soul, his parents called him. From age ten on, he'd treated Charlie like more of a son than a baby brother. Arthur aped his parents, doing everything they did since they were his models for adulthood—attending art shows and the symphony, playing polo like his father, going to auctions with his mother, lectures, board meetings... He'd avoided dating until he was eighteen because girls his age seemed far too young for him. Why should he date a teenage girl when he was trying so hard to be a man? He'd only fallen for Wendy because she'd seemed much older, having gone to schools all over the world. And Naledi had been five years older than him. They'd only had a few months together before she returned to Botswana, but those few months had convinced him he'd never be happy with someone his own age.

He'd even skipped university because he couldn't stand to extend his childhood—or at least to put off adulthood —another day longer. He'd chosen Sandhurst, the military academy, because he thought it would make him—finally— feel like a man. Except that hadn't worked either.

Then...Regan. He'd still felt he was playing the part of an adult until that night with her, and then, strangely, the very next morning, he'd woken up and felt like a man for the first time in his life.

Was it because she'd been married and widowed and seemed so impossibly mature to him? And if someone so impossibly mature had chosen him, then he must have been old enough and mature enough for her. Or was it because of the nature of the sex they'd had? That she'd chosen him to explore her fantasies?

He couldn't say, only that every time he thought about her, about the *events* of Monday night, he felt that something monumental had happened to him. A seismic shift. A memory stirred—something his father had tried to tell him and Charlie a few years ago, that they would not know what sort of men they were until they had an intimate partner in their lives. What was it he'd said? Something about being married, how it changes a man...

Arthur almost had it when the doorbell rang, and he sat up like he'd heard a gunshot.

When he opened the front door, he found the girl was there again, the blonde in the red raincoat and Wellington boots. She held out another notecard to him. The girl remained on the porch, glowering.

"So, who are you?" Arthur asked, taking the card. "Do you have a name?"

"Zoot," she said, like she was doing him a favor by telling him.

"Zoot? As in...'Zoot'? Could you spell that, please?"

"*Zed* plus *Oot*. Zoot."

"And why are you called Zoot?"

"I like spankings and oral sex."

He blinked. Then he got it. "Ah. A Monty Python reference."

"Never goes amiss," Zoot said.

"All right, *Zoot*, you can call me Arthur, if you'd like. Or Art. No pressure."

"Not *my lord*? Not *sir*?"

"Arthur's fine. Really," he said. He should make friends with this girl, he thought. Maybe he could get some dirt on Regan. "What do you do when you're not delivering messages and glaring at me? Are you Lady Ferry's dogsbody or something?"

"Second in command," she said, her East End accent on full display. "So mind your Ps and Qs."

"My Ps and Qs are in the best shape of their lives." He held the card, unopened. She was watching him. "Are you waiting for me to tip you?"

She clicked her tongue in disapproval. "The boss was right. You are a brat. Makes sense. Brat's just Art with a B, innit?"

"That's Bart."

"Close enough."

She turned and stomped off, red boots echoing on the pavement. So much for making a new friend.

Anyway, he had a card to read.

Let's play a new game. The Psyche Mirror *by Berthe Morisot is hanging over the fireplace in my bedroom.*

Have you ever fucked in front of a mirror, Brat?

Nine o'clock.

R

Arthur went into the house and closed the door behind him, resting his back against the cool of the wood. Fucked in front of a mirror? Sounded like a nightmare. As long as he could see her, why would he want to watch himself? His naked body grinding and the pained awkward horrible facial contortions? Why would she want to do something that awkward? Because she was a sadist, obviously.

So what did that make him, other than hard again? Nine o'clock was hours away. Hours away, and he was already counting the minutes.

———

ARTHUR TRIED to distract himself with a grueling workout at the gym. Walking home through Hyde Park he felt his phone ring in his jacket pocket. He wanted it to be Regan calling, though he knew it wouldn't be her.

No, not Regan. It was his father. Arthur considered ignoring the call, worried he'd let something slip, but knew he couldn't put off the inevitable.

He answered and after the usual greetings, Arthur asked about Mum.

"Missing her babies," his father said.

"Does she mean us or her houseplants?"

"I didn't ask. I'd assume both," his father said. "How's your brother?"

This question was asked in a tone that implied the answer would not be a satisfactory one.

"Fine, I think. Haven't seen him in a few days. Busy with friends."

His father scoffed. He felt the same way about Charlie's friends as Arthur did. Horrifying to agree with his father on, well, anything.

"What are you busy with?" his father asked.

"Reading. Working out. Enjoying my free time before the army takes it from me."

"Please tell me some of this free time is being spent with a girl?"

Arthur counted to three before answering with a polite, "Mind your own business."

"If I must."

"The following question has nothing to do with my love life," Arthur said, which was true enough. He didn't love Regan Ferry, and she certainly had no love of him.

"Go on," his father said.

"Do you know a woman named Regan Ferry?"

"You don't mean Lady Ferry, Sir Jack Ferry's wife?"

"Widow," Arthur said.

"Of course I know her. Not well. We spoke to her a few weeks before your sister's wedding. Are you seeing her?"

Arthur ignored that last part and concentrated on the other. Lia had gotten married in The Pearl's ballroom, held her reception at The Oyster, taken wedding photos in the old smoking lounge. No surprise his parents had chatted with the hotel owner's wife.

"I know this is strange but...do you remember what you talked about?" Arthur asked.

"Only Lia's wedding plans. And Lord Malcolm. He used to live there, you know."

"She asked about Lord Malcolm?"

"If I remember correctly. It was over six months ago. I know we talked about him, and she had quite a collection of photographs of him from the hotel's archives. Loads of dances. Loads of balls. Parties, I mean, not—"

"Not testicles. I assumed. All right. Just wondering. Did she ask to buy our portrait of Lord Malcolm?"

"I don't recall. Why do you ask?"

Arthur hated lying, especially to his family, but he had to protect Charlie.

"I ran into her, and she recognized me," he said. "We had a long talk and she asked if she could buy Lord Malcolm's portrait. You know, since he was such a fixture at The Pearl."

"I hope you told her no."

"I did."

"She's welcome to have someone make a copy of it, but never the real thing."

"Right."

"We'd sell you to her before we'd sell that painting.

Lord Malcolm would never forgive us, and I'd hate to get on his bad side."

Arthur bit his lip. "Understood."

"But if she wants to buy you and get you off our books, the price is negotiable. All reasonable offers considered. We'll toss in Charlie, too. Buy one, get one."

"Thanks, Dad. Love you, too."

"Here's your mother."

"Wait."

"Yes?"

He almost asked his father if he remembered what it was he'd said about being married, how it changes a man, but decided against it—it would be tipping his hand, and his father was the last person in the world he wanted to discuss his sex life with.

"Nothing," Arthur said. "Forgot what I was going to say."

He chatted briefly with his mother about New York, and he promised her most sincerely that he would go to Wingthorn next week to check on the renovations at the old manor house. By the time the conversation was over, Arthur was back at the townhouse and on his way to the shower.

While in the shower, he considered what his father had said, that the one conversation he'd ever had with Regan Ferry was mostly about Lord Malcolm. Was it really because he'd been such a legend at the hotel? That was eighty, ninety years ago. And Regan's animosity toward Arthur—toward the entire Godwick bloodline—made no sense either. Unless it was simply her fetish to emotionally assault the men she was attracted to. Considering how she'd treated him before and after the sex on Monday night, he could believe it. But the answer wasn't completely satisfying. Not the way she'd looked afterwards. So wounded. Almost scared.

———

IN THE HOTEL lift that evening, he reminded himself that Regan was using him and that he should under no circumstances allow himself to get emotionally involved here— not more than he already was, at least.

A note was taped to Regan's door with the letter A on the front. He assumed that was him, that he was the A. Whether that A stood for Arthur or Ass, he didn't know and wouldn't ask.

The note read, *Unlocked. Wait upstairs.*

Short. Succinct. To the point.

He did as ordered.

As soon as he stepped into the empty bedroom, he remembered in his body everything he had done and felt here Monday night. He stood at the foot of the bed and remembered how his wrists were lightly chaffed the morning after and how he'd laid in his bed at the townhouse, lifting his arms into a silver shaft of morning sunlight to stare at the redness on his skin. Seeing it had been a revelation. How right those pale welts looked on his wrists. It was like seeing himself for the first time—not the way he actually looked, but the way he was supposed to look.

He turned away from the bed and noticed a familiar face in the bedroom. Regan had hung Lord Malcolm on the wall opposite the bed.

Crossing his arms, Arthur stared at his long-dead great-grandfather. "What are you up to, old man?"

There was no answer, of course. Malcolm offered

nothing but his Mona Lisa smirk. Yet Arthur couldn't shake the feeling that somehow Lord Malcolm was a part of all this. He certainly wasn't an innocent bystander.

Arthur turned his attention to the painting above the small fireplace, the one Regan had referenced in her note. It was a delicate and diaphanous scene, a winsome young woman gazing at her profile in her cheval mirror. She was wearing a filmy white shift, falling off one shoulder. The sort of painting that would hang in the bedroom of a fine young lady. An intimate scene of a pretty girl enjoying the sight of herself.

"There's my Brat."

Regan stood in the bedroom doorway, hand on the knob, leaning casually against the frame. She wore a grey skirt and jacket to match her eyes. She looked like she'd come straight from work though it was past nine.

"You summoned me," he said.

"Like a witch summons her favorite demon." She smiled and shut the bedroom door behind her. "You like the painting?"

"This one?" He pointed at the Morisot. "It's very nice. That one, however," he said, pointing at the portrait of his great-grandfather, "has to go."

"Go where?"

He glared at her. "You're not really going to leave his painting hanging across from the bed, are you?"

"What? We don't want good old Great-Granddad Malcolm watching us fuck?"

"Would you want your great-grandfather watching you?" Arthur asked.

"It's just a painting, yes?"

"Of course it's just a painting. Still." He pleaded with his eyes. Surely she had some pity in her soul.

"If you're so sensitive about it..." She went into her closet and brought out a gauzy paisley-patterned scarf. She draped the scarf over Lord Malcolm's portrait.

"Better," Arthur said. "A bit. Thank you."

There. It was happening again. She did something cruel and cold and then stopped it upon request, forcing him to be grateful for the tiniest crumb of decency. And he ate that crumb like it was a feast for a king.

"Don't thank me," Regan said. "Lord Malcolm was a notorious pervert. If he wants to watch, he'll find a way to watch."

She came to him and put her hands on his chest. The heat of her touch permeated all the way through his t-shirt to his bare skin underneath.

She met his eyes, forcing him to meet hers. "How is my Brat tonight?"

"Fine," he said, and since he couldn't help himself, added sarcastically, "and how was your day, dear?"

"Oh, the usual. Busy. Stupid." She didn't seem to be joking.

"You don't like your work here?"

She laughed coldly. "Running a hotel was not what I expected to be doing at thirty."

"Why do it then? You have enough money to retire for a hundred years."

When she answered he heard a false note of levity in her voice. "Have to do something to keep from thinking. Managing The Pearl does the job."

He looked at her. "What are you trying so hard not to think about?"

"Stop. I'm done answering questions. Your turn. How did you feel after Monday night?"

He had to laugh a little at that. "I work out every day,"

he said. "You have to if you're going to survive Sandhurst. But after you, I was sore in places I didn't know I had places. And I had a bit of rug burn."

"On your wrists?"

He nodded. "And on my back."

"Did you like that?" she asked.

"I...don't know if I can answer that question."

"I think you can. I think you don't want to. Embarrassed you liked it so much?"

"No, it's not that."

"Then what is it?"

"Like you said. This is just sex for you. And it's just about getting our painting back for me. Let's not get personal, all right?"

If she was going to shut down his attempts to get her to open up, he would shut down hers just as swiftly, just as hard.

"Of course. We'll have very nice impersonal sex in front of a mirror tonight. And you'll hate every second of it, won't you?" She laughed softly, teasingly.

She brushed her lips lightly over his, and a shiver of pleasure passed through his body. "Do you hate this?"

She wrapped her arms around his neck and kissed him again, kissed him with hunger, real hunger. He wanted to return the kiss. He wanted to push her away. But more than anything he wanted to be punished and humbled, and if this is how the gods saw fit to punish and humble him, who was he to question their judgement?

He put his arms around her waist and pressed his mouth to hers. She opened her lips and tilted her head back, giving him silent permission to kiss her all he could.

She tasted like sugar and whisky and one kiss alone would get him drunk on her. The more he tasted her, the more he wanted. He pulled her tighter against him, felt her breasts pressed against his chest, her back arching and her arms wound round his shoulders. He grew hard, painfully hard. His cock throbbed and he wanted to shift his hips away from her so she wouldn't feel it, but it was too late... She pressed her hips into his, and he flinched with pleasure, even with all their clothes between them.

Her cheeks were bright pink, her soft lips swollen. She ran her hand from his shoulder to his chest, to his stomach and then cupped him between the thighs, pressing her palm gently but firmly onto his erection.

"Better," she said.

Her fingertips found the head under his clothes, and she lightly traced along the tender foreskin. His breath quickened. He closed his eyes.

"No." She snapped her fingers in his face. "Look at me. Watch. You aren't allowed to close your eyes and pretend this isn't happening. It is. It's happening. You chose this."

Arthur opened his eyes and looked, watching her hand touch him. He breathed in and smelled again the scent of her, which had an electric current in it. The scent of a storm.

He had always loved storms. He breathed her in again, wanting more of her.

The feeling must have been mutual because she reached for his belt and unbuckled it. She slipped her hand into his pants and took his penis out and held it in her palm.

"There we are," she said. "It's really a very beautiful cock you have, Brat."

"Penises are the least attractive part of any human being's body," he protested.

"Beauty is in the eye of the beholder. If I say it's beautiful, it's beautiful. Your Wendy was a lucky girl, wasn't she?"

"She didn't think so."

"Then she was a fool."

"Sometimes I can't tell if you hate me or you're starting to like me," Arthur said.

"Neither can I," Regan said and wrapped her entire hand around him again and held him.

A sound came out of his throat, half gasp, half sigh.

"Good Brat," she said. "I like that you like being treated like a whore." She held him in her hand a little firmer. "Even if you won't admit it."

She stroked him again, base to tip then around the head and back down. Her hand was soft and her grip strong. His head fell back. He closed his eyes.

"What did I say about that?" Regan demanded. "Eyes open. Here. Look above the fireplace."

She pointed to the painting. "Berthe Morisot," she said. "*The Psyche Mirror.* That's what they used to call cheval mirrors, because it could show you your whole self. And there she is, seeing herself and liking what she sees. You are going to see yourself tonight. You understand?"

"No."

"You will. Stand in front of the mirror. Undress," she said. "All the way."

"Do I have to?"

She gave him a look and that look answered the question so that no further words were necessary.

He didn't want to do it. He knew people found him attractive. He was twenty-one and had been doing hard military workouts for two years. Yes, he was in good shape physically, but he still didn't go around staring at his naked body in mirrors. Too much looking in mirrors was dangerous. You ran the risk of seeing someone in there you didn't want to see.

What choice did he have, though? For Charlie, he reminded himself as he pulled his t-shirt up and off. This was for Charlie.

He tossed his shirt onto the wingback chair. Then his jeans and pants and socks. And then, there he was, completely naked and standing in front of the cheval mirror. The "psyche mirror." Regan stood near him, her back to the fireplace mantel, her arms crossed over her chest, studying him again as he stared at himself in the mirror. Seeing himself there, he remembered, finally, what his father had said to him about marriage, how it changes a man...

"What do you see?" she asked, her tone cool and probing, like a psychotherapist's.

"Just me."

"Don't lie. I can tell you're thinking about something."

"Earlier today I was trying to remember something my father said to us years ago, and it finally came to me."

"What was it?" She came to him and rested her chin on his shoulder. He liked that she was tall enough to do that.

"Charlie and I were complaining to Dad one day about how he was always chasing Mum around the house. We thought it was about as disgusting as anything could get. Usually he just said, 'Put a sock in it, virgins.' That day he actually sat us down and lectured us about how important Mum was to him. 'Your wife will be like a mirror to you,' he said, 'except she'll show you your true self. A man can be the life of the party at the pub with his mates and a monster at home to his wife. Who is his real self? Not the mask he wears in public but the soul he shows only to her.'"

"Why were you trying to remember it?"

Because of Monday night, he thought but didn't say. Because that's what had felt so monumental about that night, why he'd woken up Tuesday morning feeling like a man for the first time in his life. He'd shown his face to a thousand friends. That night with Regan, he'd shared some secret part of his soul for the first time with someone. With her.

"I was just...you know, thinking about my parents when we were on the phone today. On their millionth honeymoon in New York."

"I see," she said. There was a split second when he thought she might look disappointed in his answer. He relished that look.

Regan wrapped her arm around his waist, took his cock in her hand, held it, stroked it.

"What I see is this," she said. "I see a young man who is getting harder and harder every second that passes, who chose this for a reason that has nothing to do with his brother, even if he won't admit it. Yet."

He was so hard it hurt. His erection humiliated him, that he was this easy to manipulate. Everyone thought he was some perfect son, perfect soldier, perfect angel. That's what Regan had said. But the truth was he was exactly what the mirror showed him to be. An absolute whore for this woman and the way she treated him.

She released him, stood back and undressed. Off came her grey jacket. Down went the zipper of her skirt that clung to her round hips. Then her shirt and lacy white bra, lacy white knickers. She stood before him, naked and glorious, naked but for the pearl drop earrings hanging from her ears.

In the mirror's reflection, he could see her hair,

crimped from her earlier French plait, falling in waves down her back. Her lovely bottom, so soft and round, waiting for his two hands to clench it, hold it. Long lovely naked legs. Long throat and pale olive skin. Breasts that sat high on her chest and firm, perfect handfuls. Nipples a darker brown. Just seeing them and his mouth watered at the thought of sucking them. Narrow waist and the flare of her hips, and then her vulva with the softest curls of hair.

Between her thighs, hidden from his eyes, was what he wanted to see more than anything. See and smell and taste and touch and push inside and fill. But he couldn't, not yet. He had to wait for her instructions.

She took a step to the right and revealed his body in the mirror again. Now he saw himself and her in the glass. Two of him. Two of her. His desire doubled as did his humiliation.

Regan took his hands in hers and brought them to her breasts. "Touch me," she ordered.

He held her breasts with a firm grip in both palms, held them and felt the heat of her body and the smoothness of her skin. Her nipples hardened but not enough for him. He wanted them hard as diamonds. He cupped the mounds and ran the pad of his thumbs over and around the nipples. The skin puckered and tightened. He wanted a reaction from her. He was as tired of her coolness as she was of his coyness. Lightly, he pinched both her nipples and saw in the mirror as her lips parted in a gasp.

Arthur found it was easier to let go and do what he wanted if he wasn't looking at her but at her reflection. He pinched the taut brown tips again and then tugged them gently. They grew harder against his fingertips. He pinched and plucked them and the woman in the mirror, who wasn't Regan but instead was some bewitching girl he couldn't stop staring at, gasped again, this time audibly. That strange woman in the glass...he wanted to watch someone sucking her nipples. He lowered his head and took her left breast in his mouth, latching on to the tip.

The mirror woman arched her back to give the man in the mirror more of her breast to suckle. The mirror man licked softly, licked hard, covered the areola with his lips and pulled the tip into his mouth, pulled more and harder, as her back arched even more until she seemed to hang from his mouth, as if it was all that was keeping her standing.

Whoever he was, that man in the glass, he wanted that woman. His cock was engorged, a livid red, dripping. It rubbed against her hip as he sucked her breast, massaging the nipple with his mouth and tongue, unable to get enough. In the mirror, the woman put her hands into the man's hair and held him to her breast, then wrapped her arms around his head and pushed her hips into his stiff organ.

She pulled back and took his head in her hands, forcing their lips to meet again. Arthur closed his eyes and the man in the glass was gone. He was himself again, kissing Regan, pushing his tongue into the hot cavern of her mouth, opening her lips wider to press in deeper.

She broke the kiss first, which almost broke him. But then she turned around, lifted her hair off her back with one graceful motion and draped it over her shoulder. The cheval mirror stood at an angle in the corner by the fireplace and reflected the whole room—the bed, the door, the shrouded painting of his great-grandfather. Now the mirror showed him Regan reaching out to grip the edge of the fireplace mantel. It showed her leaning forward slightly and arching her back. It showed her spreading her thighs and lifting her buttocks.

Then it showed him bringing his hand between her thighs, finding her vulva and stroking the silky soft hair he found there.

The hair was damp, and he sought for the source of the dampness. He found the sealed folds of her vulva and ran his fingers along the seam. Wetness, more wetness. He pushed into the seam and parted it, found slick bare flesh, hot against his hand and wet. Up and down he stroked along the slit. Regan said nothing, but her breaths were fast and ragged. He found the hidden little hole into her, and he slowly pushed two fingers inside. The sound that came out of her throat caused his cock to stiffen even more. His muscles were hard as steel, his cock a rod of iron.

The man in the glass did as Arthur had done—pushing two fingers into the woman in the mirror. He watched the man's hand moving in and out of her body, watched his hand turning and going in at another angle. He saw the woman's lips part and her eyes close tight as the fingers inside her spread apart, opening the hole.

Regan turned her head to meet his eyes in the mirror.

"Enough playing with me, Brat. Put your cock in. I want to see you watching yourself in the mirror while you do it."

He took his penis in his right hand and guided it to her wet and swollen seam. With a slight push of his hips, the tip went through the folds and found her entrance, resting against it.

With one hand on his cock and the other arm wrapped around her stomach, and with slow thrusts of his hips, he pushed his way into her body. Watching in the mirror, barely breathing, hardly blinking, he saw his penis disappearing into her inch by inch. Saw and felt it as her hot inner depths enfolded and drew him into her.

She moved with him and against him as he went into her, arching her back again, bowing it as they both moved in tandem to work all of his thick organ into her tight but eager cunt.

Regan spread her thighs wider, lowered her head. The woman in the mirror did the same, as the man in the glass took her hips into his hands and began to slide his cock deeper into her.

He wanted to thrust. His body screamed at him to pound her open, but he held back. He worked with the rhythms of her own movements, sliding slowly out of her to the tip, sliding in as far as he could go, taking as much as she could give and giving as much as she could take.

And in the mirror he watched it all. He watched his thick inches pulling out of her, glistening with her wetness, watched her vagina enveloping his cock, taking it inside of her until he couldn't go any farther into her.

It wasn't enough for him that they were joined, wasn't enough that he'd watched as it happened, as he'd speared that beautiful slit of hers. He had to touch her, too.

He pulled her even tighter against him, and, with the fingers of his right hand, he sought and found the place where their bodies joined. As he pushed into her, he felt himself, the hot hard length of him, now wearing her wetness as it plunged into her. He touched her folds, speared by his cock, and then went up in search of her clitoris.

He knew he'd found it when she cried out with pleasure again. The woman in the cheval glass cried out, too. A sharp intake of air followed by a gasp as his fingertip touched the small but throbbing knot where they met and melded.

"Harder," she said, and he didn't know if she wanted her clitoris rubbed harder or her cunt pounded harder, so he did both. He thrust and watched himself thrust. He rubbed and watched himself rub. And he saw the girl in the glass come undone as the man between her thighs undid her...

She lowered her head again and shuddered. He felt her orgasm as much as heard it, felt her vaginal muscles twitch and clench at his cock, fluttering madly all around him. He lost his mind then and every last bit of self-control as he rode her to his own completion. He bent over, hands on her small shoulders, splitting her like an iron nail into soft, tender wood.

He felt his own orgasm bearing down on him, unstoppable as a tsunami. It rushed over him and crashed into her. His thrusts were rapid-fire as the pleasure spiked and the dam burst, and he let go. He wrapped his arms around her stomach and pulled her back against him, holding her in place as he used her hole. His come rushed out of him in hard spurts, filling her and filling her with his semen. He wanted to fill her until there was nothing left inside him to give her. And when there was nothing left, he just held her against him and breathed.

Slowly they pulled apart and Arthur stood up straight, swallowing air, eyes closed. When he opened his eyes again, he looked in the mirror to see Regan's face. She was smiling, wickedly, triumphantly.

"Do you see what I see in the mirror?" she asked.

He looked and saw what he'd been trying not to see for years—that he was one of those men who was turned on by the power and cruelty of a woman. His cock hadn't been hard inside her—it had been solid steel. Regan had forced him to look and now that he'd seen what he'd seen in her psyche mirror, he couldn't look away. Even if it meant admitting he hadn't thrown himself on the sword to save Charlie. He'd thrown himself on the sword because she was wielding it.

"You know what I see?" she asked. "I see Lord Malcolm."

"I am *nothing* like my great-grandfather."

"You are actually," she said. "But that's not what I meant."

He followed her gaze into the mirror. She wasn't looking at him or her own reflection. She was looking at Lord Malcolm.

And Lord Malcolm was looking back.

She'd covered his portrait with the scarf, but the scarf had fallen off the frame, and the painting hung uncovered. Where was the scarf? On the floor by the door halfway across the room.

Regan laughed wickedly. "I told you if he wanted to watch, he'd find a way."

Arthur didn't tell her that she didn't know the half of it.

4

THE WALTZ

Two nights down with Regan.

Eight to go.

And in the meantime, Arthur was snooping.

On Regan, of course. He told himself it was because she had made herself an enemy of the Godwick family—finding a way to legally steal a painting from them and then practically forcing Arthur to sleep with her to get it back.

"Really," Arthur muttered to himself as he fought off another pesky erection. "How dare she."

In the back of his mind, he knew he was snooping because she fascinated him, aroused him, infuriated him, and stripped him of all his defenses. He had to get some of those defenses back.

Know thy enemy, he reminded himself. *Biblically, if necessary.*

His parents had a private service they used to vet employees and household staff, which included complete background checks and that sort of thing. Seemed rather intrusive to Arthur, so he turned instead to the internet.

He spent half the morning after his last encounter with Regan in his father's office at the townhouse, online, digging up everything Google could tell him about her.

First, he learned her maiden name was Moira Regan Pryce, but she'd always gone by Regan.

She was thirty. Her birthday was in August. Clearly her parents had found something to do on those long, cold December nights in Wales.

With a little more digging he found that Regan and Sir Jack Ferry had a grand wedding at St. Paul's. He even found a photograph of them standing on the steps afterward—Regan looking like his granddaughter in a white lace wedding gown and Sir Jack looking a little like that American actor Gene Hackman. The article mentioned a candle had been lit on the altar in honor of her mother Hannah, who'd died when Regan was only four years old.

Four? How horrid. She'd mentioned her mother had died young, but she hadn't said exactly how young. What would that do to someone, to lose their mother at four years old? He couldn't imagine life without either of his parents, even his father who drove him mad most days, but especially his mother who'd been the love of his life at that age. He remembered how she'd read to him and Charlie every night at bedtime, fairy tales and silly stories about frogs and toads, cats and hats, and bears going to the moon. She called him her Morning Star since he always woke up so early. Charlie was her Evening Star who went wild at night before bed.

He had to wonder if, subconsciously perhaps, that was why Regan had gotten married so young? To recreate in some way the family she'd lost?

He discovered only one other piece of information that seemed significant. When Regan married Sir Jack

Ferry, there were a few small write-ups in the gossip rags. The usual rubbish about a social climber marrying a rich old toff. One thing jumped out at him: she was described as a student at the time. She'd been studying painting at LOCAD, the prestigious London College of Art and Design.

Regan was an artist. Or had been once. He tried to find out if she'd ever graduated, but couldn't access any of the alumni pages.

He sat back in his father's big leather desk chair and with the toe of his shoe, swiveled the chair toward the windows that looked into the shadowy back garden and the trees shedding their autumn leaves.

Once upon a time, Regan had been a young artist. Then she'd met a rich man who'd offered her the security of money and marriage and discovered the price of both was higher than she ever expected to pay. She seemed to be paying the price now, even months after Sir Jack had died. Working late at The Pearl, still wearing her watch to cover her wrist tattoo, buying Arthur to sleep with because she wouldn't give herself time to date.

After their most recent encounter in front of her mirror, Regan had slipped on her robe and said, "You can go now. After years of sleeping with a man I loathed, it's the height of luxury to sleep alone."

He hadn't even asked to sleep in her bed...although if she'd asked him to, he would have. How was it that he could feel so close to her while they were having sex, but the moment it was over, he was dismissed like a servant? Probably, he admitted to himself, because to her, he was a servant and nothing else. And, as she'd said, he'd have to get used to it.

When he was done snooping, he knew more facts about Regan, but the truth of her still eluded him.

The doorbell rang. Arthur went to the door and there was Zoot again in her red coat and boots, holding out another notecard to him.

"We meet again," Arthur said. "I promise to mind my Ps and Qs today."

"Just read the note," she said, glaring. "I can't go until you've read it and given me your answer."

He opened the card, expecting to find another note from Regan summoning him to her bedroom.

Instead he found an invitation.

"*The Fox and Hen Hunting Club Ball*," Arthur read aloud. "A hunt ball? Brilliant. My favorite." Of course he was being sarcastic. Hunt balls were an old English tradition, hunting clubs celebrating the end of their season. He didn't hunt, and he tried to avoid balls. Regan really was a sadist.

"The boss wants to know if you've got a tux or something formal to wear," Zoot said. "She needs a date to the ball. Geezer friends of her crap dead husband are throwing it, and she wants them to see she's getting fresh young cock these days."

That statement was a lot to take in.

"Her crap dead husband," Arthur repeated. "Do I want to know what you call me behind my back?"

"Lord Dogshit. Viscount Manwhore. The Rude Baron."

"Am I a baron?" he asked solely to make Regan's underling roll her eyes. It worked. "I'll have to ask Dad. I can't remember my own titles, much less his. Anyway, I do like 'Viscount Manwhore.' I'll put that on my stationery. What should be on the crest? One big cock or three smaller cocks in a triangular formation?"

"You're not funny."

"Why are you laughing then?"

"Pity for the madman."

"I'll take all the sympathy I can get. Please tell 'the boss' that I do have formal attire, and my fresh young cock will *gleefully*—" his sarcasm was out of control by this point "—escort her to the hunt ball being thrown by the geezer friends of her crap dead husband." He shoved the invitation back into the envelope. "And you have my answer, so you may go unless you'd like to come in and call me more names over tea."

She raised her eyebrows, and he noted that her blue eyes were even bluer when they were glowing with pure venom.

"No need for airs, *my lord*," she said. "We're both on her payroll, remember?"

Laughing, she turned away and half-walked, half-skipped down the path to the iron gate. Someone—not him, but definitely someone—needed to turn her over their knee. Immediately.

Upon returning to his bedroom, Arthur checked the mantel clock. 6:30. The hunt ball began at eight. Plenty of time for a shower and shave and stealing a splash of his father's Le Labo cologne.

———

ARTHUR ARRIVED at The Pearl Hotel a few minutes before eight. On his way to the lift, he heard the strains of music from the ballroom and saw well-heeled guests streaming through the doors.

At the penthouse door he knocked and waited. He

expected Regan's redcoat to answer it, but Regan herself opened the door.

She stood there in her robe, hair tied back, make-up understated but for her full burgundy lips. Pearl drops dangled from her ears.

"Am I late?" he asked.

"You're in uniform," she said.

He glanced down as if just now noticing his own clothing.

"Mess dress," he said. "Pretty standard attire for a hunt ball. Did you want a tux instead? I can run home."

Mess dress was military party dress—in his case, a scarlet cutaway jacket with gold trim, dark waistcoat, and navy trousers with braid down the outseam.

"No, no," she said softly. "You'd said you were joining your regiment in January. I suppose I'd forgotten. I'd been picturing you in a tuxedo, that's all."

"Really, I can run home and—"

"Absolutely not. You look...very nice." She let him into the sitting room. "Have a drink if you like. I'll run up and finish dressing."

In her silk kimono, she didn't so much run up the stairs but flowed up them, robe lightly billowing behind her like a black cloud. He went to the fireplace and saw that she'd left de Morgan's *The Gilded Cage* hanging above it but had now added a new work of art to the mantel.

A small bronze sculpture of a dancing couple. The man was nude, but the female form wore a sort of skirt from the waist down. They were dancing so close their lower bodies merged into one.

"It's *The Waltz* by Camille Claudel," Regan said.

Arthur turned and looked up at her as she came down the stairs. She wore a low-cut gown of ice blue, the skirt fitting her hips like a glove and then falling in soft folds to the floor. The words "Old Hollywood" came to Arthur's mind, especially with her hair parted on the side and laying on her shoulder in thick dark waves.

"You look stunning," Arthur said simply.

"I *am* stunning." It seemed she'd recovered from the shock of seeing him in uniform. He still didn't know if it was a good shock or a bad shock, but he was hoping for good.

"Is this sculpture the artwork we're 'playing' tonight in honor of old Malcolm?" he asked. "Are you going to make me waltz nude with you?"

"Can you waltz?"

"Well enough not to humiliate myself or break your toes."

"Good." She took a heavy breath.

"Nervous?"

"Why should I be?" She gave him a look that told him quite clearly that wasn't a question he was supposed to answer out loud.

She turned to the mantel. "She was originally nude, too." Regan stroked the bronze folds on the skirt of the woman in *The Waltz* sculpture. "Art critics savaged her for that. Can you believe it? Male sculptors had been portraying female nudes since Zeus ran the world, but God forbid a woman in 1905 sculpted a female nude. They excoriated Camille, and she added the skirt so as not to offend their wounded male sensibilities."

"Men are fools," Arthur said, nodding. "You don't have to tell me. My mother and sister have me well-informed on the matter."

"Perhaps I'm reminding myself."

"Why would you need reminding?"

"Oh, what do they say? I'm a sucker for a man in uniform."

Flirting? He knew he shouldn't press his luck. He did it anyway.

"I keep thinking about you," he said. "I can't seem to stop."

"What do you think about?"

"Trying to figure you out. One second you hate me. The next second you seem to almost like me. *Almost*. It's like you want to hate me but can't. You work constantly, until nine at night, too busy to date, but you admit you hate the work. And practically blackmailing me to sleep with you when you could have anyone you wanted... I don't know. Nothing fits."

"Everything fits," she said. "You just can't see the big picture. I can."

"I wish I could."

"No, you don't. I wish I couldn't..." She sighed and her grey eyes looked suddenly sorrowful. Then she turned them on the sculpture of the couple waltzing. "But we have no say in which cards are dealt to us at birth. We can only decide how to play the hand we're given. And I've decided to play for high stakes. Why not? We all lose everything in the end anyway."

Her words were so pessimistic, so dark, he wanted to shake sense into her. "Regan—"

"I'm fine," she said, then smiled widely. "Don't mind me."

"Your first officer mentioned the hunt ball was being thrown by friends of your husband's. Are you nervous about seeing them again?"

"Lord and Lady Somers. The wife, Caroline, is fine. She's a harmless gossip. But Sir Jack and Nigel were close.

They always hold the ball at The Pearl. This is the first time in ten years I'm not there with Sir Jack. I'm expecting *commentary*."

"I won't embarrass you."

"No, you won't. But I fully intend to embarrass you. Come on. Let's go and get this over with, shall we?

He held out his arm to her, but she ignored it and walked alone to the door. He followed and held it open for her. They said nothing to each other in the lift on their way down, and Arthur was wounded by the silence until it occurred to him there was a very good chance Regan was simply sick with nerves.

"They won't expect me to bring a date," she said when the lift arrived at the main floor. "That's all." It was as if she were answering a question he hadn't asked but was clearly on her mind.

"It's not the Victorian era," he said as the doors opened. "Widows are allowed to date after six months."

"Tell that to them."

"If you want me to," Arthur said, "I will."

When he held out his arm to her this time, she took it.

'

THEY WALKED arm in arm to the open double doors of The Pearl's ballroom, an Art Deco addition to the hotel, all crimson and chrome.

The ball was in full swing already, but there was no hope of an anonymous entrance, what with an actual herald at the door who blew a hunting horn as every guest entered and shouted their name to small, medium, or great acclaim.

And so it was their turn to be—loudly—announced as Lady Ferry and Lieutenant Arthur Godwick.

Heads turned at her name.

Jaws dropped at his.

They *really* hadn't been expecting Regan to bring a date, Arthur thought. Especially not another member of the peerage. The shocked expressions he saw reminded him of Munch's famous *Scream*.

He placed his hand over Regan's and escorted her into the throng of guests who stared and smiled awkwardly at them. Of course, it made sense they'd be shocked if this was her dead husband's crowd. It would be like bringing a date to your dead spouse's annual family reunion a mere six months after their funeral.

Arthur chuckled softly when he realized how audacious she was being.

"What?" she said, playing innocent.

"You really did hate your husband, didn't you?"

"When we waltz tonight, I'll imagine we're waltzing on his grave."

"The sooner the better, then."

Arthur took her by the arm and led her not to the bar or to a table or toward a group of ladies who'd waved at her but straight into the dance floor as a waltz began to play.

Regan's eyes slightly widened as they took their first steps together. Arthur hadn't waltzed since his sister's wedding, but he'd had to practice so much when Lia was younger than he could have done it in his sleep. He could still hear her muttering instructions in his ear—*slow, quick, quick, slow, quick, quick, right foot forward, left foot side, right foot closed*. The music was unfamiliar but pretty, played by a small yet loud orchestra.

"You're very good at this," she said, her hand clinging to his shoulder.

He felt the heat of her body all the way through her gown and his uniform. "Learning to waltz with your sister is a rite of passage."

"For you toffs, maybe," she said. "Not for us poor unwashed commoners."

"Right, *Lady* Ferry. Of course, *Lady* Ferry."

"I was born in the stable, married into the castle. And they've never let me forget where I came from." She glanced around the room at the other toffs.

"You're good enough for me," he said. "I'm one-half American, remember? That's as common as it comes."

"Ugh. Forgot that. Excuse me."

She tried to turn away from him, but he grabbed her and pulled her back to him, laughing.

"Snob," he said.

"Brat," she said.

And on and on they waltzed until the dance ended. Arthur escorted Regan to the bar where they ordered cocktails. A man approached, older, about seventy. Florid face, bristle brush mustache, and a barrel chest stuffed into a white waistcoat about to burst and send the buttons flying into the crowd like a hail of bullets.

"Reggie," the man said and mashed his mustache against Regan's cheek. "Good to see you out and about, old girl."

"Nigel," she said with a tight smile. "Nice to be out."

"Who's this lad now? Godwick? Must be Spencer's boy, yes?"

"You know my father, sir?" Arthur asked, his tone neutral.

"Thrashes me at Sotheby's every time we turn up for

the same sale. I keep trying to get him in the Hunt Club, but he's certain I'll set the dogs on him and call it an accident."

"You wouldn't be the first to plot his murder," Arthur said gamely. "That would be my mother."

The big man laughed a big laugh. "Good lad. Still at Sandhurst, are you?"

"Not anymore. I begin my training as a medical support officer in January."

"This one's quite a switch from old Jack," Lord Nigel said to Regan. "Was this one even born when you married Jack?"

"Yes," Regan said. "Arthur's older than ten."

"Ah, well, pendulums always swing the other direction eventually, they say."

Did they say that? Arthur wanted to ask.

"Jack wouldn't want me to be lonely," Regan said. She was doing a good job of keeping a straight face.

"Suppose not. Suppose not," the man said. "This one's an earl sooner or later. You're reaching even higher this time around, aren't you, girl?"

"You assume I have nothing going for me but my rank?" Arthur asked.

Lord Nigel turned to him. "No offense, lad, but you're just a boy. What else would she want you for?"

Regan spoke up for him. "He's not a cruel, possessive controlling old fart, for starters."

"And I do have a fresh young cock," Arthur added, as Lord Nigel's eyes went wide.

"It's true, Nige," Regan said, straight-faced. "It's really quite massive."

Arthur held out his hand to her. "Shall we dance, my lady?"

"You won't trip over your cock, will you?"

"I make no promises, so watch your step."

They set their drinks down as the music swelled. They returned to the dance floor, leaving Lord Nigel Somers sputtering like a car that had just run out of petrol.

Once they were in step, Regan started to laugh. "Did we really say all that out loud to the husband of the biggest gossip in London?"

"We did. Wonder how long before I'll be hearing from my family about that."

"The speed of posh gossip is faster than the speed of light."

She appeared to be right. Arthur saw, as they spun around the floor, that more eyes were on them than even before, that what they'd said to Nigel had been overheard and was now being passed around.

"Why didn't I keep my mouth shut?" Regan said. "Standing up to these people is more trouble than it's worth."

"I like your mouth open," Arthur said, dropping a kiss onto her lips.

She looked up at him, startled, then laughed.

"What are you laughing at?" he asked.

"At you, at me, at the mad, mad world. That's all. Can you believe that the waltz used to be considered the height of scandalous dancing? The couple held each other in their arms like lovers. The man's foot could disappear under his partner's gown. His knee sometimes slipped between her thighs... Claudel's sculpture was the last time the waltz caused a scandal. Until tonight."

"We're only dancing. Not very scandalous."

"I can make it scandalous," she said. "Do you want to hear about when and how I lost my virginity?"

"Right now?"

"I was eighteen years and needed money for art school. I'd been accepted, but the scholarship wouldn't cover rent in London or supplies. So I came to The Pearl and found the madam, asked her how much I could get for my virginity if I sold it."

"Regan, if you tell me—"

"You'll get hard on the dance floor. That's the plan."

———

As they spun around the room, she spun the story, so clearly that he could envision it as if it were happening before him...

The client's name was Giles Russell. He'd played rugby in his youth and inherited a fortune from his father and now owned his own team. Built like a rugby player gone to seed. He'd been handsome twenty years earlier and still had the charm.

Giles rented the Diamond Suite at The Pearl and Regan was summoned to his room around nine. The madam had dressed her in a little white frock, white lace-trimmed ankle socks and Mary Jane shoes. Giles laughed when he saw her at the door. He didn't care about virgins. He just preferred it in the raw and didn't want to catch anything. The dress was overkill but that was fine by him. She looked sweet enough to eat, he said. So he did.

"Right on the rug," Regan said. "He ate me like a starving man at a feast. Dress up to my neck, face in my cunt. I could feel his tongue in my stomach, I swear."

"Regan."

"I was so nervous that I think I came from pure adrenaline, but I did come. Hard. He had these thick fat fingers," she said. "I still think about those thick fingers sometimes."

After she came, he picked her up off the rug and took her into the bedroom, stripped her naked—except for her little white lace-edged socks—and laid her out on the big white bed. He stuck his fingers in her and declared her still too tight. Didn't want to tear her, or he'd only get one turn on her before she'd tap out.

"One turn, he called it." Regan's eyes glinted. "He really was a wicked man."

He'd brought all these lovely weighted metal balls, about the size of large marbles, and he used them to open Regan's vagina. She remembered him putting her over his lap and spanking her good and hard until her bottom was burning and red as fire. He worked one large metal ball into her, then another. She felt them nestling into the hollow in the front wall of her vagina so they would hit her g-spot and clit.

"He let me get close to coming... I was really panting for it, but instead of putting his cock in me, he spanked me again. I had to keep my legs shut tight so the balls wouldn't come out. And the wicked part was, squeezing my legs together so tightly and being spanked like that...I came so hard I screamed. Then he took the balls out and fucked me."

He had to go slow as she was tender, and his cock fat and blunt like a Cuban cigar. She was gripping the headboard as he worked himself into her, playing with her nipples with his free hand, playing rough—pinching and tugging on them. Her breasts ached and felt so heavy on her chest. It wasn't enough for him to put his cock in her. He had a clitoris vibrator he used on her when he was fucking her. When she came, she said, it was like being turned inside out. Her muscles clamped down on the shaft so hard she nearly pushed it out.

"After I came, he really let himself have at me," Regan went on. "He took my tits in his big hands and just rode me into the bed."

All this was said as if she were reciting a recipe for scones or telling an anecdote about the time the butler lost the lid to her favorite teapot.

It was quick and hard but good. She was shocked by how good it felt to have his cock in her and him rutting on her like an animal. She even came a third time, her clit was so swollen and her vagina so open...and then the come, shooting into her, filling her until it spilled out and coated her young thighs.

Arthur's cock was stiff inside his trousers.

"He paid for a whole week before he had to return to Sydney," she said. "I spent most of that week naked and coming. Mouth. Arse. Every hole. I was fully debauched in one night. Lovely man. Invited him to our wedding. Told Sir Jack I was a rugby fan."

The herald blew his trumpet and all eyes turned to the front doors, where new guests were arriving. Thank God.

Arthur grabbed Regan by the wrist and dragged her toward the staff exit. She owned the hotel. She counted as staff, right? And he was certainly at full-staff.

As he dragged her away, she laughed. "Where are you taking me? Or are you just taking me?"

"I don't know, and yes." The staff exit led to the kitchen, but there was another door to the lobby.

"Follow me," she said. She pulled him across the lobby toward the old smoking lounge, now a private area for VIP guests. "All of our VIPs are at the ball," she said, as took a keycard from her bodice and unlocked the lounge doors.

As soon as they were alone inside, Regan turned the deadbolts. Arthur took control, pushing her onto her back on a hunter green leather sofa. He opened his trousers and pulled her gown to her waist. She was naked underneath her skirt.

"You planned this," he said.

"I wanted the waltz to be scandalous again. That's all. And this," she said, taking his cock in her hand. "I wanted this."

She pulled him down onto her. As soon as the head kissed her opening, he felt her wetness and knew she was as aroused as he was. He entered her with a thrust and her slick walls parted to receive him. He came up on his knees and with one hand on the arm of the sofa to brace himself, he rode her with quick rough thrusts. She was wet, soaking wet.

She bathed his aching organ with her slick fluids. He looked at her face, eyes closed and mouth open as she took it, took him. Her breaths were shallow, fast, her breasts rising and falling, straining against the bodice of her gown. He tugged the fabric down, freed one breast and latched immediately onto her nipple, sucking it, rubbing it with his tongue. It grew stiff in his mouth and he pulled on it, licked it to make it stiffer.

Regan lifted her hips in need—a miscalculation. Arthur grabbed them, held them and yanked her against him, splitting her on his cock and forcing a cry from her throat that revelers at the ball had to have heard. Her vagina spasmed on his as she came on him. While she was lost in her own pleasure, he let himself have his own, ramming her hard. He didn't want to hurt her. He just wanted to give it all to her, all of him—every inch, every thrust, every drop of come, all into her grasping little hole.

Regan's eyes opened as they were still moving together, slowing now, riding the wave of orgasm down, down, all the way down until they were still. Still, and still joined.

She winced as Arthur pulled out of her. "My gown."

He pulled a handkerchief from his pocket, pressed it to her vulva to catch his come before it left a stain on her dress. Gently he cleaned his sperm off and out of her and wished the smoking lounge wasn't so dark. He would have liked to have seen her in better light, open like this, dripping with his semen.

"That's enough," she said. "I think we've gotten most of it."

"My father taught me to never leave home without a handkerchief. I have to wonder now," Arthur said as he wadded up the linen square, "if this is why."

"From what I've heard about your father, yes."

Arthur half-laughed, half-groaned as he tidied his uniform as best he could. "Please don't remind me what whores my parents are."

"Happy whores from what I hear." Regan stood. She smoothed her gown back into place. "Madly in lust with each other, even now." She went to the liquor cabinet and poured herself a finger of whisky, neat.

"I walked in on them in the kitchen once," Arthur said. "Scarred for life."

"What were they doing?"

"Something less than seventy and more than sixty-eight."

"Ah. Poor Brat." She drank her whisky, then poured another. "You really aren't a typical Godwick, are you?"

"Why do you say that?" he asked as he walked around the lounge, contemplating how many uniform codes he'd just violated. The smoking lounge was every inch the Victorian gentleman's paradise. Dark wood paneling ornately carved with stags and boars and foxes and other noble beasts old men liked to murder.

"Oh, let's see. Your parents are rather notorious for being in a lust-filled yet open marriage. Your sister, if the rumors are true—"

"Whatever you've heard...it's probably true."

"She ran a little escort service of her own while at King's, didn't she?" When he didn't respond, she continued, "We've got Lord Malcolm, of course—as notorious as it gets. Even your grandmother was a bit of a lush, wasn't she? And Charlie's certainly following in the Godwick footsteps."

"My grandfather, the fourteenth Earl of Godwick, was notorious for not being notorious," he said, thinking of his namesake, Lord Arthur. "Dad says he was as stodgy, humorless, and pompous as they come. Until me."

"You aren't any of those things. You're..." She looked at him through narrowed eyes. "You're self-disciplined, strict with yourself. Unusual in someone your age. You're only twenty-one. Why aren't you out drinking all night in pubs and going to parties and clubs and all that?"

He turned his back to the bookshelves and leaned against them, arms crossed over his chest. "Because of Charlie."

She eyed him skeptically.

He continued, "When we were kids, ten and eight... there was a little winding river in the woods behind Wingthorn. I was mature enough, Mum and Dad trusted me to keep an eye on Charlie when we went out adventuring. One day in June, we were by the river and a tree had fallen across the water. Genius me decided to cross the tree trunk to the other side. It was mossy, slick. I fell in. Got my foot trapped under a branch. Nearly drowned."

"Good God."

He could still remember the panic, the immediate terror, thrashing in the ice-cold water, choking on it.

"Charlie was only eight," he said. "Just eight and he didn't hesitate one second. Went right in the river and worked my foot free. Did I mention he was only eight?"

"You mentioned it."

"Someone had heard us shouting and came running. When Mum got there, Charlie immediately lied and said he was the one who fell in and I'd saved him. I was too shocked to say anything, so I went along with it. Later that night I asked him why he'd lied. He said he didn't want me to get into trouble because if I did, Mum and Dad wouldn't trust me to watch him anymore. He'd rather get into trouble than lose me. Our parents still don't know the true story. Nobody does but Charlie and me. And now you."

"And you never did anything foolish or childish again in

your life, did you? Until me, that is." She raised her eyebrows.

He didn't argue. "You nearly get your baby brother killed, you'll never let your guard down again."

"So now it's your turn to save him from drowning."

"You'd do the same if you were me," Arthur said.

"It's not your fault if he drowns this time." Her voice was surprisingly kind coming from the woman who was holding Charlie's fate in her hands.

"Maybe it is and maybe it isn't, but that isn't going to stop me from diving in after him like he did for me."

She didn't argue further, only said, softly, "The moment you realize you're going to die someday is the moment your childhood ends."

That was it. He'd been ten years old when he'd learned that terrible truth, learned it with a bellyful of river water. That had been the end of his childhood, the end of even wanting to be a child, since to him it always meant letting his brother down.

"When did your childhood end?" Arthur asked.

"My mother died when I was four," she reminded him. "I never got to be a child."

The door handle rattled. Someone wanted in.

Arthur froze, looked at Regan. "Should we unlock the door?" he mouthed.

"No," she whispered. "I may make you fuck me again."

"Shouldn't we go back to the ball?"

"After." Then she called out, "Lounge closed for private party."

The door handle stopped rattling. They waited until the footsteps faded.

"So, are you going to force me to listen to another story about your sex life?" he said.

"I'll tell you one right now, if you'd like."

———

SHE SAT on the sofa and Arthur took the club chair opposite her. She was an absolute mystery to him, despite being a seemingly open book. He'd found photographs of her online from every year of her marriage to Sir Jack Ferry. Their hotels. Their charitable functions. A few high society weddings in Milan and Rome and New York. But something was amiss. Something beyond the trauma of a bad marriage, beyond the unconventional way she'd lost her virginity. Something that made her work too hard and drink too much.

"I cheated on Sir Jack only once in our entire marriage," she said, swirling her drink in her glass. "We were in New York dining at one of his hotels there. I saw a painting on the wall near our table and it was very good. I asked the waiter if he knew the artist, and he said it was one of their servers, a young woman. He told me a bit about her work, how she was in art school. That's all. When he stepped away from our table, Sir Jack quietly and calmly called me a disgusting tart for throwing myself at our waiter in front of my own husband." She laughed to herself. "All for something as innocent as asking the name of a painter."

Arthur wanted to hold her but didn't dare move. Her eyes told him she had only just begun her story.

"It was Fleet Week. Do you know what that is?"

He nodded. "When the U.S. Navy docks its ships in New York and other ports."

"Five years into our marriage...I thought I was immune to Sir Jack's insults," she said. "Apparently not. I ran from the restaurant, really ran and ran straight into a white wall."

"A white wall?"

"A Naval officer. Full dress whites, cap and everything. Executive officer on the *U.S.S. Something or Other.* An officer and a gentleman. I had never seen a more handsome man in my life. I don't even know if he was handsome or if he was just so kind that he might as well have been wearing a golden halo. He offered to take me up to my room. I said I couldn't go there, never wanted to go there again. We went to his room instead."

She took a sip of her drink.

"I seduced him," she said. "It was easy enough. He asked what he could do to help me. I said he could make love to me."

Another drink.

"He knew I was married. I didn't lie to him. He said a man who would treat a woman that badly didn't deserve to be married. Maybe it was a line, but it was a line I needed to hear. After the sex, he gave me a bath so I wouldn't go back to Sir Jack 'smelling like a sailor,' he said. That evening with him was the first tenderness I'd felt in years. I can still see him in the lobby of the hotel, like something out of a dream. When I saw you in your uniform at my door, it brought it all back in an instant."

She put her elbow on the sofa arm and leaned her head against her hand. "I suppose that's not a very sexy story though," she continued. She smiled but Arthur saw through it. "No virgin girls in white socks getting spanked with Ben Wa balls inside of them."

"What can I do to help you?" he said.

"You can't help me."

"Why not?"

She looked away and he followed her eyes to a painting hanging on the wall by the door. Nothing special, just a ship sailing away from the shore. "Because no one can help me. Not even King Arthur. Not even Lieutenant Godwick."

"Regan, what's wrong?"

She smiled at him. "Nothing. Nothing and everything."

"That's not helpful."

"You're not here to help me."

"Then what am I here for?"

"To make me forget for a few minutes that no one can help me."

"Then I'll do that," he said.

Slowly she stood and set her empty glass on the side table. She came to him and stood in front of the chair, where she gathered her gown and lifted it. Arthur pulled her down onto his lap. Clothes were pushed aside, his cock hardened, and he slipped easily inside her still-damp cleft.

Regan rested her chin on his shoulder and wrapped her arms around his neck. He unzipped her gown and lowered it to her waist. He licked her nipples, sucked them, as she moved on him slowly, slow enough he could count her breaths. And from the ballroom came the sounds of a Viennese waltz as she sunk down onto him and rose in time with the music.

One, two, three... One, two, three...

5

_____

BLACK IRIS

Arthur woke from heavy sleep Monday morning. His phone on the bedside table vibrated loud as a jackhammer in his ear. He saw it was his sister, declined the call and shoved his phone under his pillow.

He wasn't surprised to hear it beep a few moments later, warning him he had a text message.

The message was simple. Only two words, all caps, plus punctuation.

REGAN FERRY?!?!

Arthur groaned and rubbed his forehead. The hunt ball had only been two nights ago. Gossip really did fly faster than the speed of light.

He replied with two words. No punctuation.

Regan Ferry.

The next text summed up his sister's thoughts on the matter—two thumbs-up emojis.

Arthur tried to return to the dream he'd been having before Lia's call woke him. In the dream Regan was on his old bed at Wingthorn, naked but for white lace-trimmed socks on his white sheets with the red pinstripes. She'd been on her hands and knees and he was in her from behind. All good. All very good. Except while they were having sex, she said something to him like, "Don't stop or I'll die."

He'd laughed at that, but she hadn't laughed. She'd said it again, like she meant it. *Don't stop or I'll die.* So he'd fucked her harder, deeper, as if he would never stop.

Arthur wanted to go back to sleep and find out what she meant by that, but now it was too late. The bloody front doorbell was ringing. First the phone. Then the doorbell. Why did the universe not want him to finish the most intensely erotic dream he'd had in his life?

Quickly he yanked on his jeans and a t-shirt and went down to the front door. He knew exactly who he'd find there, and he was right. Regan's redcoat was waiting on the front steps.

"Can't she send an email?" Arthur said to Zoot. "A text? A carrier pigeon?"

"She says to come at eight tonight, and you can pick the painting."

"I can pick the painting?"

"That's what she said."

"Anything else?"

"Your shirt's on inside out."

Arthur looked down. Yes. His t-shirt was definitely on inside-out. Seams for miles.

"It's a viscount thing," he said. "You wouldn't understand."

"I understand you're a daft prick, but the boss likes you, so sod me and my opinions from now to next Thursday, I guess."

"That's an extraordinary amount of sodomy," Arthur said.

"I can take it," she said, and spun on her red Wellie to leave.

Arthur stopped her on the steps by calling her name.

"What?" she asked, facing him again.

"Is Regan...okay?" he asked.

Zoot scrunched up her face, looking confused as if she'd asked him if Regan occasionally transformed into a werewolf. "She's all right, far as I know."

"You're sure? I'm not asking for gossip."

She grinned. "Yeah you are."

"Fine. So I am. But only because she sometimes says things that make me wonder. She's not depressed or anything?" He wasn't sure what he was asking. All he had was a hunch that there was something moving under the surface of Regan's tough exterior, a deep current of sorrow or maybe even fear?

"She's been in a better mood than I've seen her in a long time. Hasn't threatened to sack me all week."

"And that's unusual?"

"I usually get the boot twice a day."

"Only twice?"

Zoot pointed at his face. "Brat," she said, then turned and stalked off again.

Arthur called after her, "I like your coat."

The reply came in the form of her two fingers in the shape of a V.

Eight o'clock was a full day away. And the sun was out —a rarity in London in November. Arthur went for a long run followed by a full English breakfast. Buoyed by the knowledge he'd get to see Regan again tonight, he decided to brave texting Charlie.

THAT AFTERNOON, Arthur put on his black jacket and boots and set out across Hyde Park. Not only had his brother texted him back, but Charlie had agreed to meet him for tea.

The plane trees that filled the park were in full color— a mottled yellow and red. The oaks had gone red and orange and the paths were littered with fallen leaves, every color of autumn. They crunched under his boots as he strode past tourists taking photographs on their phones.

His dream had cast a strange pall over the day. It was erotic, yes, and he'd liked it (of course), but it had left him unsettled, the way too-vivid dreams could. In the dream, Regan had spoken with such honesty that he'd believed her, that she really would die the second their bodies parted. And it hadn't been erotic exaggeration on her part. It had been the truth.

At that moment, he realized he hadn't been having a dream but a nightmare. What unsettled him wasn't that it was a nightmare, but that it was a nightmare from which he hadn't wanted to awake.

He blamed the dream on the conversation they'd had in The Pearl's old smoking lounge, about how learning about death was the end of childhood. That was all. Fitting that the dream took place at Wingthorn Hall. She was just like their famous roses, loved not for their petals but their enormous thorns.

A young couple from Japan interrupted his reverie, and he was glad for the chance to shake off the dream. Smiling kindly, they asked if he would take their photo in front of the Serpentine, the bridge in the background. The Serpentine had been a pet project of Queen Caroline, one of Arthur's many exalted ancestors on his father's side. Could they imagine that the random man they'd asked to take their picture shared DNA with kings and queens, lords and knights?

They didn't. They couldn't. And he liked them the better for it. They might have found someone else to ask if they'd known he was the titled son of a wealthy earl and not, as he appeared, just a lad in his early twenties, probably a university student, out for a walk.

He had never taken his "noble" ancestry seriously. His paternal grandmother had been quite a genealogist and kept the family tree updated. To Arthur, his ancestors had nothing to do with him. Yes, so a great-grand-great-whatever grandfather had fought beside King Henry the Eighth in the Battle of the Spurs. Meanwhile, his mother's grandmother had worked as a typist at a publisher in New York City. She'd moved up from typist to editorial assistant to editor-in-chief by her death and imbued a working-class family with a love of the arts and literature.

That impressed Arthur much more than his rich and titled relatives on his father's side. They'd been born rich, stayed rich, and died rich. Or, in the case of Lord Malcolm's generation, had been born land rich and cash poor, which inspired his great-great grandmother to force Malcolm into a marriage to the daughter of a war profiteer with blood money to spare.

Was that noble? Really? Did someone who'd sell a free-spirited son into a loveless marriage to the daughter of a man who'd made his fortune manufacturing mustard gas really deserve the title of "Lady"? Did Malcolm, a man who'd spent the last of his family's fortune on paintings and prostitutes really deserve the title of "Lord"?

They were all whores, weren't they? No wonder Arthur took so naturally to selling himself. It was a Godwick family tradition.

Charlie was waiting for him at a table in the corner at The Tea Room. Arthur was glad to see he looked well-rested, much better than he had last time he saw him, even flirting with a girl at another table. Charlie was a good-looking lad, a "pretty boy" as girls had said. Rust-colored hair—he took after their father in that—and blue eyes. He'd already ordered scones with jam and clotted cream, and they were mostly gone when Arthur sat down.

"How're the scones here?" Arthur asked as he reached for the teapot.

Charlie shrugged. "What did you want?"

"Didn't want anything. I'm allowed to see if you're all right, right?"

"Fine."

"You sure?"

"I said I was."

Arthur sighed. How had it gotten like this between them? They'd been best mates for sixteen years. Then, suddenly, it was as if someone flipped a switch and Charlie decided to hate him, hate himself, hate everyone and everything.

"I did want to ask you something," Arthur said. "Did Regan ever—"

"Who?"

"Regan Ferry? The lady you're in hock to for a hundred grand?"

"The girls just called her the boss."

"Right. So. Did the boss ever say anything to you about our family? She made it clear to me she's got a grudge against us that has nothing to do with your 'hotel' tab."

"We didn't talk much." Charlie stared at his plate. "She just said I had to pay my bill. When I told her I didn't have the money and it would take me forever to get it, she said she'd take the painting of old Malcolm. I told her Mum and Dad loved that painting. You know why."

Yes, Arthur knew why...not that he believed it. Not really. Except he never loved being alone in a room with Lord Malcolm's painting, the feeling that he was always being watched by those dark eyes far too much like his own.

"You offered her a Degas? A Picasso?"

"I offered her the bloody Rembrandt, Art. She wanted Malcolm. I knew Mum and Dad would kill me later when they found out, but if I didn't give her what she wanted...I was afraid, okay? I thought it would at least buy me some time to figure out an alternative."

Charlie played with the crumbs on his plate, piling them into a little hill.

"Anything else?" Arthur asked.

Charlie shook his head. He picked up the tea pot, but it was empty.

"I can get us more tea," Arthur said.

"Don't bother."

"No, I'll get it."

"We could go to a pub."

"At three in the afternoon? Can you not manage one day sober?"

"Can you not manage one day without treating me like a child?"

Arthur stared at him for a beat. Then he said, "What did I ever do to you except clean up all your disasters? Do you have any idea what I'm doing for you to keep you out of trouble?"

"Shagging her, right? Poor you."

Arthur scoffed. "It's a little more than that."

"You want me to give you a medal?"

"You could at least say thank you."

"Don't pretend you're doing me any favors," Charlie said. "You got exactly what you wanted—one more reason to hate me."

Charlie got up and left without another word.

The waitress brought Arthur the bill. As usual, he paid for them both.

WHEN ZOOT ANSWERED the penthouse door, she dropped into a low and surprisingly graceful curtsy. "Good evening, my lord," she said. "You're early."

"Good evening, my lady," Arthur said with an equally sarcastic but well-executed bow. "I am."

That got a small, almost sincere smile out of Zoot. He entered, carrying a small framed art print wrapped in canvas. It was seven-thirty. Traffic had been light, and he didn't feel like waiting in the lobby now that he'd been seen waltzing with Regan. He hoped she'd forgive him being early this once.

"The boss lady's in her private office. This way," Zoot said, showing him to a small room down the hall to the left of the fireplace. She knocked on the door, but didn't wait for an answer before opening it. "Lady Ferry, Lord Dogshit here to see you," she announced.

Regan was seated behind an enormous ornately carved mahogany desk. A lion's head was carved into the front panel, with lion's paws for the feet.

"Thank you, Zoot," Regan said, barely glancing up from her papers. "Is it eight already?"

"He's early, Boss," she said before slipping out the door, leaving them alone.

Regan's hair was in a French plait again, falling elegantly over her shoulder. She wore a black dress, short with a deep V neckline. A long strand of pearls was looped twice around her neck, first flush with her throat and then dangling between her breasts. He couldn't stop staring at her. The dream of them endlessly fucking came back to him in a rush that left his heart racing. If she'd let him, he'd have her on her desk right that second.

"Nice desk," he said, trying to focus on anything but sex.

"Your great-grandfather's," she said. "When he died, the hotel seized his belongings since he owed The Pearl so much money. Unfortunately he didn't leave the keys to the desk. You don't have his old keys, do you? I've been trying to get into the bottom drawer for years."

He heard her toeing the drawer with the tip of her shoe.

"I'll ask Dad, but I don't think so," he said.

Zoot stuck her head in the door. "Going now unless you need anything more?" She pointed a thumb at Arthur. "Want me to show this one out?"

"No, thank you," Regan said breezily.

"You sure?"

"Very sure."

"You sure you're sure?"

"Zoot. Goodnight."

"Night, Boss." In an exaggerated posh accent, she added to Arthur, "And prithee goodnight, my lord and liege."

"Ta," Arthur said. When he heard the penthouse door close, he turned back to Regan. "I don't think she likes me very much."

"What was your first clue?" Regan said, flipping through some files.

"Any particular reason why or just general animosity toward men and/or the nobility?"

"It's your average everyday case of jealousy," Regan replied. "She likes me. She thinks I like you more."

"You treat me like a whore," he said.

"Yes, but you like being treated like a whore. Therefore, I treat you the way you want to be treated, so you can hardly complain, can you?"

He thought for a moment, but had no comeback.

"I would apologize that you have to watch me finish up my work for the day, but that's what happens when you don't follow instructions," she said, closing her laptop. "Finished. Or close enough. Wine?"

"Please."

She left to fetch a bottle. Arthur took a book from the shelf and flipped through it. Regan returned with a Rosanella Syrah and two glasses. She took a corkscrew out of her desk drawer.

"Were these all your textbooks from LOCAD?" Arthur asked, showing her the cover of the book he held. *A History of Modern Art*. Every last book on her shelves was about art or a famous artist, technique guides, art histories...There were even large padded envelopes sitting on the floor by the shelves, recent purchases. One had a label from Prestel, another from Phaidon. Famous art book publishers. New additions to her collection, apparently.

He looked at Regan. She pulled the cork from the bottle, and didn't meet his eyes when she replied. "How did you know I went to LOCAD?"

"I Googled you."

She shook her head. "A few are old textbooks," she

said, pouring two glasses. "The rest I've bought over the years."

"Why did you quit art school?"

"Got married."

"Did you want to quit, or did Sir Jack make you?"

"He didn't make me do anything. I always had a choice. Either do what he wanted and stay married, or I could do what I wanted and get tossed out on my arse. My decision."

He might have argued with that but knew better than to try. "Do you still paint?"

"Haven't in years. What little talent I had is long gone. If you don't feed your muses, they'll find someone else who will."

"You have a tattoo of a quote about art being eternal on your wrist. And you just...quit?"

"I got the tattoo at seventeen. How many people grow up to do what they wanted to do when they were seventeen?"

That was a fair point. At seventeen, he'd considered moving to New York and working at The Red Gallery. At twenty-one, now, he was freshly out of Sandhurst and off to join the British Army in two months.

"Do you have any of your old paintings still? I'd love to see your work."

Before she could answer, they were interrupted by an odd tapping sound. Arthur looked past Regan at the window. The raven was perched on the windowsill.

"The baby's home. Eight on the dot as usual," Regan said, glancing at the slim gold watch on her wrist. She seemed relieved to have the distraction. "He'll want his supper. You can wait here."

She strode past him just as Arthur felt his phone buzz in his trouser pocket. He took it out. A text from Charlie.

I forgot something. When Regan got the painting, she stared at it for like forever and I asked her what was wrong, and she said something about how she'd had a very strange dream about Malcolm once and he was wearing the same suit in her dream as he was in the portrait.

Regan had dreamed about Lord Malcolm? She was staying in his old flat now, and had to have seen photographs of him in the hotel archives. Surely it was just a dream, as his dream this morning had been nothing but a dream.

Arthur replied to his brother. *You didn't mention anything to her about how Mum and Dad think the painting's haunted, right?*

Charlie wrote back, *I'm a fuck-up, not an idiot. Course not.*

Arthur replied with a simple, *Thank you.*

No surprise when he didn't get a reply to that.

Arthur went out to the garden terrace to find Regan. He followed a lantern-lit path to the bird perch, where Gloom was happily dipping his enormous black beak into a bowl of raw and bloody meat.

"I begin to understand," Arthur said, "the origins of the term 'raven-ously.'"

"Hungry little buggers, aren't they? Ravens originally came to London from the country, drawn to the carcasses of animals that used to float along the Thames from the slaughterhouses."

"But a *pet* raven," Arthur said. "How does that happen?"

Regan looked over her shoulder, smiled at him. She held out her arm and let the bird climb onto her wrist. "Gloom landed on the terrace with a bent wing, and I brought in a wildlife rehabilitator to help him. Ravens have wonderful memories for humans who help them."

"Does he bite?"

"Of course. Better to get bitten by a hawk than a raven. See?" She held out her right hand to show a pale white scar near her wrist. "He nipped me good and hard when I had to catch him that first day he landed with the broken wing."

"That must have hurt." He touched the scar, gently caressing it. "But you kept him anyway."

"He was scared. Animals bite when they're scared."

"Is that why you bite, because you're scared?"

She stroked Gloom lightly across the back of his head. Then she turned to Arthur. Her stare was dark, cold. "I know you're trying to make me like you," she said. "It won't happen."

"I think it's happening."

"It will *never* happen."

He lowered his voice to a haunted house whisper. "It's already begun..."

That got her to laugh, a little. A very little, but still he counted it as a win.

"Come on, Brat," she said. "Time to work off more of your brother's debt." She left her bird to his bloody feast and went back into the suite.

SHE OPENED the door to the red and gold bedroom and let him inside. The first thing he saw was his great-grandfather's portrait hanging across from the bed, uncovered. He groaned.

"Don't ask me to cover him up again," Regan said. She

went to the fireplace and turned on the gas. "You'll simply have to get used to having an audience."

"He's my great-grandfather. Having him here is the exact opposite of taking Viagra."

"He's a man you've never even met, who has been dead for over eighty years."

"Fine. Leave it," Arthur said. "Let's put on a show."

"He'd appreciate that. Loved to watch other people fucking almost as much as he loved being watched, I hear."

"This is not helping me to get aroused here," Arthur reminded her.

"You're already half-hard in your jeans. Don't deny it."

"Half? Maybe a third."

She pointed at the parcel he was still clutching. "Is that the artwork you brought to play in honor of dear old Great-Granddad?"

"I did. Sort of. It's only a signed lithograph. We have a Georgia O'Keeffe, but skulls aren't nearly as erotic as her flowers."

He unwrapped it and Regan set it atop the fireplace mantel. The painting was called *Black Iris III*—an iris, painted in extreme closeup, its petals a lurid purple, so dark they almost look black. And the flower was open, blooming, wide and trembling.

"A boy never forgets his first O'Keeffe," he said.

"Yes, because it looks like an enormous engorged cunt."

"It's a very nice enormous engorged cunt."

She looked at him, eyebrow slightly raised. "I think that's the first time I've heard you say the word 'cunt' in my presence."

"Might be the first time I've ever said it out loud.

When you're the son of Spencer Godwick, you rebel by *not* being rude."

"I like it. You should say it more. Use it in a sentence."

"Now?"

She nodded.

"Ah...I would like to do very nice things to your cunt."

"Now a question."

"May I please do very nice things to your cunt?"

Regan came to him, stood in front of him. "Yes," she said. "You may do very nice things to my cunt."

"I serve at your pleasure," he said almost reflexively.

"Yes, yes you do." She put her hands on his shoulders and leaned back, smiling at the portrait of Lord Malcolm. "Did you hear that, Malcolm? I've turned your great-grandson into a whore. Who are you prouder of? Him or me?"

Arthur sighed. He really wished she would stop talking to the painting. It wouldn't be good if it started talking back...

She cupped Arthur's crotch. "That's more than a third. I suppose having Great-Granddad here isn't as much of a mood-killer as you thought."

She kissed him, and no amount of wounded male pride could keep from kissing her back. She wasn't cruel to him so much as she was just...cold. And the colder she was to him, the more he wanted to warm her. And the more he wanted to warm her, the colder she was to him. Even this, hanging his great-grandfather's portrait was cruel, made him feel vulnerable, exposed. She alone knew how much he loved being exposed.

He returned the kiss, pushing his tongue into her mouth, tasting her.

"You like this so much," she murmured against his lips,

laughing between kisses. "You like being treated like this and I love it. I love it and you hate it."

"I hate that I love it," he said soft as a penitent giving his confession. He wrapped his fingers around her long pearl necklace and lightly, lightly, oh-so lightly tugging on it to make sure he had her attention. "But I like that you like it."

If only she liked him a little. Maybe? She smiled, a real one, not mocking and it was gone as fast as it had come. "Get on your knees," she commanded.

She said it, so he did it. He released his grip on her pearls and went down onto his knees. As soon as he was there, he realized this is where he'd wanted to be all along.

"You whore," she said, tilting his chin up so he faced her. "Did I make you like this? Or were you like this before me?"

"I was like this before you, but I don't want to be like this after you."

"Why not? You're enjoying it as much as I am."

"I just... I don't." If he could have waved a wand to make it go away, he would have waved it like a drowning man signaling for help. Once Regan was done with him, who would treat him like this? Who could he trust to tell that he needed it? How would he find someone who made him feel the things Regan made him feel?

"Who told you this was wrong?" she asked him.

He shot her a confused look. "I don't understand."

"Someone must have gotten it in your head that this, what we're doing, is wrong, bad, the sort of thing real men don't do? Who was it?"

"Nobody. You know the Godwicks. We're one big happy whoring family."

Regan stared him down, but he refused to be goaded

into answering. "Do you want to keep glaring at me," he asked, "or do you want me to make you come?"

"Well, when you put it that way," she said and finally smiled. Then she grabbed him hard by the chin, hard enough he knew she'd leave red marks from the rough grip of her fingers. "But make it good."

He met her eyes. "I'll make it good."

GENTLY, he pressed his mouth to her stomach and felt the soft muscles fluttering. His hands found her ankles, fragile and birdlike. He stroked up her bare legs, up her calves, up her thighs, under her little black dress to her little black lace pants underneath. He held her soft small arse in his hands, kissed her stomach through her dress and slowly pulled her knickers down. When they were at her ankles, she lightly kicked them aside. Then she stepped back and sat on the edge of the bed.

She crooked her finger and he crawled across the floor. It was only a yard, but it felt like a mile on a public street, just from the humiliation of it. The delicious humiliation.

It was worth it for the reward at the finish line, to push her thighs apart and press between them. He lifted the skirt of her dress and tucked it under her to keep it out of his way. There she was, the soft light brown hair on her mound and the seam he'd touched and fucked but hadn't tasted yet. He buried his face against her warm thighs, inhaling the light musky scent of her arousal. He kissed the curls of her sex as he pushed her legs wider. His fingers found the slit of her vulva and he stroked it slowly, carefully. Then he opened the folds, parting them like petals. And they *were* like petals, silky and warm as if in sunlight.

He spread the folds of her labia wider. His mouth watered. Lowering his head, he pressed his tongue to her vulva, tasting his first drop of her. One drop wasn't enough, so he licked her, drawing his tongue up and receiving as his reward Regan's arm around the back of his head, her hand in his hair.

"More," she said, a quiet and gentle order. She wanted more, and she would get more.

Arthur cupped her bottom again and tilted her toward him. She accommodated, spreading her legs farther apart on the bed so that her thighs fell wide, wide open.

The light from the bedside lamp showed her cunt in all its glory as he pulled the labia apart again, spreading them open. Regan's breathing quickened. She liked this, being opened, being seen. Had her old husband even been able to fuck her, or had he just kept her on his arm to make the world think he could satisfy a woman like Regan?

Her clitoris was hidden under a little shield of skin. He lightly rubbed around it, the tips of his two fingers on either side, kneading it in circles. She inhaled a long breath and held it. The tight knot of flesh swelled under his touch and in the lamplight he could see the clitoris itself starting to come out from hiding. As carefully as he could, he pulled that hood of flesh back, exposing the tiny knot. He brought the very, very tip of his tongue to it. Regan gasped at the gentle contact. He licked it again, a little harder and then again, again, again. Her clitoris swelled more, blooming before his eyes.

He pushed a finger inside her. She was slick and scalding hot. He needed more of that heat on him. He pushed in a second finger, then a third. Was there anything more exquisite than her open cunt wrapped around his hand? If she'd been more open, he might have tried working his entire fist inside of her. But she was too taut, too tight. He pushed against the clenching muscles inside her and they pushed back.

"Are you seeing this, Lord Malcolm?" Regan said. She was speaking to the painting, but her gaze was locked on Arthur's eyes. "You see how your family has fallen? You used to buy women for your pleasure like a boy in a candy shop, and now your heir is worshipping at the cunt of the great-granddaughter of a whore."

Her arrogant tone was like petrol tossed on a fire. Arthur's cock throbbed inside his pants. As he licked her cunt, he unzipped his jeans, freed his erection from the confines of his clothes. He wanted to climb on her, mount and enter her...but he didn't, of course, though the urge to fill her was painfully strong, to release into her ropes of thick white come and then to pull out and watch his own semen drip out of her...

Arthur kissed a path up her body, up her belly, coming up high on his knees and kissing her neck. He took the long string of pearls around her neck and started to take them off of her.

"What are you doing?" she asked.

"You told me to make it good."

She gave him a look but didn't argue and surrendered her pearls to him. Her face was flushed. Her pupils were so wide and dilated, she had black irises, just as she'd wanted.

He kissed her once on the mouth, letting her taste herself before going down on his knees again.

The pearls were heavy in his hand. True saltwater pearls, a fortune in pearls. He poured them into his hand, and they filled his entire fist.

He pushed her thighs open again, kissed and licked her

clitoris until she was moaning. But it wasn't enough to make her moan. He wanted her to scream.

Arthur began to push the pearls into her cunt.

At first it was clear she didn't understand what he was doing. Then at once, she rose up on her elbows. She didn't say anything, didn't stop him, just watched. He glanced at her and saw her face, her eyes, looking at her own open cunt, her thighs wide, heels braced on the edge of the bed.

Pearl by pearl, inch by inch, he pushed the strand into her, filling her hole with enough pearls to pay a year's rent on a two-bedroom flat in Mayfair. And she let him.

She lay back as more pearls filled her, too many to count. She lay back and let him push the entire long strand into her. It took time. God knows how long, but she lay there and panted while he did it, panted and pulled at the bedcovers. He saw her fingers nearly tearing the silk as she twisted her hands into the fabric.

"Too much?" he asked.

"Too much. It's perfect."

And that was Regan. Enough was not enough. Too much was perfect. He pushed in the last of the loop. Her lips were wide apart, her hole as dilated as her eyes. The small shining white beads were visible inside her, her inner muscles expanding and contracting to accommodate them. He pressed his hand flat over her opening to keep them from being pushed out.

Then he licked her clitoris again. It was so swollen he didn't even have to hold the hood back to get to the naked organ. Regan's hips rose in tight and tiny undulations. She was coming undone, utterly undone. Her breathing grew louder, and her head writhed on the bed. She made sounds, lovely pained sounds. She didn't ask him to stop, instead spreading her legs wider.

He licked her hard. She was long gone now. He thought about stopping—to punish her, to turn the tables. But it would have punished him more to stop licking her, kneading her pulsing little clit with his tongue as she pushed her hips up and into his mouth.

She came with a sudden jerk of her body and a loud cry. Her head rose off the bed, head and shoulders, before she fell back panting, still softly moaning. She went limp and Arthur let the pearls begin to fall out of her body, one loop dangling out a few inches. He caught the loop in his finger —the pearls were damp—and gently he pulled on them, emptying her out. Her vagina gave little gasps, little twitches. He gathered the long string of her pearls into his hands as he pulled them out of her and then she was empty. He stood and gazed down on her, her dress ruched up to her waist, her eyes closed, her body listless and spent.

Arthur pushed his cock into her dripping opening and when she didn't stop him, he entered her with a stroke. Her cunt was open now, supple and soft against his cock. It was ecstasy to feel her body taking every inch of him without any resistance. He was bathed in heat and wetness. She lay motionless under him, insensate, eyes half-closed, letting him have her. He pounded fast, rutting on her, ashamed of his lack of self-control but not ashamed enough to stop. His thrusts were pistons firing fast and hard and it was only seconds before he started to come. He pulled out. Gripping his cock in his hand, he came on Regan's neck. Spurts of semen landed white and wet on her glistening olive skin, on her chest, in the hollow of her throat, and each spurt harder and stronger than the last.

When he'd finished emptying himself out onto her, he

looked at her, at what he'd done, he decided he'd seen no work of art in the world more magnificent than this woman wearing his come.

"I'll clean you off," he said. "Lay there."

"No," she said. "Leave it."

He slid to his knees again and rested his head on her lower stomach. Regan slowly moved her legs, spreading them again. She sat up, still wearing his come and opened her vulva wide open for him. Her cunt was a livid red, almost purple, tender from how hard he'd used her and supple enough to spread out wide as an iris in bloom.

She touched his burning face. "Well done, Brat."

He kissed her thigh. She dug her hands into his hair and stroked it tenderly. Then she picked up the pearls and examined them.

"I'll clean your pearls," he said, smiling sheepishly. "I promise."

She put them on over her head and let them settle around her glistening neck and tits.

"No," she said. "I think I'll wear them just like this."

6

WOMAN WITH A PEARL NECKLACE

R egan sent him to fetch their wine from her office while she cleaned herself—and, presumably, her pearls as well.

Arthur winced slightly as he took the winding staircase. His still-damp penis was tender from the rough fucking. Though it was painful, it wasn't entirely unpleasant. His body was alive with feeling, right down to the bottoms of his naked feet on the cool, polished wood of the steps. He liked this new awareness of his body, this new sensation of having a body for a reason other than carrying his brain around town. To please Regan, that's what his body was for—his fingers, his tongue, his hands, his lips and his cock and come—all for her. And what he'd just done to her to please her...

He couldn't believe that had been him in her bedroom. In this place, in this private little world of theirs in The Pearl, no one could see him or mock him or judge him or laugh at him. No one but Regan. Regan, the woman whom he wanted to see him, to mock him, to judge him, to laugh at him. He would have to thank Charlie down the road for his bad decisions. Some good had finally come of them.

The penthouse was dark and quiet. When he found the door to Regan's office, he switched on her desk lamp to see where they'd left their abandoned bottle of wine.

A heavy art book lay on the floor next to one of the bookshelves. It was open, having landed on its spine. Had he knocked it off earlier? He bent to pick it up, but stopped, when he saw it had fallen open to a painting.

His peace, his contentment, his afterglow...it all evaporated in an instant.

"Are you hungry, Brat? I can call—" Regan was standing in the doorway to her office. She had slipped on her kimono and followed him down. She looked at the book on the floor, then back at him kneeling beside it. "Were you reading? You were supposed to be getting—"

"I turned on the light, and found this book on the floor open to this page."

Regan stepped into the office and bent down to pick up the book. She drew her hand back, gasping, as if the book had burned her.

"Arthur." Not Brat. *Arthur*.

The book lay open to a full-color, full-page reproduction of a Mary Cassatt painting, a painting of a beautiful woman sitting in a box at the opera. Beautiful hair, beautiful gown.

Beautiful pearl necklace. That was the name of the painting—*Woman with a Pearl Necklace.*

"Is this a joke?" she asked. "It's not very funny."

"I was about to ask you the same question," he said, but he could already tell she hadn't left it out for him as some sort of prank or mind game. The confusion in her eyes was too real. Either she was scared to her bones or she was an actress worthy of both a BAFTA and an Oscar.

"Was someone watching us?" Her voice was low, scared and her eyes were wide, clouded with grey fear. "Someone had to have been watching us. How else would they know..."

How else would they know Arthur had, moments earlier, given Regan a very special "pearl necklace" of his very own?

Arthur scooped up the book. It was heavy. Too heavy to simply flutter off a shelf. He closed the book and handed it to Regan.

"Call hotel security," he said. "I'll look around."

HEART RACING, Arthur left her in the office and began a sweep of the penthouse. Regan had money, jewelry, expensive artworks. And hotels weren't known for their air-tight security, what with half the staff having keys to get into every room. But if someone had broken in while they'd been upstairs, why taunt them? Unless it was personal...

His first stop was the galley kitchen, where he picked up a knife. No one in the kitchen or the butler's pantry. No one in the bathroom downstairs. No one in the sitting room or dining room. He returned to her bedroom, where he snagged his clothes—no one there either.

What if they were overreacting? Books fell off shelves all the time, of course. Not by themselves, but he could have bumped it when he was talking to Charlie. He'd had a little wine by then. But for the book to land open to a painting of a woman in a pearl necklace? It couldn't be a coincidence.

Arthur started for the French doors to the garden terrace, determined to search every corner of the penthouse.

"No," Regan said. She'd come into the sitting room. "Don't go out there. Security's on their way up."

He hesitated. He was certain if someone was still here, they would be on the darkened terrace, where there were plenty of hiding places behind the plants and trees.

"I need to check—"

"No," she said, her tone stern. "Stay with me. That's an order." Then desperately, she said, "Please. Please stay."

Regan still had the Cassatt book clutched to her chest. He sat on the arm of the club chair and took her by the hips, pulling her close to him. "Could it have been Zoot?"

"She left," Regan said, shaking her head. Not so much to say no, but to show she was baffled. "I was in the office with you when I sent her home, remember?"

"I heard the door close, but that doesn't mean—"

"She follows orders. If I tell her to go, she goes. And she doesn't have a key."

A knock sounded on the door, strong and steady. "Ma'am? Security."

"I'll get it," Arthur said. He went and opened the door. Two large male security officers in blue uniforms, one white and in his forties, one Black and in his twenties, entered the penthouse.

"Lady Ferry?" the young Black man said. His name tag read DAVID J. "Someone was in here, you say?"

Arthur watched as Regan quickly transformed herself from a frightened young woman and back into the boss lady. Her spine straightened and she dropped her arms to her side. Her voice was calm as she explained the situation, leaving out a few salient points about exactly what they'd been doing upstairs—although in their state of dishevelment, it wasn't much of a mystery.

As the guards searched the suite and the garden terrace, Arthur poured a drink for Regan, two fingers of whisky neat, and sat with her on the chaise in front of the fireplace.

She took a sip of her drink and stared at him over top the rim of the glass. "You were alone in my office when I went out to feed Gloom."

"For about thirty seconds, texting with Charlie. Not reading..." He glanced at the book's cover. "Not reading *The School of Paris—A Survey of Nineteenth Century Female Painters*. I couldn't even tell you where it came from on your shelves."

"You were texting with Charlie?"

"Yes. I wasn't flipping through that book, planning to..." He lowered his voice to a whisper and leaned closer. "...*violate* you with your own pearl necklace and then—"

"Give me one?"

He saw a flash of light on the terrace, the guard David out there with his torch.

"Show me your phone," she said.

"Regan, I would never—"

"Just show me."

He'd left his jacket on the arm of the club chair. He found it and took his mobile out. She extended her hand and he gave her his phone, praying there was nothing too embarrassing on there. He told her his code and she read his messages with a blank expression on her face.

Then she returned the phone to him.

"Gloom was at the window at eight," he said. "You said so yourself. You checked your watch and said, 'eight on the dot.' The messages were also at eight—"

"Relax, Brat," she said. She took another drink of her whisky. "I just wanted to make sure you were telling him good things about me."

The guards returned. David, the young guard, looked tense.

"Nobody around," he said. He spoke quickly in a strong Northern accent. "Didn't find anything and we searched every inch. No one's taken the lift up here but us in the past hour. Nobody on the cams in the halls either."

"No one on the cameras?" Regan repeated. "You're absolutely certain?"

"Not a soul," David said. "It was just the book, right? Nothing taken?"

"Not that I could tell," she said, bunching her necklace nervously in her palm. "It's only...it seemed like a threat or a message, you see. Arthur and I were discussing my pearl necklace in one room and in the other room, someone left a book open to a woman with a pearl necklace. It sounds mad when I say it out loud." She gave a weak smile.

"You sure you didn't knock it off accidentally? Or maybe the walls were shaking? From the wind maybe?"

It wasn't windy and Arthur thought the guard deserved a raise for keeping a straight face when he asked that.

"Well, there's nobody here but us, ma'am," the young guard continued. "So if there was someone here, they either jumped off the terrace, or you got a ghost."

Arthur glanced upstairs. Regan nodded, and dismissed the guards with thanks. They promised to check the perimeter and keep an eye on the cameras, even post a guard if she wanted. She didn't want that. They left.

When they were gone and Arthur and Regan were alone again, she looked and him and said, "Tell me everything about that painting of Lord Malcolm. Now."

BACK IN HER BEDROOM, Regan stood at the fireplace while Arthur sat on the edge of the bed facing her. She still held the book in her arms, clutching it to her chest like a child, one finger in the page as a bookmark.

"I guess it starts twenty-five years ago, when my parents met," he began. "My mother owned a gallery in New York in the nineties—The Red. The way she tells the story, she had a dream about a man with black hair and black eyes in a three-piece suit who told her to check the bed knobs in the brass bed in storage at the gallery. She did, and inside the bedposts were a few paintings. One Picasso, some sketches, but also Lord Malcolm's official family portrait."

They both glanced toward the portrait on the wall.

Arthur continued, "Finding a lost Picasso worth millions rolled up in the post of an old bed is the sort of thing that makes international news. My father saw the story in the paper. It included a photograph of Lord Malcolm's portrait, too. Dad hopped on the first flight to New York. Mum refused to sell the painting to him. No matter how much he offered, she wouldn't accept it. Said she'd never give the painting up. Where she went, it went —the end.

"She was young and beautiful, and he was, well, my father. He picked Mum up, threw her over his shoulder, and carried both her and the painting out to his car. He said he intended to marry her, and that everything she owned—including the painting—would be his, and all that was his would be hers. They eloped. Nine months later my sister was born."

"What was Lord Malcolm to her?"

"She said she'd dreamed about him."

Regan opened the book again to the page of the Cassatt pearl necklace painting. She shook her head, then slammed the book shut and tossed it onto the bed.

"I dreamed about David Cameron giving me a haircut once," she said. "If I had a painting of him, I'd *give* it away. Why was she so attached to a painting of a dead lord she'd never met?"

"You'd have to ask her that."

She pointed at him. "I'm asking you."

Arthur thought about what to tell her that wouldn't sound completely mad.

"Mum has nicknames for us all," he said. "My father's her Sun, my sister's her Moon. That's what she always called them, her Sun and her Moon. And me and Charlie are her Morning Star and Evening Star."

"Very sweet. What's your point?"

"I remember when I was little, and we were out star-gazing and she showed me the Evening Star. Then she showed me the North Star and I asked who that was? She said it was Lord Malcolm, but she didn't say why."

"Malcolm?"

He met her eyes, nodded. The whisky in her glass was shaking. "You're scared," he said.

"Terrified. And you're not, which scares me even more. There's more, isn't there? In your texts, you told Charlie that your parents joke about the painting being haunted. All because your mother had one dream about Lord Malcolm?"

Arthur studied the floor. "No," he finally said. "Not just that."

"Well?" She raised her hand, waiting not very patiently.

"There's an old family story about Lord Malcolm. His

mother forced him into a marriage he didn't want. The second his wife was gave him an heir, he ran off with some girl he was lusting after. Her father followed them and caught them in bed together—so he shot Malcolm.

"That should be the end of the story, but it's not. While he was dying, he allegedly sold his soul to the devil —not to avenge his own murder, but to get revenge on his family for forcing him to marry someone he despised. The other rumor is he sold his soul so he could keep on whoring after he was dead. Maybe both. Maybe neither. It's all third- and fourth-hand gossip.

"Anyway, the bed he died in was the bed my mother found the painting in. The bed she was sleeping in when she dreamed about him—supposedly." Arthur sighed. "And..."

"Go on. Tell me everything."

"You'll think we're all starkers."

"You're a Godwick—I already do."

"He seems to *interfere*, for lack of a better word, with the family sometimes. For good. Only for good so far. My father didn't know what to get Lia for a graduation present. He swears a wind blew through his office though all the doors were shut and all the windows down, and it opened a sales catalogue to a page for an Ancient Greek *kylix*. She loves Greek mythology, so he thought this would be perfect. He found one for Lia, and then a collector came and tried to buy it from her. Now she and that art collector are married."

"So Lord Malcolm plays matchmaker. Anything else?"

"Mum's not the only one who's had dreams about him that have come true. Dad dreamed Lord Malcolm came to him and said, 'Ditch that girl you're after. She only wants you for your title.' Turns out that was all she wanted. Then

Dad met Mum. Like I said, Mum's dreamed about him and...I've had my own encounter with him."

"You dreamed about him, too?"

"When I was very little, about four or five, I think? My parents had a party and the house was full of people. I snuck out of the nursery and wandered to the landing on the stairs to watch what was happening. Just a load of people drinking and talking and laughing. This man saw me and walked up the stairs and asked if he could hide up there with me. I remember the two of us putting our faces up to the balusters, looking down at the people below."

Arthur put his hands to his face, miming a small boy's face pressed between the spindles on the landing.

"The man asked me questions about Mum and Dad and Lia and Charlie," Arthur sad. "He asked if I liked Wingthorn and what I wanted to be when I grew up. The sort of questions any adult asks a child to get them talking."

Arthur took a breath. He didn't want to tell the rest of this story or Regan might never speak to him again. She'd call the men in white coats to take him away.

But he went on.

"After a few minutes the man said he had to leave. At breakfast, I told Mum and Dad I'd met a nice man in a black suit called Malcolm, and I thought they should invite him back because I liked him so much. Mum dropped her coffee cup. It shattered everywhere. Dad didn't hesitate. He took me immediately into the picture gallery and showed me the painting." Arthur looked over his shoulder at Lord Malcolm. "I said that was him. Dad said I must have dreamed the whole thing since that man had been dead a long time."

"But you didn't dream it."

Arthur shrugged. "Maybe I did. More likely than I had a nice long talk with a man who's been dead since 1939."

"When that young man from security joked we had a ghost in the suite, your eyes flicked upstairs."

"I don't believe in ghosts," Arthur said. "Do you?"

"No, but you still looked."

"I looked," Arthur admitted. "And you're still shaking."

She lifted her whisky to her lips but didn't drink. She turned, set the glass on the mantel, didn't turn back.

"You told Charlie you dreamed about him, too," Arthur said.

She sighed, but didn't turn around. "It was the night after Sir Jack's funeral. Soon as he died, I moved into the hotel. Couldn't stand to spend another night in our house at Ferry Hill. This suite, Lord Malcolm's old flat. Supposedly it looked just like this when he lived here."

She gestured with her hand at the fireplace, the bed, the wingback chair.

"In the dream, I was in a beautifully decorated room," she continued. "Like a lady's morning salon. There was a breakfast table with a pink and white chintz tea set on it and a..."

She shook her head, as if trying to dislodge her memories.

"A small roll top desk, antique. A red sofa and a fireplace with a white mantel. Lord Malcolm was there, and I knew him. I knew who he was the way you know who people are in dreams. He was standing in front of the fireplace looking up at something. When he saw me in the doorway, he smiled and invited me in. I went to stand beside him and there was an empty frame on the wall, a large gilt frame, right above the mantel. Like this."

She waved her hand to show the painting of *The Psyche Mirror* still hanging over her bedroom fireplace.

"That's what we were looking at, this empty frame," she said. "I asked him whose painting was going into the frame. He smiled and said, 'Yours.' Then I woke up."

"'Yours'? So a painting of you?" Arthur asked.

She nodded. "I think. Or a painting I'd painted. But I hadn't painted in years."

"What color were the walls?"

"White," she said. "White...wallpaper, I think. Green vines and red and pink roses. Why?"

Traditionally, the Earl of Godwicks' portraits hung over the fireplace in the sitting room, while the Countesses' portraits hung over the fireplace in the morning room. His mother's portrait was there now, but...no. There'd never been white wallpaper there. He knew that for a fact. His mother was always complaining about the ancient red wallpaper and how shabby it looked, how it had been there since King Edward's reign.

"My mother has a roll top desk in the morning room and a chintz tea set," Arthur said. "But the walls are some sort of red damask wallpaper."

"It was only a dream," Regan said, trying to sound dismissive and failing. "But it's stayed with me like no other dream ever has. And when Charlie brought me Malcolm's portrait and I saw it the first time, I was shocked his suit matched what I'd seen in my dream. Like he'd stepped right out of the frame."

"Let's say it was real," Arthur said. "Let's say, for the sake of argument, my great-grandfather did sell his soul and now it's bound to his painting *á la* Dorian Gray. Why would he come to you in a dream?"

"He lived here at The Pearl, in this suite. I'm sleeping

in his bed. Maybe he's taken a liking to me." She was mocking him again. "And, if you think about it, Lord Malcolm and I are on the same side," she said. "He wanted revenge against the Godwicks, too."

Was that all their arrangement was, atonement for some perceived slight? Now wasn't the time nor the place to pry it out of her, but the acrimony she felt for the Godwicks was fueled by more than a single unpaid hotel bill.

He decided to keep things light for the moment. "You weren't complaining about the Godwicks when you were coming on my tongue an hour ago."

She smiled. He was relieved to see it. "What are we going to tell ourselves?" Regan asked. "Shall we start believing in haunted paintings that can throw scarves across rooms and knock books off shelves? Or are we going to tell ourselves a book just fell of its own accord and landed on this painting, that it's all a big coincidence?"

"I think we're better off sticking to your original theory—that someone was in the suite. Someone saw us together, saw the necklace. Someone who's trying to scare us."

"And they, what? Jumped off the terrace?"

He could think of a half dozen different scenarios, none of which would comfort her. None of which he himself believed.

"God," she said, exhaling hard. She stared at Lord Malcolm. "When I was talking to the painting, I was only joking. Never thought for one second...I was only trying to goad you."

"Whatever's going on," he said, "I don't want you to sleep here tonight. Not alone, anyway. I'll stay if you won't go."

"You're not in charge."

"I am if and when you put yourself in danger."

A small smile flitted across her mouth. "You can stay," she said softly. "But you'll sleep on the floor. You're still a Godwick, after all."

ARTHUR MADE one more sweep of the suite, kitchen knife in hand, and found no one. Then again, he didn't know all the hiding places in the penthouse. Ceiling tiles? False fronts? Bookcases that spun to reveal secret rooms? Highly doubtful. This wasn't a hotel in a horror film.

He returned to the bedroom and Regan gave him one blanket but no pillow. Fine. He didn't need a pillow. He lay the blanket down and folded it in half, making a pseudo-sleeping bag. He took off his jeans but kept on his pants and t-shirt. Regan locked the bedroom door, and Arthur lodged a chair in front of it.

She set the book on the mantel. "There," she said. "If it falls off, it'll fall on you. You can wake up and fight the ghost. Let me sleep through it."

The carpet was soft and plush but a floor was a floor. Arthur turned onto his side toward the fire which was still burning low and let the heat settle into him. He ignored the sounds of Regan moving in her bed, getting comfortable, ignored the image of her in her black silk slip and nothing else pulling back the covers and sliding into the bed.

The room was dark but for the firelight dancing. Regan was quiet and her breathing steady, but he sensed her alertness. She was as awake as he.

"If you tell me what my family did to you," Arthur said, "I'll do anything I can to make it right."

"Only a time machine could make it right," she said. "Why would you help me anyway? I've already put you and your brother through hell."

"Charlie puts himself through hell. And if this is Hell, sign me up for eternity."

"I'm going to have to hurt you more so you'll stop liking this so much."

"Do your worst," he said.

A joke, but he heard her toss the covers off and leave her bed. He rolled onto his back and she stood before him in her black kimono. Regan sat at his hip, and threw the blanket off of him. The silk of her robe tickled him as it brushed his thigh.

"Why are you wearing clothes?" she demanded.

"I didn't want to have to fight off an intruder naked."

"You should be more worried about me than him."

Message received. He stripped bare.

She took his cock in her hand at the base, fingers wrapped firmly around it. He'd been half-hard until she touched him, but he stiffened and lengthened at once when he was in her hand.

She brought the head to her mouth and licked a white pearl of come off the slit at the tip. The pleasure of the little lick shot up his spine. His hips and stomach tensed. She drew the head into her mouth, all the way in and she sucked him, her pale peach lips stroking his burning red flesh.

Watching his cock disappear into her mouth was a fantasy come to life. She'd bought him to service her. Never had he dreamed that she'd reciprocate. The urge to thrust up and into her mouth was powerful, but he forced his hips to lie still on the floor, though his thighs contracted hard as if they wanted to move on their own.

She nestled between his legs and forced them wider. She pulled up for a moment and he saw in the firelight she had a small bottle of lubricant in her hand.

She poured it onto her fingertips. "If I were really cruel," she said, "I would do this without the lube."

"Do what?" he asked, but got no answer.

He lay his head back onto the rug and tried not to tense as Regan began to slowly, painstakingly work her wet fingers over and into him, opening him slightly though not going in very deep, not as deeply as he craved, but he didn't say that, afraid she'd stop. As it was, the massage on that tender private part of his body felt incredibly good. Intimate. He thought he'd feel shame or embarrassment and he waited for those feelings to come but they never did.

As she massaged his anus, she took his penis into her mouth again, drawing it slowly to her throat until he was hard as a rod of hot iron in her mouth.

Then he felt something on him, something cold and round. She had the string of pearls again and he knew at once she was going to put them inside him as he'd done to her.

"Don't," he said, tensing. "Please?"

"Don't what? Don't do anything I want to the whore I paid for?" She gazed down on him, there on his back, subject to her entirely. Softly, almost—but not quite— tenderly, she said, "Are we still pretending you don't want this?"

He couldn't. He wouldn't. It was too much to ask of him. Except she wasn't asking, was she?

"Let me do it or tell me about you and Wendy and Charlie," she said. "Your choice."

Arthur slowly spread his legs wider. He lay there on the floor, burning for the reason anything burns—because someone had set it on fire.

Carefully, she pushed the first of the pearls inside of him. The first few felt small and strange but not painful. More and more and then even more. The tight hole opened to take them, stretching as she filled it. She took his cock into her mouth again, drawing it in deep, then deeper. More and more pearls. He'd lost count of how many were inside of him. Ten? Twelve? The sensation changed. He felt an oddly pleasant fullness. His hips were tighter than ever. The deep inner muscles inside of him were clenching at the pearls, gripping and releasing them and gripping them again. He breathed fast breaths, quick pants as one bead after another entered and stretched him.

Regan's mouth was on his cock, sucking and pulling. He felt assaulted on two fronts. It was almost more than he could take, the pleasure so sharp it almost hurt. His head fell back as a bead rubbed against that little organ inside of him, that sensitive nub of tissue that pulsed as the pearls pushed and kneaded it.

More pearls. He had to spread his legs wider. His head came up in a sudden spasm of pleasure. The most beautiful woman in the world had his cock in her mouth and his arse was filled to the brim with a king's ransom in rare pearls. Nothing in the history of the world ever felt so decadent.

His head fell back again, and he came with a powerful release that rose from the depths. He ejaculated hard into Regan's mouth, and as she swallowed it, she withdrew the pearls steadily, stoking his orgasm on and on and on...

He emptied himself into her as she emptied him out, a dual release that felt obscene even as it was happening to his own body. When it was over and the pearls were out of him, he felt like a hollow shell. His quick breathing slowed, and he melted into the floor. His strength was gone, his will, his ego. He was a body spent, well-used, finished off.

Regan leaned forward and kissed him on his bare stomach. He hardly felt her lips.

A long time passed, or maybe only a few seconds before she rose up over him, her hands and knees on either side of his shoulders and thighs.

"You liked that," she said, meeting his eyes. "The correct answer is 'Yes, I liked it.'"

"Yes," he said with a sigh, "I liked it."

He laughed at himself, at how much he'd like it. God, he was a whore, wasn't he? Or was he just a Godwick? Regan wrapped the pearls into a tissue.

"Those are officially the most expensive anal beads in the world," he said.

"Sir Jack gave them to me," she said. "He liked me to wear pearls. Tarts, he said, wear diamonds. Ladies wear pearls. I disagreed but didn't want to argue the point."

"Why still wear them?"

"Old habits die hard, I suppose. I really can't tell you how much I enjoyed shoving them up your arse."

"If only you could have shoved them up his."

She smiled, almost laughed, and it was the truest, sincerest, most honest smile he'd seen on her face yet. Unguarded, open, happy.

Arthur wrapped his arms around her and pulled her to his chest, kissing her mouth, tasting himself on her tongue. When the kiss stopped, she smiled down at him again.

"Go to sleep," she said.

"Yes, ma'am."

One more kiss, then she rose up off of him leaving him on the floor, wet and shivering from the power of the orgasm she'd given him. He heard her in her bathroom, heard her come back to the room, heard the hushed rush of the sheets and the sigh of the mattress as she lay in her bed again.

Arthur said softly, "If Lord Malcolm *is* trying to play matchmaker, are we going to let him?"

Say yes, he thought. Say yes, say yes, say yes. Please say yes.

After a tense silence, Regan finally answered, "Over my dead body."

The one small, miserable comfort Arthur took in those words was how unhappy she sounded when she'd said them.

7

AFTERNOON TEA

Almost a week passed before Regan summoned Arthur again. It felt like the longest week of his life.

He waited for the doorbell all day Tuesday and Wednesday, but it never rang. Eventually, he got stir-crazy. When Charlie didn't answer his messages, Arthur met up with friends from Sandhurst instead. They lifted weights at the gym until they were almost sick. He continued to tax himself all week, running in Hyde Park in the cold rain. At night, he visited every last one of the Godwicks' art galleries in Greater London on the pretense of "checking on things" for his parents.

The more time that passed since that strange night with Regan, the more he managed to convince himself what had happened with the book was nothing but a coincidence. Arthur and Regan had been having intense sex. Maybe the walls had rattled, jostling the book from the shelves as the guard had intimated. No denying it was strange that it fell open to a painting of a woman in a pearl necklace, but life was strange sometimes.

And, yes, those "sometimes" often involved Lord Malcolm's portrait...but still. No need to go mad. Yet.

When he arrived home from his Saturday morning run, he was halfway to the shower when his phone buzzed in his hand. He didn't recognize the number. Usually, he wouldn't have answered it. Only the hope it was Regan made him accept the call.

"Hello?"

"Tea at four on my terrace," Regan said.

Arthur sat down on the second storey landing, sunk down really, so relieved to hear her voice it was humiliating. He'd been aching all week to hear from her. And now she was on the end of the line and he knew he would have waited a year if she'd made him.

She continued, "If the weather's nice enough we might fuck *al fresco*, but as it's London, I wouldn't count on it."

"I don't know anyone named Al Fresco, and I have no interest in fucking him on your terrace."

"Did I give you permission to be funny? I don't recall."

Arthur gave a cocky laugh. "You haven't even asked me what I'm wearing."

The silence at the other end of the line was potent. Needling Regan was his new favorite pastime.

"White tee, in case you were wondering," he went on. "Been running. Very sweaty. I turned the heads of many women and gay men between the ages of forty-seven and ninety-eight. Want a pic? I'll text you."

"Why are you in a good mood? It's annoying me," she said.

"Why are you so cross? You're the one who gets to fuck me tonight."

"Are all the Godwicks like you?"

"Clever? Charming? Desperately attractive?"

"Obnoxious. Sardonic. Insufferably arrogant."

"I get it from my father," Arthur said.

"Give it back."

"What happened to your redcoat? Zoot? She who lives to insult me to my face at my front door?"

"She has today off. Do you think I'm a monster?"

"Do you want me to answer that honestly?"

She was silent on the line, silent but for a soft exhalation that he almost felt in his ear.

"Four. Tea. Terrace," she finally said. "Don't be late. We have a brief window of good weather, and we're going to enjoy it."

"I won't be late." Before Regan hung up, Arthur said her name.

"What, Brat?"

"Have we decided to pretend the thing with the painting of the pearl necklace was just a coincidence?"

When he'd woken up on her floor on Tuesday morning, she was already gone. He hadn't had a chance to discuss it with her yet.

"Have you ever heard the name Violet Jessop?" she asked.

"No. Should I know her?"

"She was on the ship the *HMS Olympic* when it accidentally hit the *HMS Hawke*. She was on the *HMHS Britannic* when it hit a mine. And she was also on the *RMS Titanic* when it hit the iceberg. Coincidences happen. I'll see you at four."

She ended the call. Arthur stripped and while showering, decided to never go boating with Violet Jessop.

———

He arrived at The Pearl a few minutes before four. Traffic had nearly made him late this time. He ran to the lift and urged it upward as fast as it could carry him. Being early was one thing, but being late... He marveled at how well-trained he was. She'd broken him down faster than he'd imagined possible; now, on their fifth date—if you could call it a date—Arthur was powerless against her.

And he loved it.

He was being foolish. What would happen to him once their pact was over? Every time he considered asking her if she thought there could be something more between them, he remembered her words—*over my dead body*—and gave up on that dream. It was easier for both of them to keep their emotional distance. Their relationship had an expiry date, anyway, regardless of the ten nights they'd negotiated for. When January rolled around, he would be leaving to serve his country.

The door to the penthouse was open. Immediately, the hair on the nape of his neck picked up. Another intruder? He called out for Regan, but there was no answer.

When he stepped inside, he saw that she was sitting on the terrace. He breathed a deep sigh and locked the door behind him.

Hanging above the fireplace mantel was a new painting —a woman in a fine blue afternoon gown, sitting at a table on a garden terrace, looking at the viewer, an invitation to have tea with her.

The same scene Regan had set up on her own terrace.

Regan was sitting at a small round table outside, a white tea set before her. Her dark-blue dress was ankle-length, but it had a slit that revealed her lovely thighs. He opened the door and let himself onto the terrace.

The sun was out, though clouds threatened in the east.

And it was warm, warm enough he was more than comfortable in his light jacket. The garden terrace was far more welcoming by day and without a bloodthirsty raven perched on the railing. The small trees and ferns out here were so thickly clustered, he and Regan could have sex out here without anyone seeing. Like a little sky-high Garden of Eden.

Regan took her sunglasses off and pushed them up onto her head. She glanced at her watch. "One minute late," she said. "You'll be punished for that. You may pour."

"Whatever happened to 'Hello, how do you do?'" he asked playfully.

"Hello," she said. "You're late. Sit."

With a graceful—yet somehow still sarcastic—wave of her hand, she indicated that she would allow him the honor of sitting in the chair opposite her.

He was about to apologize, but something in her grey glinting eyes told him it would only mean digging himself a deeper hole. Arthur sat and picked up the teapot, poured two cups. He had to admit he liked seeing her like this, full of mischief and malice. Even if it was directed at him. Who was he kidding? Especially if it was directed at him.

"I saw the painting you hung over the fireplace," he said. "That's our artwork we're role-playing today?"

"Eva Gonzalèz," she said. "French Impressionist painter. She studied under Manet, his only formal student, he saw such promise in her." Regan lifted her teacup and took a sip. "Died at age thirty-four—in childbirth."

"That's tragic," Arthur said. "I imagine that was the fate of a lot of female artists."

"We could spend all afternoon listing the names of talented women who died in childbirth before they could make their mark on the world, but that wouldn't make for very pleasant conversation."

"I didn't know you were capable of pleasant conversation," Arthur said. "Not complaining. Just stating a fact."

"Only because you like when I torment you."

"Tea and sandwiches and cake aren't my idea of torment," he said. "Maybe you should take some lessons from Vlad the Impaler or the Spanish Inquisition."

"Your girlfriend Wendy fucked your brother, didn't she?"

Arthur sat back in his chair, but didn't answer.

"There's a girl here, Lily," Regan went on. "She was Charlie's favorite. She and I had a talk this morning about some things he'd said to her. My God...that must have hurt, didn't it? Your first girlfriend takes your virginity and then fucks your baby brother."

"Maybe the Spanish Inquisition could take lessons from you," he said.

She rested her elbow on the chair arm, her chin on her hand, the picture of beauty and innocence. A picture that was worth a thousand lies.

He'd been stupidly happy to hear from her today. God, he was an idiot. Did he really think he could make her like him by sheer charm and willpower?

She smiled at him. "Do you think I wanted you here just for afternoon tea?" she said. "I'm tired of knowing everything about you but still knowing nothing."

"Imagine how I feel."

"I don't care how *you* feel, only how *I* feel."

"Just when I'm starting to think you're human."

"I can't afford to be human," she said. "Tell me. What happened with Wendy? Is it worse than I think?"

Arthur's stomach knotted up and lodged in his throat.

"She was the daughter of the old curator at one of Mum and Dad's galleries," he said. "I met her at a party. My parents threw us together, thought we'd get on. We did. I found out later she'd asked my mother to introduce us. Wendy's short for—"

"Gwenivere, yes?"

"Gwendolyn actually, but close enough. Really, I should have known better, but Mum's a romantic. She thought it was sweet."

"Very sweet. Social climber, I imagine?"

"Did Charlie say that?"

"Educated guess. When a girl asks a countess to introduce her to her eldest son, she's probably not trying to sell him a timeshare in the Maldives."

Regan held out her cup, demanding he pour again. He did so and felt a flash of real anger at her. Was it because he didn't want to dredge up the old agony? Or because he didn't want to slander Charlie to her? Maybe he just didn't want Wendy here, with them. And now she was. The clouds moved in. The day was ruined.

"She was beautiful," he said, remembering how his sister had said she looked like a younger Billie Piper with brown hair. "And smart. Funny. Mature. She worked at the gallery, too, so it was like she was already an adult. I don't know if I was in love with her or just sick of being a virgin."

"Bit of both I would guess."

He shrugged and went on: "We spent hours on the phone, talking, texting. When we had sex the first time two weeks later, it didn't feel like two weeks. I felt like I'd known her for years. She wasn't even upset when I was hurting her. We laughed about it. It doesn't hurt a bloke's feelings when your girl teases you over having a cock too big. Eventually we made it work."

"What went wrong?" Regan's voice was smooth and cool and clinical, the voice of a psychologist examining a patient.

"I loved her. First mistake. I trusted her. Second mistake. We spent time with Charlie together. Biggest mistake."

"Trusted her with what? Wait." She lifted her chin off her hand, narrowed her eyes at him. "You told her, didn't you? What you like?"

"She asked."

"She asked about your sexual fantasies?"

He nodded.

"What did you tell her?"

"I...tried to explain it like knights and ladies. How a knight would swear to do anything for his lady, serve her in any way she asked. Basically worship her. I was trying to come around to, you know—being treated the way you treat me. Tied up or blindfolded or just...servicing her. She said that was very interesting, and she would think about that."

"Did she pat you on your head?"

He turned his teacup on the saucer, turned it round and round but didn't drink from it. "On her birthday I decided to surprise her, go over to her house, take her flowers. Her Mum let me in, let me sneak upstairs with my stupid bouquet. I was in the hall, outside her door, and heard her in her bedroom, talking to a friend on the phone."

He was back in that hallway again, flowers in hand— honeysuckle and roses, the scent of their cloying sweetness tickling his nose.

God, fuck, why did I have to go and pick the pervert? I think he wants me to tie him up and spank him or something. Should have known. That entire family is just a load of whores. Even the mother. Especially the mother.

Silence followed as her friend on the phone said something in reply. Then Wendy laughed and spoke again.

Yes, he's gorgeous but no one's that gorgeous. Nearly killed me not to laugh in his face. Like, really?

Silence again.

You're right. The brother seems normal, at least. And he's mad about me already. Boys that age are so easy. You give them one smile, and they think you want to have their babies. At least if I ever need cash, I have something I can blackmail a future earl with. "Hand it over, Arthur, or I'm telling the world you like being spanked by girls."

"Then she laughed," Arthur said. "She laughed and laughed and laughed."

Regan stared at him without expression.

"For the record," Arthur continued, trying to make light of it so she wouldn't see how mortified he'd been, "I have no interest in being spanked. Slapped, maybe, but not spanked."

"What did you do?"

"I left. Couldn't face her. Later that night, I called her. She didn't pick up so I left a message calling her a pathetic chav, a shameless social climber who didn't deserve to lick the bottom of my brother's shoe. Didn't take that well, did she? I knew she'd be angry, but I didn't think she'd be so vindictive.

"She called Charlie crying and told him a sob story about how I'd broken up with her because she wasn't good enough for our family. Charlie fell right for it, little idiot.

She asked him to come over and talk to her in person about it.

"A few hours later I get a text message from her that says, *I did a little more than just lick your brother's shoe.* She'd attached a picture of him asleep in her bed."

"My God..." Regan shook her head. "I'm almost impressed."

"Gets worse," Arthur said. "After he woke up, she told him he had to go, because what I said about her was true, that she wasn't good enough to be with a Godwick. She laid it on very, *very* thick. Genius maneuver on her part. Not only did she fuck my brother, she turned him against me. Bad enough I insulted her, but I'd also ruined his chances to be with her."

"You never told him what you'd overheard? What she said? Never mentioned the picture she'd sent you of him sleeping?"

"Of course not. He would have been crushed to find out she was just using him to get back at me. He'd never been with a girl before, either. You've seen what a wreck he is right now. Can you imagine how bad it would be if he knew?"

He was sick at his stomach just thinking of it.

Regan picked up the sugar bowl, sweetened her cup. "If I were you, I'd tell him. Then I'd punch him in the face for fucking my girlfriend the day I'd broken up with her. Would do him a world of good."

"I would never—"

Regan leaned forward. "Do you want to know why he behaves like he does? I'll tell you whether you do or not."

She sipped her tea, set her cup down. Despite himself, he leaned forward in his chair.

Regan continued, "Until you've fought, you can't make

up, can you? What do you think he's been doing when he goes drinking and whoring and brawling outside pubs at four in the morning? He's trying to pick a fight with you. One good row would clear the air. Instead of treating him like a poor wounded lamb, a victim, treat him like a man, like an equal. Call him out. Have a duel. Bloody his nose at the very least, and you'll have your brother back."

"Physically assault my own brother? You don't know anything about it, anything about us. You don't know anything about my family."

She sat back in her chair, arms crossed over her chest, legs crossed, everything crossed as if to X him out. "I don't know anything about your family?"

"Your turn in the dock. What did the Godwicks ever do to you, Regan? Steal your parking space? Outbid you on some priceless painting? Or are you pissed that Mum married a man with a title and money like you did, except she's happy and you're a miserable b—"

"Bitch?"

"Widow. I was going to say a miserable bitter widow."

She narrowed her eyes at him.

"Enjoy Lord Malcolm," Arthur said. "I hope he's as fun to have in your bedroom as I was."

He tossed the linen napkin on the table and stood up, started to leave.

"You want to know what your family did to me?" she said, freezing him in place. She met his eyes. "Do you know the name Hannah Howell-Griffiths?"

He furrowed his brow. "Hannah? Your mother?"

"Right. My mother. And you selfish, entitled bastards killed her."

ARTHUR'S BLOOD WENT COLD. He couldn't feel his feet. Everything in him wanted to deny what she said, what she was about to say...but he could see that, whether it was true or not, Regan wasn't lying. *She* believed it.

"There's a letter," she said, "in the top of my desk. You'll know it when you see it. It's been read a billion times. It's got my name on the envelope. Bring it out here."

He stared at her a moment longer, but then did as she said.

In her office he went straight to the desk, opened the drawer and there it was—a plain white envelope with REGAN written on it in a woman's shaky hand.

The urge to tear open the envelope and read the letter was almost overwhelming but he carried it back to her.

She pointed at the chair. He sat down again.

He thought he'd die in those five seconds it took for Regan to slip the letter out and unfold it.

"*My Darling Regan,*" she read, her voice steady but cold.

You're too young to understand what's happening right now. I need to tell you a few things before I'm gone. My own mother died when I was about your age, and every unanswered question in my heart is an open wound.

It's no one's fault that I have cancer. I was dealt a bad hand of cards just like my own mother. That's life, I'm afraid, and a lesson you need to learn. But I also want you to know that I did literally everything I could to save myself so I could watch you grow up. I'm afraid "literally everything" won't be enough.

Regan cleared her throat.

There is a clinical trial in America for people with my sort of cancer. I was accepted into the trial, but as it's in New York, I needed money for the airfare and a few months of funds to cover a long recovery. We didn't have it, not even close enough to get me halfway there. Desperate, I went to see Lord Arthur Godwick—

"I never—"
"I know she means your grandfather, not you."
"Sorry. Go on," he said.

...I went to see Lord Arthur Godwick who my father told me on more than one occasion I should go to if I was ever in need of help. He couldn't tell me why there was a connection between our families, only that he was certain the Godwicks would help if I gave them his name. Lord Godwick agreed to see me at his private home, Wingthorn Hall. The meeting was short and pointless. Even though I told him my name, my father's name, and that I had a young daughter at home, that I needed only a modest loan so I could possibly live to see you grow up, he refused me.

I begged him, on my knees. I reminded him that my father was a friend of his family, and that even his least valuable painting hanging on the walls of his picture gallery could mean the difference between life and death for me.

He sent me away and told me to never show my face there again.

And now I'm in hospital and there's no chance anymore. But I did try, my darling. I did try everything I could for you. Please forgive me for not being there to see you grow

up. And whatever you do, stay away from the Godwick
family. No matter what your grandfather believed, they
cannot and should not be trusted. My life was worth less
to them than the price of one of their precious paintings.

Regan slowly folded the letter and slipped it back into
the envelope that had gone soft as cotton with age and a
thousand readings.

"There's more," she said, "But I'll spare you the rest
where she tells me how much she loved me."

Arthur buried his head in his hands, his elbows on the
little tea table. Slowly he looked up. "Why us?"

"She guessed my grandfather had done something for
your family years ago—a gift, some good deed during the
war. Something that meant we were owed a favor," Regan
said. "He was wrong."

"Doesn't matter though, does it?" Arthur sat back in
his chair. "Your mother was right. Even our least valuable
painting could have paid for her to travel first-class around
the world ten times over."

"He tossed a dying woman, a mother with a young
child, out on her arse for the price of an airplane ticket
and three months in a cheap hotel. She died two weeks
after she wrote that."

Regan blinked and a tear fell down her face. Or started
to. As soon as it left her eye she swatted it off like it was a
fly that landed on her and not proof of her humanity, her
deepest hurt.

"I'm—" he began.

"Don't say you're sorry if it won't bring her back."

And so Arthur said nothing, because nothing could
bring her back.

"I had no grand plan to avenge her," Regan said. "But

when young Master Charles Godwick was suddenly in hock to me up to his eyeballs, I remembered a conversation I'd had with your mother at your sister's wedding. A conversation about art. My favorite paintings. Her favorite paintings..."

"She told you their favorite painting in the house was the portrait of Lord Malcolm's."

"She didn't say why," Regan said, "only that if the house were burning down, that was the only painting she'd risk her life to pull from the fire. Now every time I see him hanging on the wall of my bedroom where I've been fucking his great-grandson, it makes me feel a little better. Petty revenge, yes. But not for a petty crime."

Arthur couldn't begin to think of anything to say to her. What could he say? That it wasn't his fault? Not his doing? True but useless. He might as well toss money onto her mother's grave.

"Get out," she said coldly, quietly, which was so much worse than ordering him out screaming and shouting. "Get out of my hotel. You and everyone else with Godwick blood in your veins are forever banned from The Pearl. It will not be your playground anymore. And I will keep that painting of Lord Malcolm. Your family's attorneys can pry it out of my cold dead hands. If your father's anything like *his* father, I'm sure he'll have that arranged."

She picked up her teacup again, took a sip, then set it on the saucer and continued: "You act like I'm some sort of monster for taking one painting from your family, meanwhile your family took my mother from me. This is rather a moot point considering everything that's happened between us, but I'd be remiss if I didn't say it— fuck you and every Godwick who's ever walked the face of this horrid little Earth."

Now her tears did fall and she let them, hot angry tears. She stared at him through them, like a veil.

"It's my fault," she said. "I never should have...what is it they say about sleeping with the enemy? This was a mistake, and it was *my* mistake. You were attractive and desperate, and I was lonely and bored." She wiped her eyes and sighed. "Your brother will survive whatever your parents do to him, and he'll be the better for it. You'll see."

"Of all the awful things you've said to me, that's the only thing that hurts," he said quietly. "This happened between us because you were bored? Insult me all you want, but don't lie to me. You were dripping wet the first time I touched you."

"Why shouldn't I lie? You won't even admit you like it."

"I admitted it. Eventually. I know it took—"

"This is why you won't tell your brother what really happened with you and Wendy, isn't it? You're too embarrassed to tell him that it all started when she mocked you for being a submissive? Your brother is destroying himself with self-loathing and all you care about is your worthless male pride."

"You don't care about Charlie," Arthur said. "If you did, you wouldn't have backed him into a corner he couldn't escape."

"He could have escaped by being honest and accepting the consequences for his actions."

"Why should he when you won't."

She looked at him like he'd grown a second head.

"You can try to hate me, hate us, all you want, but I know the truth," Arthur said. "You hate yourself. You hate yourself for being just like us, *Lady* Ferry. And you hate yourself for giving up on your art and your freedom and choosing money over your own happiness. You've been a rich widow for six months and you're still working a job you hate, still wearing a watch over your tattoo because Sir Jack made you, still wearing the pearls your dead husband made you wear instead of picking up a bloody paintbrush and daring to do something that makes you happy instead of wallowing in your self-pity.

"If you want me to, I'll apologize on my hands and knees for what my grandfather—who died before I was born, let me remind you—did to your mother. But if you want someone to blame for your own misery, go into the bedroom and look into your psyche mirror, Regan. You chose it, remember? Nobody else but *you*."

"Are you finished now?" she asked. She sounded tired. "Because I am."

For a terrible moment, he was back in the river again, in that ice-cold water and drowning. He wanted to love her, he realized just now, far too late. He wanted to love her and would never get the chance.

"Why are you doing this to me?" he asked, his voice a hoarse whisper.

She picked up her teacup, brought it to her lips. "It's for your own good," she said. "Really."

She sipped her tea and looked away into the distance. That was the last he might ever see of her. She stared off at the silver clouds over London, and just like the woman in the painting, she sat there, dressed in blue, drinking her tea all alone.

PART II

8

JUDITH SLAYING HOLOFERNES

Arthur was gone and Regan was alone and that was exactly how she wanted it.

There was a little tea left in the pot. No use letting good oolong go to waste. She poured the rest, added milk, added one lump of sugar and drank. Regan coughed, unable to get the tea down for some reason. Her throat was tight. Obviously, she'd been outside too long in the brisk air.

A tear streaked down her cheek. The cool air, again. Time to go in for the day. She'd leave the tea things for later. She'd leave everything for later.

Regan rose from the table, shocked by how tired she felt all of a sudden. Arthur's fault, she decided. She hadn't meant to tell him about her mother and what his grandfather had done to her. But what was she supposed to have done when he sat there smug and steaming, furious at her for daring to suggest she knew anything at all about his family?

Oh, she knew everything there was to know about the Godwicks. Everything that mattered. She'd done the right thing by sending him packing, by reneging on their agreement. Charlie didn't deserve to get pulled out of the fire, and Arthur certainly didn't deserve her.

When she closed the terrace doors behind her, the pictures rattled on the wall. She hadn't meant to shut the doors so hard. Arthur somehow brought out the worst in her.

Especially in bed. For all the years of her marriage to Sir Jack, she'd survived sleeping with him by retreating into a fantasy world where she was in charge, where no man ever told her what she could and couldn't do.

Only with Arthur, it hadn't been fantasy anymore. During their nights together, she'd let herself live out her dreams, her deepest fantasies. She never should have let that side out to play. After all, look what had happened. She'd started to care for the stupid boy. For a Godwick, of all people. She was starting to care for a Godwick, all because he'd made her dreams come true. Those dreams should have stayed dreams. Instead, they'd turned into nightmares.

She went straight up to her bedroom, threw herself across the bed and closed her eyes. It had begun when she'd brought the first red ripe strawberry to his lips, and he'd eaten it out of her hand. That willingness...that trust...giving so much of himself up to her...

That was the first time she'd felt something for him other than loathing and vengeance, something like tenderness.

And then he'd shown up at her door in uniform, looking like every delicious dream she'd never let herself have...and when he'd waltzed her out of the hunt ball to make love to her so roughly in the smoking lounge...

And finally, worst of all, when they'd found the book

lying open to the painting of the woman in the pearl neck-lace, and Regan worried there'd been an intruder, Arthur transformed in front of her eyes from whore to hero, searching the penthouse with no weapon other than a kitchen knife, and sleeping on her floor to guard her all night...

What would her mother think of her, sleeping with a Godwick, giving him her body? Bad enough. But giving him her heart? A true betrayal.

She'd always admired the art of the Italian Renaissance painter Artemisia Gentileschi. Her most famous work had been an oil painting titled *Judith Slaying Holofernes,* a graphic rendering of the Biblical story of Judith, a brave and beautiful widow, who'd played seductress to the enemy general Holofernes, tricking him into lowering his guard so that she might cut off his head and save her city.

Imagine if instead of Judith killing General Holofernes, she'd fallen in love with him. Judith would never have done something so stupid. Sleep with the enemy? Maybe...but never fall for him.

And neither would Regan.

Banishing Arthur and his whole wretched family from The Pearl was the right thing to do. Keeping the painting was the right thing to do. Making Charlie suffer for his actions was the right thing to do. Never seeing Arthur again, never calling him Brat again, never coming on his cock again, never feeding him out of her hand again, never letting him take her pearls off her neck and slip them one by one into her cunt again, never letting him protect her again, dance with her again, touch her again, fill her with his come again...

That was the right thing to do.

She knew it was right, even if the very thought of never

seeing him again made her want to sleep until the end of the world.

Emotions exhausted her, which is why she tried never to have them.

She'd simply take a little nap and when she woke up, she would feel fine. She'd put Lord Malcolm's portrait into storage and never give the Godwicks another thought.

———————

WHEN REGAN OPENED her eyes again, it was dark. She smelled incense and woodsmoke. She rose from her bed only to find the bed was gone, and she lay instead on a pile of silk pillows. A rustle of heavy fabric and a woman appeared, an older woman, with lines deep as furrows on her face. She carried a dripping candle in her hand.

Regan was dreaming. She knew it. Now, she would wake up as she always did when she realized she was dreaming.

Yet she stayed asleep and the dream played on...

"He's ready for you," the old woman said. "If you still have the stomach for it."

Words came to Regan's mouth, and she spoke them like she belonged to the dream, to this tent, to this story. "I have the stomach, the heart, and the will if you have the blade."

The old woman nodded, touched her billowing skirt and said, "I have the blade."

Regan could only nod as the old woman ran a wooden comb through her long dark hair, parted it in the center and let it fall in waves down her back. This wasn't her hair anymore; this wasn't her body.

Regan wasn't her name.

Her name was Judith.

The old woman helped her into a loose silk gown of red, a harlot's color. This was a harlot's task, but General Holofernes had taken no interest in the harlots of the city. Only she, Judith, had caught his eye. For days, she'd put him off, playing the grieving widow and so far it had worked. But now she had to go to him. The word had come that day that the general's army had their orders to sack her city tomorrow. If she wanted to save herself and her people, she must go to him.

"There, that's done," the old woman said. "No man would turn you away from his tent."

Regan hoped it was true. Regan? No. These were Judith's thoughts. The how and the why could wait, because it was time for her to see the general.

They walked along the city streets under the light of a full white moon. At the gates, the keeper took one look at her and spat at her feet, thinking she'd gone to sell herself to the enemy.

"We have to take care of ourselves," she said, playing her role in case any of the enemy Assyrian soldiers were watching the gates.

Once out of the city, she and the old woman headed deep into the center of the army camp, past a hundred tents filled with soldiers. She felt as if she were walking through a den of sleeping vipers and with one wrong step, one sound, she would wake them all and they would swarm...

And there ahead was the tent of the king of those vipers.

Holofernes.

The man she'd come to kill.

A young soldier stood watch outside his general's tent. He held up his hand to stop her.

"Don't bother," the soldier said. "There's no mercy to be had."

"Tell him Judith is here," Regan said. "And tell him I'm not here for mercy."

The soldier seemingly knew her name, because recognition flashed in his eyes. The general must have mentioned her. He slipped into the tent. Muffled male voices spoke. The soldier reemerged, coming through the flap like a baby being born, headfirst.

"Wait here," he said.

They waited. There came the sound of male laughter, deep and cruel from inside the tent. Another soldier, older, grey-haired, emerged from the tent and gave Judith a look. He liked what he saw, but it was not for him. He walked off.

The young soldier nodded. "You may go in now," he said. "Only you."

The old woman did not complain. She dropped down at the side of the tent, at the very edge of it, making exaggerated sounds of pain as she planted herself on the hard ground.

Judith gave the old woman one last look. The old woman nodded, and then Judith went inside.

General Holofernes lay draped over a thick pile of silk cushions, a cup of red wine in his hand. His eyes gleamed and his cheeks were flushed. He'd been drinking deep. Good.

He lifted his cup to her. "Judith. Finally. You came to your senses."

"I've come to claim your protection, if you will have me."

He stared at her and she dropped her eyes demurely. It was said, far and wide, that General Holofernes prized nothing so much as meekness and submission. And if a woman or a city were not meek and submissive when he came to them, they would be ever after.

The general was an enormous man—tall, broad-chested, arms and legs thick and corded with muscle. He wore a beard and his brown hair was short. If he hadn't been her enemy, the man who would burn her city down in the morning, she might have found him handsome.

He gave her a leering smile. "I will have you."

The tent was large and lit by three oil lamps hanging from the beams. A large tent, almost grand with comforts. Fine wool blankets, thick cushions for sleeping and more. A table laden with bread and oil and wine. He hefted the wine skin and filled a wooden cup for her. She cradled the large wine cup in her two hands, lifted it to her lips, and feigned drinking from it. Even though the table sat between them, she could smell his body—the sweat and heat and musky maleness of it.

He drank deep from his cup before setting it down, empty. If his fighting prowess were anything like his drinking prowess, her city would be ashes by this time tomorrow.

"More wine, sir?" she asked, her voice low and respectful.

"You first. Wine after." He waved his hand lazily, beckoning her to him. She prayed her God would forgive her when she sinned this night. She sinned to save her people. She offered another prayer that she would live long enough to repent.

She rose from the floor and went to him, head down. If she'd thought he was deep enough in his cups to be weak and yielding, she was sorely mistaken. When she neared him, he grabbed for her, his Goliath hands circling her waist almost entirely. He pulled her down to him and thrust his hand into her hair, holding her head and assaulting her mouth with rough, wine-sweetened kisses. He pushed his tongue between her lips, and she allowed herself a soft moan.

She'd been a widow too long, she thought, which is why she didn't recoil as she should. But perhaps if she could feign pleasure well enough it would fool him into letting down his guard.

His hand moved from her back to her belly, then to the bodice of her gown. He yanked on the fabric, baring her breast. The kiss ceased but only so he could gaze on her body.

As if she weighed no more than a child, he hefted her in his massive arms and brought her breast to his mouth. He latched onto her nipple and sucked it hungrily, greedily, and to her horror it hardened in the hot cavern. He let it go but only to kiss her mouth again, as hungrily as he'd sucked her. He held her breast in his hand and kneaded it, hard, but not too hard. His large palm cupped it and his thumb rolled the nipple, which sent waves of pleasure— unwanted and unwelcome—rolling through her belly.

"Better than dying at dawn, isn't it?" he taunted as he pulled her red gown up to her hips, exposing her to his eyes under the soft flickering light of the oil lamps. He wedged his hand between her quivering thighs and forced them apart. He cupped her between the legs, his hand buried in her soft curls.

"Burning hot," he said. "I hope you burn my fingers off."

Roughly he rubbed her, pushing through the folds of

swollen flesh until he found her wetness. And she was wet and it did shame her. Worse, when he stroked her along the slit of her body, she released another moan, shameless this time. He pushed a thick and calloused finger into her sex, then a second. She cried out softly at the invasion, even as her body contracted around his fingers. He spread them apart inside her, opening her almost painfully wide. Her hips moved into his hand. He held her cupped in his palm and he was so strong he lifted her lower body by the fingers inside her, lifted and moved her so that he could cover her with his own body.

He tore his tunic off. When he was naked, he hovered over her on his knees, letting her see his organ, dripping from the tip, big as another man's forearm and purple-red in its eagerness to have her.

He grabbed her by the hips again and yanked her to him, settling her in place so that she lay splayed open before him, thighs wide, gown bunched at her waist and her breast bare. He tore at the shoulder of her gown to bare her other breast. He gripped it, squeezed it, all the while watching her face contort with pleasure and fear.

In the back of her brain, Regan knew this was a dream —she wasn't Judith, and Judith wasn't her. Still, she quivered with true fear. She could smell his sweat and the olive oil burning in the bowl of the lamp. This was no ordinary dream. She was damp with sweat and wet inside. Her skin prickled on the rough fabric beneath her. And she desired this man who she knew she should hate, and so hated herself.

He brought his massive organ to the entrance of her body and pushed it to her opening. His arm wound round her back and lifted her. When her hips rose off the cushion, he impaled her.

Judith cried out in ecstasy, which she would later tell her servant was feigned. It was their signal after all, that cry of pleasure. A small sword would soon be slipping under the edge of the tent, even as the general loomed over her, spearing her again and again...

He pounded at her womb, driving into her with brutal thrusts. His body was heavy on top of hers and his male organ split her, taking the breath from her body. Her female juices poured out of her, bathing his rod and wetting the cushion under her so that she felt it on her back as he ground down into her.

His face flushed red, his breathing loud and fast. Every few thrusts he'd release a loud lusty grunt of pleasure. He rutted on her, driving into the core of her. She had been holding tight to his shoulders, clinging to him, but now she lay back in total surrender as he rode her. She slipped her hand under a cushion and felt the cold iron blade against her fingers. Relief. She only touched it and let it go. It would be there when the time came.

He took her by the hips with a brutal grip. Her breasts bounced on her chest, and he laughed at the sight of her body so helpless under his.

It wouldn't work. He was too strong and had the leverage on top of her. She had to get him on his back.

"Please," she said, her breathing labored. "Let me take you. It'll be a release like you've never known."

"Then go on and take me," he said, a sneer on his mouth.

He held her by the waist and rolled them, putting her on top of him. Light-headed from panting and shocked by her body's reaction to this giant wicked man, she put her hands on his broad chest to steady herself. Then she began to move her hips. This pleased him, she could tell.

He groaned again as the thick organ inside of her worked its way in deeper and deeper into the hot, tight cleft.

Judith's husband, long dead, had been a skilled and tender lover who had taught her all the ways a man could please a woman and all the ways a woman could please a man. She remembered one such way. Closing her eyes, she concentrated, and clenched her inner passage hard around the general's rod, squeezing it tight.

He gasped and looked at her wide-eyed with wonder. "Again," he said, and she did it again, clenching hard around him as he writhed underneath her.

His thick fingers held her in an iron grasp. She would have bruises on her hips tomorrow and on her nipples and inside her womb. But even as she tried to unman him, she was undone herself. She moved faster on him, snapping her hips against his until she came with a powerful release.

"You whore," he said. "No virtuous widow are you." Then he laughed, his head falling back, and she laughed too, laughed as she bent to kiss him, laughed as she grasped the slim short sword under the cushion, laughed as she slid the sharp blade out...

Her old maidservant had been waiting outside for her to take the blade's handle, and she lifted the edge of the tent and slipped under. As Judith raised the sword, her maidservant grabbed the general's hair and pulled his head back, baring his throat.

Holofernes, lost in his own pleasure, began to release inside Judith, spurting scalding hot seed against her womb.

The sword gleamed red in the lamplight. She had to act fast, before the last shudders of his orgasm passed and he regained his senses—

Too late. He snapped free from the maidservant's

grasp, his head bolting upright...and she saw it wasn't Holofernes.

It was Arthur. Her beautiful Brat, his eyes wide with terror.

"I'm not your enemy," he said as she brought the blade down on his neck...

REGAN WOKE UP SCREAMING, her lover's last words ringing in her ears.

I'm not your enemy.

A NIGHT and a day passed and by Sunday afternoon, Regan was calm again. Not calm, no, but empty, which was better in her books. Calm meant that peace and contentment were present. Emptiness meant that everything, including loneliness, regret, and pain were absent.

It had only been a dream, of course. A particularly vivid dream, true, but Regan was well-versed with the popular art subject *Judith Slaying Holofernes*. She'd studied various incarnations of the story during her first and only year in art school. Her first oil painting she'd ever attempted had been a modern version of that theme, with her playing Judith and playing Holofernes was a man who vaguely resembled Lord Arthur Godwick—not her Arthur, of course, but his grandfather, the man who'd killed her mother.

Of course talking about her mother with her Brat would bring that memory back to her, conjuring up a dream of the original "sleeping with the enemy" myth. That's all it had been.

Same with the dream where Lord Malcolm had stood at her side, tender toward her as if she were his own child, and shown her the empty frame and promised that someday a portrait of hers would hang in it.

Mad, stupid dreams. Not worth the sand the Sandman scattered on her pillow.

And yet, for the first time in a decade, she'd taken out her old sketchbook and begun to sketch Judith slaying Holofernes. Without lust this time and without mercy.

She sat on the garden terrace in the last of the golden rays of the late afternoon sun as she sketched, hating how horribly amateur her drawing looked and hating even more how happy it made her to be sketching again. As absorbed as she was in her work, she didn't hear the doors to the terrace open.

"Boss?"

Startled, Regan looked up.

"Cold out, Boss," Zoot said. "You want to freeze?"

"I have my coat on," she said. "But I'll be in soon. This is good light for sketching."

"Didn't know you sketched. When did you start doing that?"

"Years ago," she said. "I just haven't done it in a long time."

Zoot craned her neck, shamelessly peeking.

"A nice murder you done there," she said, approving of the drawing of a blade going through a man's throat. "Who we murdering?"

"General Holofernes. Biblical story. Can't compete with Artemisia Gentileschi though. She did the definitive portrait." Regan closed the sketchbook and rested it on her lap. She stared out at the waning sunlight, gathering clouds turning it silver. "Artemisia was raped in her art studio by one of her father's art students."

Zoot's eyes widened. "Hope she murdered him, too."

"No, but they took him to court and won." Regan looked at Zoot. "Do you know what she did after that?"

"Murdered him, then."

Regan smiled. "She went back into the studio and painted."

Hard to believe, a teenage girl in the seventeenth century, raped by her father's student who swore after the attack he'd marry her to take the stigma away from her... then he reneged on his promise and during his trial for breach of promise, she was literally tortured with the thumbscrews to verify her testimony. Eighteen years old. Raped and tortured.

And when it was all over...she went back into her studio and painted incredible scenes of women murdering men. Judith and Holofernes. Salome and John the Baptist. Jael and Sisera. One of Regan's favorite paintings, a young woman pounding a tent peg into the skull of a sleeping enemy soldier. She was one of Regan's very few heroes.

"I like her," Zoot said, nodding. "My sort of girl. She's got balls."

Regan laughed. It felt good to laugh at someone or something other than her own sorry self.

"All it took to get me to stop painting was one black look from my husband. Meanwhile, Artemisia..."

Not only had she continued to paint after the rape and trial, she'd become a famous painter, belle of the Baroque, painter to dukes and duchesses, kings and queens.

Regan continued, "What would Artemisia think of me, letting Sir Jack completely destroy my love of painting."

"Doubt that highly," Zoot said. "Sir Jack was a wrinkled old bellend. Only person I know tough enough to put a dent in you is *you*." She laughed, because it was a joke but it sounded painfully close to Arthur's accusation that it was Regan who chose to make herself miserable. Well, he didn't know a thing about her and her misery. Not a bloody thing.

Zoot shrugged. "If you want to paint again, Boss, I'll let you paint me. Always fancied having my picture done. Maybe on the back of a horse? Suit of armor, Joan of Arc-style? Loads of dead Tommies all around me on the ground? Buckets of blood? You see it?"

Zoot feigned raising a sword above her head, composed her face into a mask of determination and godly rage. It was a surprisingly impressive sight. Regan almost did want to paint that scene.

"A little beyond my skillset at the moment, but I'll keep that image in mind," Regan said. "Did you need something?"

"Message for you," she said, lowering her imaginary sword and sheathing it. "He said he would've hand-delivered it to you personally, but he said you banished him from The Pearl."

Regan sighed. "I told him never to come back," she said. "I suppose I should have told him never to contact me either."

"What he do? Piss in your umbrella?"

Regan glared at Zoot. "He was rude."

"Were you rude first? Never mind. Already know the answer."

"Do you remember who you work for?"

"Yes, and she's a proper harpy sometimes though that's part of her charm."

"You don't even like Arthur. You think he's a brat, too."

"A rich titled brat, face of a god, body of a soldier, cock of a horse, who eats your cunt on command. You think those grow on trees? I wouldn't be working for you if they did, believe me. I'd be a bloody forest ranger."

Regan really was going to have to get a new assistant soon, someone who knew how to take orders and keep her opinions to herself.

Zoot kept on, "I know you're miffed at him, Boss— Christ knows why, still think it's your fault—but you've actually been something almost like happy the last two weeks, and it's not because you're one of those daft American bints who gets wet when the leaves change colors and Starbucks brings the pumpkin spice latte back."

"Didn't I tell you that you could go? If not, I'm telling you now."

"He's funny," Zoot said. "And he'll take the piss. He worries about you though, and I can tell he's decent all the way down."

"Godwicks aren't decent. They're indecent."

"Right there, but it's the best kind of indecent if you ask me."

"I didn't—" Regan's voice broke as tears suddenly filled her eyes and a knot formed in her throat. She forced herself past it. "—*ask* you."

Zoot was staring at her, wide-eyed with shock. "I didn't know you had it in you," Zoot said, laughing softly. "I saw you snap your ankle two years ago falling off your Jimmy Choo's, and you didn't shed one bloody tear. You better call the boy back."

"I believe I told you—"

"Going. Have fun freezing your tits off out here, Boss."

Regan waited until she was inside to wipe her tears, but

they were already dried on her cheeks. She opened the note to read whatever worthless message he'd left for her. Probably another *I'm sorry* that didn't help anything or save anyone.

It wasn't an apology. It wasn't worthless. It was, simply, three words.

Judith Slaying Holofernes.

She closed her eyes. Did he know about her dream? Impossible, and yet the impossible seemed to be happening more and more often these days. She felt something like relief, actually. Now she had an excuse to see him again.

When she went inside, Zoot was putting on her red coat to leave.

"Have my car brought round, please," Regan said. "And I'll need Arthur's address." Zoot opened her mouth, but Regan shushed her. "And not a word from you about it."

9

THE WOUNDED DOVE

The last of the evening light was fading as Regan walked slowly toward the Godwicks' red brick townhouse. The facade was imposing—five or six stories, she couldn't tell from the exterior. The street was quiet, exclusive. Old money and older titles lived here.

The house was set back a few feet from the walk and she had to open a small iron gate to reach the front door. Her heart was in her throat when she rang the bell. She fully expected a servant to answer the door, but no, it was Arthur.

"Regan," he said. From the look in his dark eyes, she knew she was the last person he expected to see standing there and yet the person he was most glad to see.

"I got your note and—"

"Could you come with me to the garden, please? I need your help."

She was too surprised by his strange urgency to ask any questions. She followed him into the entryway and down a corridor toward the back of the house. He wore jeans and a white t-shirt with red specks on it that looked like blood.

"Are you all right? Is that blood on your shirt?"

"Just a scratch," he said. "I'm fine."

Physically, maybe. But emotionally? She'd hurt him. She wanted to tell him she was sorry, but the words stuck in her throat.

They passed a formal dining room, blue wallpaper and a grand oak table, and then into a gleaming white kitchen that looked like it hadn't been updated since Queen Victoria's reign.

He opened the back door and led her into a dark garden overshadowed by a tall rowan tree, its crimson leaves raining down with every breeze. Arthur brought her to a shoebox sitting on top of an iron garden table. He opened it.

"Oh no," she said, peering inside. "Poor darling. What's wrong?"

A dove, pale grey feathers with a black band around its neck, rested in a nest of shredded newspaper.

"He's got something wrong with his foot," Arthur said. "Saw something moving in the garden and saw him—her, maybe—hopping around. I caught him, but he nicked me on the arm."

Gingerly, Regan gathered the dove into her hands to examine it. She spotted the problem at once, a bit of wire around its leg, caught tight and cutting into the twig-like limb.

"Just a case of string foot," Regan said. "Can you go into the kitchen and fetch a bowl of water. He'll need some food—grains, seeds, lettuce, carrots. Whatever you have. Antibiotic ointment if you have it, too."

Regan held the bird near her body to keep it calm while she gently eased the ragged bit of wire off the bird's leg.

Arthur returned quickly with a bowl of water, a bowl of sesame seeds and lettuce.

"He'll be fine," Regan said as she placed the bird into the box with the food and water. She showed him the bit of shiny wire that had been caught on the dove's leg. "Nesting birds sometimes confuse good nesting material with bad. Leave the box open, and he'll probably fly off when he's filled his belly."

Already the collared dove was dipping his beak into the water between taking bites out of the lettuce leaf.

"When I saw the bird I wished you were here," Arthur said. "Then you were. Magic."

Regan lightly stroked the back of the dove's head before letting him alone to eat and drink his fill.

"I got your note," she said. "I'm curious to know why you sent me the name of *that* painting."

"Wild stab in the dark—no pun intended." He looked toward the house. "My parents have a gallery near here, on Half Moon Street."

Regan knew of it—The Half Moon Arthouse. One of many galleries and museums owned or patronized by the Godwick Family Arts Trust.

"We're opening a new exhibit next week, female artists of the Baroque period. The Gentileschi is the star of the show. My parents asked me to stop by, to make sure everything was up to snuff. I was looking right at the painting when it just...fell off the wall."

"A priceless Renaissance masterpiece fell off your wall."

"Our paintings don't fall. They wouldn't fall if there was an earthquake. But this one fell as if it jumped off its hook. If you're worried, the painting is fine. The frame, too, but...it wasn't like the hooks fell out of the plaster. It shouldn't have fallen. It felt like a sign or a..."

"A message?"

He nodded. Another breeze blew and more red rowan leaves fell into the darkening garden.

"I had a dream," she said, "yesterday afternoon, after you left."

"After you sent me packing."

She shrugged, looked at the dove rooting around in the box. "I dreamed I was Judith and I was in the tent of Holofernes. And right before I was about to cut his head off, he turned into you."

"Me?"

She smiled, met his searching gaze. "Then I cut his head off."

They looked at each other as the last of the evening light faded to grey and the lamps along the garden paths turned themselves on. The collared dove hopped once, twice, then out of the box. With another hop, he spread his wings and flew up into the rowan tree. The temperature seemed to plummet all at once.

Regan shivered, but it wasn't from the autumn breeze. This was a winter wind and it came from inside of her.

"Let's go in," she said. "I want to look at that bite on your arm."

He lifted his left arm, glanced at the wound. "It's only a scratch."

"Doves can carry disease," she said.

He looked at her, then gave her a slight smile. "Anything you say."

He led her back into the house, and she gave up her coat to him. He hung it on the hook by the back-garden door, next to his. It gave her a strange feeling of *déjà vu* as if this had happened before—their coats hanging here side-by-side like they lived together in this house, which made no sense unless, maybe, it was *déjà vu* for a time yet to come.

"You look beautiful," Arthur said, staring at her.

She had dressed as nicely as she could without being too obvious about it—a fashionable grey shirt dress and black boots, all very smart and expensive. This was one of the finest townhouses in all of London, however. She felt like a street urchin playing posh.

"Thank you," she said simply, as he led her into the kitchen.

They went to the sink and Arthur held out his arm with obvious reluctance. Clearly he was the sort of man who didn't like being fussed over. The cut—and it was a cut, not a scratch—was fairly deep. If he behaved, though, it would heal quickly.

"Just a flesh wound," she taunted. He smiled. As Zoot liked to say, a Monty Python reference never went amiss.

She washed the bite out with soap and warm water and felt Arthur's eyes on her the entire time.

"Why are you being so nice to me?" he asked.

"I should have been nicer before."

"Why start now?"

Two days ago she would have shot him a dirty look. Now she laughed at herself softly. "I have some bad news," she said. "Or depending on how much you hate me, it'll be good news. Do you hate me?"

"No."

He said it softly, and she felt the word as much as heard it, felt it like a stroking of fingers across her cheek or the gentle press of a kiss on the top of her foot.

Behind the sink was a window that looked out onto the back garden. The trees and plants were listing sideways. The wind was picking up. The house was eerily quiet and the tile floor of the kitchen and the cold porcelain sink echoed the quiet. She could hear her own heart beating.

"Regan? What's the bad news?"

She dried his arm, put on the plaster, and met his eyes. "I think we both could use a drink, don't you?"

"Definitely," he said. "If you'll go down the hall to the front room, I'll bring wine. Or would you like something stronger?"

"Wine will do. Red if you have it."

Regan dried her hands and walked down the hall to the front sitting room where a fire burned behind the grate. The walls were white, the trim black and the furniture Hepplewhite and Chippendale. On either side of the fireplace stood floor-to-ceiling bookcases. She had been prepared for the Godwicks' shelves to be filled with antiques and bric-a-brac, something she could sneer at, but no, they were stuffed solid to bursting with books. Books about art, and nothing but. Many of the same books she had in her office.

Was Arthur right? Was she just like them?

Or were they just like her?

Arthur entered wearing a clean grey t-shirt, V-neck, and holding two glasses—a glass of red wine and a glass of whisky, neat.

"The whisky's for me," he said, handing her the wine. "I have a bad feeling I'm going to need it."

"And maybe you should sit down, too," she said.

Arthur sat on the black-and-white striped sofa. A gust of wind blew loudly outside the house. Regan went to the front bow window and looked out just in time to see a newspaper cartwheeling down the street like a tumbleweed out of a Western.

"It's strange being here," she said, "at your house."

Strange and nice, too nice. That same sense of *déjà vu* returned. A cruel tease. There was a world where she didn't hold back, where she let her feelings for him take root. A world where she and Arthur fell madly in love and lived together in this stunning London townhouse full of art and books and good wine and soft chairs. Marriage to Arthur would be passionate and private, just the two of them, sitting here in this room talking or not talking, up in their bedroom, making love or sleeping. Art galleries, art shows, art auctions... She could have a studio upstairs in a room with north-facing light. They could start a charity, free art lessons for children whose poorly-funded state schools didn't have art classes. And in the evenings, dinners out, the theater, home again, laughing, a little drunk but only on each other.

God, she wanted it so badly she could taste it. But it could never be. She drank her wine instead.

"Not really my house," he said. "It's my parents'."

She turned around to face him though she stayed at the window, holding the wine glass in her hand. "It will be yours. You're the heir. The townhouse. Wingthorn. The paintings."

"Not the paintings. They belong to the trust, which belongs to everyone in the family. But you're right. I do inherit the bulk of everything, which I know is massively unfair. You don't have to tell me. Dad would have left everything to Lia if he could have."

"How does Charlie feel about that, being the spare?"

"He's never said anything."

"Are you sure? He did sleep with your girlfriend the day you broke up with her. Sounds like he was trying to tell you something."

Arthur exhaled loudly. "Maybe. He had to know I'd give him anything he wants or needs. Except Wingthorn," he said with a tight smile. "It's mine."

"Why are you here if you prefer it there?"

"Renovations. We've all had to clear out. Charlie and I were staying here until he got sick of me and moved in with a friend. Mum and Dad are in New York on an art shopping expedition."

"So we're completely alone here?"

"Yes," he said, "and I have to confess something incredibly stupid."

"What?"

"I like hearing you say 'we.'"

To hide her smile she raised her wine glass but didn't drink. She lowered it and held it with two hands, staring into the crimson liquid as if trying to divine from it what the future held.

"Are you all right?" he asked her.

The answer was no. She wasn't all right and hadn't been for possibly her entire life. Certainly not since her mother died.

"In the dream," she said, "right before I cut your head off...you looked at me and said, 'I'm not your enemy.'"

"I'm not your enemy."

Hearing him say those words sent a shiver through her entire body. That uncanny feeling of a dream being real and the real world being a dream.

"I wish you were," she said. "I don't want to think I wasted all these years hating your family for nothing."

"What my grandfather did to your mother was unconscionable. If he had some obligation to her and he refused...God, even if she were a total stranger..." He met her eyes. "We can still be enemies if you prefer."

"No." She shook her head. "Friends, then?"

"You know we could never be friends."

It was becoming almost painful, the space between them. She wanted to sit on the sofa at his side, to pull his head into her lap and stroke his hair, black as a raven's wing. His dark eyes studied her. He seemed to intuit what she was feeling, or perhaps he simply felt the same, just as strongly, this aching need to touch each other.

He said, "You banished me, remember? I can't come to you. You have to come to me. Or make me come to you."

It was true. This was how it had to be if she was to be his master and he was to be her servant. She had to make the first move. She had to open the door. She had to tap the first domino. She had to say the magic word.

"I need a little time."

"Take all the time you need," he said.

Outside another wind blew hard against the house, rattling the old windows. The evening darkened deeper. The air was electric with waiting, heavy with possibilities. She'd broken their deal by sending him away, and if things were to continue with them, the rules would be different... and so would be the prize.

But the stakes were much higher now. Someone else was playing the game with them.

"I'm terrified," she said. A sinister November wind crept in under a door. She shivered.

"If it is him—if it's Lord Malcolm knocking paintings and books onto the floor, to get our attention—I don't think he'd hurt you."

"It's not him who terrifies me."

"What then? Who?"

"You know. You know perfectly well."

He did know. She saw it in his eyes as he stared at her. He knew she was afraid of him, of them.

"When you've been ice all your life," she said, "nothing is more terrifying than seeing yourself start to melt."

"Ice doesn't die when it melts. It just gets wet."

She smiled. "I know, but I'm still afraid."

"I'll protect you."

Had he slapped her in the face it would have hurt less than hearing those three words. It hurt the way mercy hurts when you know you don't deserve it. Regan turned back to the bow window, to the streets going wild with wind. Any moment now, rain would explode from the sky.

With her back to him she said, "Don't say that to a woman like me if you don't mean it." A woman like her...a woman who's had to protect herself her entire life.

"I'll protect you," he said again.

"I won't protect you."

"I'll protect you," he said a third time and with finality.

She turned back around. The fire behind the grate danced as fresh air fed it. It feasted on the wind in the room. Where was it coming from?

Regan walked toward Arthur but at the last moment, forced herself to sit in the armchair opposite him by the fire. She sipped her wine and set the glass on the table.

"I've had to be cold for so long," she said, "I don't know if I can remember how to be warm."

"November is cold," he said, "And wet and brutal. It's my favorite month of the year."

"Mine, too."

The wind gusted louder. A siren sounded in the distance. A storm was rising.

"Are you falling in love with me?" she asked.

"Yes."

She nodded, wishing she could celebrate that. Instead she was like someone who'd won the lottery but was forbidden from spending a single penny.

"Why?" she asked.

"I need to protect someone, and I've never met anyone who needed protecting more than you do."

"I don't have any enemies."

"You sure about that?"

"My own worst enemy? Is that what you're saying?"

He only met her eyes and waited.

"You can't love me," she said.

"Try to stop me."

"All right. I will." She met his eyes. "I told you the first night we slept together I couldn't have children. That was true. I don't mean I'm on birth control, I mean..."

She steeled herself to say her secret out loud, the one she'd kept even from Sir Jack.

She continued, "Both my mother and grandmother died of a rare and incredibly lethal glioma before they were thirty-five. That's a form of brain cancer, if you've never heard of it. I hope you haven't," she said. "The thing is, Arthur...it can be hereditary."

His eyes widened. "Hereditary."

"They can test for the genes now," she went on. "They know. *I* know." She shrugged. "When the geneticist gave me my results, I asked him what he would do if he were me. Do you know what he said?"

Arthur shook his head. His hands trembled.

"His exact words were, 'I would make my will.'" She gave a cold little laugh. "I did make my will. And then I...I chose to be sterilized to avoid passing it on to, you know, any children I might have had with Sir Jack. Or anyone else."

Arthur glanced away, looked anywhere but at her.

She could have told him more, that as soon as she was diagnosed—likely in the next five to ten years—a clock would start, the end-of-her-life clock, and she would have fifteen months, no more, left to live. And those last fifteen months of her life would be spent in agony.

"That's the only reason I married Sir Jack," she said. "So I'd never end up like my mother, begging strangers to pay for experimental medical treatments. And I don't regret it, even now."

"I know you don't want me to say I'm sorry," he said.

"No, don't say you're sorry. I know you are. I know I am."

He exhaled heavily. "So that's what..." He stopped, shot his whisky. "This explains a lot," he said.

She knew what he meant. It explained why she drank too much and had unprotected sex with him from their first night together, why she worked twelve-hour days to avoid thinking. It explained why she'd pushed him away so viciously yesterday on the terrace. She couldn't bring herself to hate him or anyone enough to let them fall in love with a woman condemned.

"I'm thirty," she said. "It's going to happen any day now. I won't see forty, Arthur. That...that treatment my mother wanted to try in America? Ninety percent of the participants died after two years anyway."

"Ninety," he said. "Not one-hundred. And that was over two decades ago. Who knows what they can do now, what treatments—"

"I know," she said. "I know it all."

"Is this supposed to stop me from loving you? If so, it

won't work." His voice broke and Regan had to look away from him. She couldn't bear to see how much she was hurting him.

"Maybe this will work," she said. "Sir Jack was mostly impotent in the last few years of our marriage. He would use powerful vibrators on me to force me to come even when I didn't want to. It would just...happen. I couldn't control my own responses. I had to learn how to separate my body from my heart and mind, from my...my *self*. I don't think I can put them back together.

"They've been separated too long and both halves have healed, like when you set a bird's broken wing badly... It will heal. It will live. But it won't ever fly. What I mean is... I don't think I can love you, Brat. And even if I could, I wouldn't let myself."

He looked away from her again, at the windows, rattling softly in their frames. She'd wounded him. He wanted the possibility of love, of a life together. She didn't have it to give.

"But," she said, "selfishly, I do want you to love me. Is that enough?"

He looked at her again, and he smiled the same way he had when the dove had taken flight. "Just hearing you call me Brat again is enough."

"Enough for now," she said. "I can't love you, and I can't have your children. And here you are, the heir to one of the last titles in the kingdom that means something. You know how it works—even if we adopted a son, he couldn't inherit your titles."

"I don't give a damn about my titles, Regan. I never have."

"I care about dying and leaving a child motherless," she said. "God, Arthur, don't you understand I am literally the last woman in London you should be falling in love with? I thought you were the smart one in the Godwick family?"

"Maybe." At least he admitted it. "Maybe you are the last woman I should love, but you're the only one I want."

The lights flickered. And during that flash of darkness, she wiped the tears off her face. When the lights came on again, her cheeks were dry.

"You beautiful fool," she said, then laughed coldly at herself. "Do you want to know something? After Sir Jack died, I told myself I wouldn't date anyone at all ever again. No dating. No remarrying. No sex even. I couldn't bear to think of someone caring about me and then finding out the truth...except you. I liked the thought of hurting you. That's why I made that stupid bloody offer. You were the one man in the world I hated enough to sleep with, because I didn't care at all how badly I hurt you."

"I've never been so happy to be hated in my life."

She stood up and Arthur looked at her. "Are you leaving?" he asked.

"I can't. It's raining, and I didn't bring my umbrella."

"Then you should stay."

"You have a bedroom in this house, I assume," she said.

"I do. Do you want to sleep in it tonight?"

"Yes," she said. "With you."

Arthur rose from the sofa and just as he was coming to her, the lights flickered again and went out.

She reached for his hand in the dark and found it. The wind gusted. The house shook. His hand was warm and steady and strong.

Something thumped on the floor close to them in the dark. The lights flickered on again.

They turned and saw a book on the floor, fallen off the shelf. It had landed face down, the pages open.

Both she and Arthur stared at it as if a snake had suddenly slithered into the sitting room to warm itself at the fire.

"Leave it," Regan said. "We'll look at it in the morning."

ARTHUR TOOK her by the hand and led her into the entryway, to the stairs and up, up, up to his bedroom. As they ascended, the wind grew louder. Leaves blew past the windows and cast strange shadows on the walls like a thousand shadow birds.

When they reached the landing, the lights flickered off again. Arthur was able to guide her to his room in the dark. Inside the doorway, he said, "Stay here. I don't want you to trip over anything and hurt yourself. I'll find candles."

He started to leave her and she grabbed him by the wrist and pulled him back to her. On the threshold of his bedroom, in a house gone dark and the storm suddenly quiet, their mouths found each other in an electric kiss. It was a kiss on the edge of a knife, a kiss at the edge of the world. His mouth was hot and hungry and charged with meaning and need. She opened her lips to his tongue and tasted him, the taste that was just him, only him.

"We don't need candles," she said, "if we stay here."

Arthur reached under her dress, lifting it to her waist to find her knickers. He hooked his thumbs under the lacy edges and pulled them down her legs and over her boots. Where they landed, she didn't care. On his knees, he lifted her dress higher, kissed her stomach, quivering and taut, then her naked hips. His lips brushed over the sensitive skin, teasing and tickling. His hands cupped her bottom and kneaded her there.

His head came to rest against her stomach and she found his hair, black silk, and wound her fingers into it and held him there.

"Last night," he breathed, "was the longest night of my life. And today was the longest day."

"You shouldn't feel this much for me. You're only going to lose me sooner or later."

"I pick later, then."

She might have chided him for his naiveté—spoken just like a twenty-year-old half-grown man—thinking they could build something on this alone. She didn't mock him, though. She wanted to believe it, too.

He kissed her again, all over her thighs and sides and down her legs all the way to her knees and back up again. She reached between her thighs and found the folds of her labia, spread them and pushed her hips forward. He brought his mouth to her cunt and lapped at it, licking her clitoris as he held her against the doorframe by her waist. The heat from his tongue, the wetness warmed her to her core. Each flick of his tongue sent waves of pleasure shooting up her spine and down the backs of her legs. And this, him on his knees in front of her, his head in her hands, his heart and soul and life in her hands...

The hollowness inside of her ached to be filled. The need to touch him grew unbearably strong. Regan tugged on his hair, pulling him off his knees. She reached for his shirt and almost tore it from him in her rush to reach his body. Finally she had his flesh under her fingers—hard chest, flat firm stomach, strong broad shoulders. She touched him everywhere front and back, and drew him against her so she could run her hands up and down the long furrow of his spine. She trailed her fingers around his sides and to the front, to his stomach, to his jeans, the button, the zipper.

His cock was brutally hard. He inhaled sharply as she wrapped her fingers around it and stroked. He rested his head on her shoulder while she rubbed him with both hands, making slow long explorations with her fingers. She circled the head and gathered the pearls of come and massaged them into the tip so that he would be as wet as she was when he entered her.

She brought his cock between her legs, the tip against her clitoris. He took himself in hand and stroked that aching knot.

"No more," she said. "Now."

What she said, he did. Regan was suddenly pushed hard against the doorframe, and his arms wound round her. He lifted her and brought her down, impaling her. A cry escaped her lips as she sunk down onto him. She was pinned to the frame as he pulled her legs around his waist. She locked them at the ankles, trapping him inside of her.

She clung to his shoulders and felt his mouth at her ear. Her vagina clenched around the thick organ inside her.

Her thighs strained to hold herself. She had to move so she put one booted foot on the floor and the other on the opposite side of the doorframe, waist high so that she could let him slide in and out of her wetness freely. Between her open thighs, Arthur fucked her, pushing into her open hole with long, rough thrusts. She moved to meet him and felt every inch as it entered her, split her, speared her.

It became a frenzy. They panted together, mouths close but not touching. Her inner muscles clenched and released, clenched and tightened, clenched and fluttered.

Arthur's hands gripped her arse so hard she knew his fingers were leaving bruises. She wanted the bruises. She cried out as he yanked her against him, spearing her again just as her orgasm hit and exploded. She came with a lusty loud release. Even as her climax waned, he was still pumping into her.

She whispered, "I need your come," into his ear and it was enough to finish him.

His head fell back and he lifted her off the floor and brought her down on him a final time as he filled her.

It was over. Though they broke apart, they clung together.

Arthur caught his breath before she did. She leaned back against the door and panted, her hands on his shoulders to steady herself. His come slicked her thighs.

"I'll get the candles," he said and she nodded, kissed his cheek, and let him go with an order.

"Hurry."

Hurry, she'd said, as if she couldn't bear one minute, two minutes apart from him.

He came back to her down the long narrow hall, lit candle in hand, hand shielding the flame. She followed him into the bedroom and to the bed.

He set the candle in its brass holder on the bedside table. She watched from the foot of the bed as he pulled back the covers and made a place for her.

"I should wash," she said.

"I'll do it for you."

Regan let him raise her dress and pull it off her. He laid it neatly over the back of a chair. He unhooked her bra and slid the straps down her arms, laid it over her dress.

He whispered he would be back. Regan rested against the cool smooth wood of the bedpost. Arthur returned with a warm, wet flannel. He knelt again and washed his own semen off her thighs and ran it between her legs. It was the act of a body servant, bathing his mistress. The wind was wild again outside but inside everything was calm, serene.

Except it wasn't. Arthur's mouth was tight with tension. The book downstairs that had fallen off the shelf unsettled them both. They could only pretend for so long that what was happening wasn't really happening.

But...they could pretend a little longer.

ARTHUR UNZIPPED her boots and tossed them onto the floor. He stood up and finished undressing as she watched, his body more beautiful than ever bathed in the candlelight.

She laid back and settled against a pillow. Cotton sheets, with pale red stripes against white. The candle flickered and Arthur bent over it and blew it out. In that split second his face was bathed in golden light, Regan knew his was the last face she wanted to see before bed every night of her life and the face she wanted to see first thing in the morning.

But she didn't tell him that. She couldn't. Gently, he lay down next to her, on his side facing her.

"There are other rooms in the house," he said. "If you decide you want to sleep alone. I know you said—"

She put a finger over his lips. "Forget what I said."

He wrapped his hand around hers, kissed the finger that silenced him. She rested back onto the pillow, Arthur on his side pressed close. His hands found the enormous pearl drop she wore on a chain around her neck and lightly toyed with it.

"Some masters give collars to their pets," she said.

He gently tugged the pearl on the chain. "Are you going to do that to me?"

She rolled onto her side to face him. "I think you're like a collared dove. The collar's already a part of you, born on you."

His black eyes gleamed in the dark.

She put her finger over his lips again, then moved close to kiss him, to silence him for good, at least for now. He obeyed her silent order and as he lay there, she explored his body with her hands. She rested her head on his shoulder and stroked his chest and his flat hard stomach. She cupped his testicles and held them, then wrapped her hand gently around his soft penis which began to stiffen as soon as she held it. "Mine," she said. "All mine."

"Yours," he said. "All yours."

He wrapped his arms around her.

"You were right, you know," he said. "When you said you can't make up with someone until you've had the fight."

"Are you going to talk to Charlie? Have a good old-fashioned row with him?"

"He barely speaks to me."

"Give it time." She touched his face.

"You know, my grandfather," he said, "died of heart disease at only fifty-six. My father's already sixty-one, and his cardiologist says—"

"Stop," she said. "You can't save me by wishing."

"I can still try."

"Either make love to me again or go to sleep," she said. "Just don't make me talk about it anymore."

His fingers tightened around the pearl that dangled on the end of the chain.

"Killing you, isn't it? That I have something you can't fix?" she asked.

"I could sell my soul to the devil like my great-grandfather."

"No, you can't."

"Why not?"

Wickedly, she grinned up at him. "Your soul already belongs to me. You can't give away what you don't own."

He kissed her once and pulled back, looking down at her as if drinking in the sight of her in his bed. She drank in the sight of him drinking in the sight of her. Nothing had ever tasted better. Not whisky, not wine.

Arthur pulled gently until the clasp of the silver chain holding the large pearl broke in his hand.

"There, that's better," he said.

"What are you doing?" she demanded.

"You said I could either make love to you or go to sleep. I've chosen the first option."

The room was so dark she couldn't quite see what he did to her necklace but it seemed to her like he was taking the large pearl drop off the chain.

He held up the pearl drop in his fingers. It shimmered in the light, the size of a robin's egg but a silvery white.

"This is the largest pearl I've ever seen."

"It's costume jewelry," she said.

"It's perfect."

She almost asked *For what?*, but there was no need.

He moved his hand between her thighs and pressed the pearl against her vulva. Curious and curiously aroused, Regan opened her legs wider. With one finger, Arthur pushed the large round pearl through her folds and into her body, still slick from their earlier lovemaking.

Arthur maneuvered the pearl inside of her until it was nestled under her pubic bone, into the hollow of her g-spot. It fit there snugly, as if it belonged. Regan's heart beat harder as Arthur used the pearl to knead that hollow, rolling it against that patch of tender nerve-endings.

"Oh, God," Regan said, catching her breath. Her head fell back and her legs fell open even as every muscle in her thighs and back tensed. Arthur held the pearl inside her with one finger and yet with that pearl and his one finger, he was in control of her entire body. Wave after wave of pleasure passed through her belly. Her fingers tangled in the sheets. The pressure was ecstasy, the slight and tight pressure right there in that cleft just inside her...and if that wasn't incredible enough, Arthur pushed two then three then four fingers inside of her, filling her even as he gently ground the fat smooth pearl into her.

She'd never been brought to orgasm so quickly in her life, not even when she was a hormone-addled teenager. She came with a sudden cry as an electric current spiked through her body. Her vagina contracted sharply around Arthur's fingers, and it seemed an eternity her shoulders hovered off the bed, her body frozen in place, before she collapsed back onto the pillow.

As she lay there, utterly spent and insensate, Arthur pushed the pearl deep into her cunt, all the way to her cervix. Then he rose over her, mounted and entered her. He fucked her slowly with long deep strokes and every time the tip of his cock touched the pearl she felt a sweet spasm of pleasure again.

She lay on her back and watched Arthur lose himself inside of her in the candlelight, watched his lips part and his face tighten, watched his muscles move and the long strong cords of his neck and shoulders tense.

She ran her hands over his chest as he moved inside of her and she memorized every second of this moment, this gorgeous young man making love to her as if he'd die if he didn't.

A sob escaped her throat and at once Arthur's arms were around her clinging to her. "Regan."

"Don't stop." She wrapped her legs around his back. "I'll die if you stop."

"Then I'll never stop," he said and it seemed he wouldn't. He rode her with long and tender strokes. It felt like the pearl inside her touched the tip of her spine. Her body tensed again, tingling and when he came she came with him. The one part of her brain still thinking rationally reminded her that the French called orgasm "the little death." Every time she came she died in Arthur's arms. That's how she wanted to go when the time came, in his arms.

When it was over and done, he lay on top of her, cradling her against his heart.

She wanted to live.

She'd thought she'd accepted the inevitable end, but now, in his arms, she knew she'd only accepted dying in her old life, with Sir Jack, when death might have been a relief.

Not with Arthur. With Arthur, a thousand years in his arms wouldn't be enough.

She said into his ear, quietly but sternly, "You aren't allowed to ask me to marry you. We can keep going like this, but not forever. I don't have forever to give you but I'll give you what I can."

What she could give him was until he went away to join his regiment and she went...somewhere, somewhere away from him so he could get on with his life and forget she existed.

"Do you understand?" she said.

He nodded. "Should we go and look at the book?"

She knew he was trying to distract her and she appreciated it. She also appreciated how gently he pushed his fingers into her to extract the large pearl from her vagina.

"Not yet," she said. "Let's have one last night of sanity before we both go mad in the morning."

"I always wanted to go mad," he said. "Now I have an excuse."

He rolled onto his back and brought her with him. Regan lay her head on his chest. He wrapped his arms around her.

The winds died down. The storm passed. Regan slept like the dead.

REGAN WOKE early and saw the bedroom for the first time in daylight. A teenage boy's room. Massive Union Jack hanging down the wall. Concert posters. A rugby ball on a shelf. A polo mallet tucked into a corner. She knew he was only staying here while Wingthorn underwent renovations, that of course the room still held all his old things, but it served as a bitter reminder of their age difference. She was a woman of thirty, already widowed, and if he hadn't been joining the army soon, he'd still be at university. His life was beginning. Hers felt almost over.

He was too young to commit himself to a woman who was certain to face a brutal fate sooner rather than later, just as she'd been too young to marry Sir Jack. She couldn't do to Arthur what she'd done to herself.

But she didn't have to tell him that.

She kissed his cheek and his eyes fluttered open. In wordless agreement, they got out of bed. Arthur put on his jeans, nothing else. She found her knickers and he gave her one of his t-shirts to wear—clean, soft, grey, comforting.

They went down, down, down to the sitting room where the book still lay open on the floor face down in front of the cold fireplace.

Arthur picked up the book and showed her the page it was open to—a painting of a pretty young girl holding a dove against her chest, a dove with a broken wing.

The Wounded Dove by the Jewish Victorian-era painter Rebecca Solomon.

Regan stared at it, then knew they couldn't deny it any longer.

"So this is it," Regan said. "We both believe and accept that the ghost of a dead lord is trying to tell us something, and we're willing to listen. Yes?"

Arthur nodded. "Yes."

So it had happened. They'd both gone mad.

10

THE HAUNTED WOOD

They'd planned to meet in her penthouse at The Pearl around eight that evening. At five 'til, Regan sat on the chaise in the sitting room to wait for Arthur. Upstairs in her bedroom hung the possibly haunted portrait of Lord Malcolm, which was why she waited in the sitting room, not wanting to be alone with it.

A knock on the door. She went to it at once, certain it was Arthur. She opened the door to find a waiter in a white jacket, carrying wine in a bucket.

"Lord Godwick ordered wine," the young man said.

"Wonderful," Regan said, "bring it in."

He carried in the bottle and two glasses from the hotel kitchen with little faux pearl charms on the stems. The waiter set the glasses on the fireplace mantel and uncorked the bottle.

"Interesting artwork," the waiter said.

Hanging above the fireplace was a print reproduction of an oil painting—an uncanny scene of a woman running through a dark forest, a vague ghostly figure behind her, imprisoned in a tree but escaping it, seemingly following her.

"A Lizzie Siddal print," she said. "She was Dante Gabriel Rossetti's muse, working class but very beautiful. She could have been a painter in her own right if she hadn't...ah, well. Rossetti rather took over her life."

The waiter nodded. "Such a shame."

"Rossetti once gave the poor woman pneumonia by making her lie in a bath of cold water for hours while he painted her. They married eventually, but she died very young. Only thirty-three. Painter, poet...she was terribly talented. And then snuffed out like a candle. I think that's supposed to be Death in her painting. That's what's haunting her."

The young man gazed on the painting and she saw he had darkly intelligent eyes.

"No," he said, "it's not Death. It's her. That ghost looks like a shadow of her. She's haunting herself."

Regan moved closer to the print, studied it carefully. The ghost did somewhat resemble the running woman.

He smiled and met her eyes. "But what do I know? I'm only here to pour the wine." He offered her a glass. "Enjoy, Lady Ferry," he said with an elegant bow then made his way to the door.

"Thank you... I'm sorry, you must be new, and I haven't learned your name yet."

"John," he said and flipped his lapel over to show her his name tag. JOHN NOONE.

"Welcome to The Pearl, John."

"Thank you very much, ma'am," he said, opening the door. He turned back and glanced at the painting over the fireplace again. "You've got a bit of Lizzie Siddal in you, I think."

"You do?"

"Both of you were painters. Same eyes, too. As Rossetti said, 'Eyes as of the sea and sky on a grey day.'"

She stared at him. "Never expected a waiter to quote Dante Gabriel Rossetti poetry at me."

"Yes, but I'm not your ordinary waiter, Lady Ferry. Enjoy. It's pomegranate wine," he said. "If you've never had it before, you're in for a treat."

He bowed again and left, shutting the door behind him.

Regan had never had pomegranate wine before, but as soon as she heard the name she knew she wanted to try it. Very romantic of Arthur to send wine up to her. She lifted the glass to her nose and sniffed. The scent was strong but not too powerful, velvety and seductive, sweet but too sweet and utterly delicious. She took a sip and it tasted as good as it smelled. She took another sip and sighed with pleasure. Arthur had excellent taste in wine. Surprising, since he so rarely drank in her presence.

She was about to take another drink when she heard a familiar buzzing sound. Her phone. She had a message.

Almost there, Arthur had written. *Hit accident traffic. So sorry. Don't start the madness without me.*

She smiled. She would never start the madness without him. Only the drinking.

Take your time. Thank you for the wine. It's wonderful.

She moved to set the phone back down on the table when it began to ring in her hand. Arthur was calling.

"What wine?" he said, as soon as she answered.

"The bottle you sent up."

"It wasn't me."

"The waiter said Lord Godwick sent up—"

Arthur swore violently. "I'm not the only Lord Godwick."

Regan's body went cold. Her hands shook. She set the wine glass down before she dropped it.

"I didn't tell him I used to be a painter," she said.

"What?"

"The waiter. He knew I'd been a painter, but I never mentioned that to him."

"I'm on my way," Arthur said. She could hear the fear in his voice. "I'll be there as fast as I can. Don't drink another drop of that wine."

"Malcolm wouldn't poison me. I know that."

"How do you know that?" Arthur demanded. "You don't know him. Neither do I. We don't know what he wants from us or—"

Her head was starting to swim. The world went water-colored. She wasn't sure what Arthur was saying. Regan collapsed onto the chaise lounge.

"Regan? Are you there? Regan?"

Tiredly, she brought the phone to her ear. "In the dream."

"What?"

"In the dream I had about Malcolm," she said. Her tongue felt thick in her mouth. "The one with the rose vine wallpaper and the empty frame...I didn't tell you that in the dream, Lord Malcolm loved me."

"He loved all pretty women."

"Not like that. I don't know why or how but he...*cared* about me."

"Regan, listen. You should probably call 999. If it wasn't him, someone might be trying to hurt you—"

"No one's hurting me. No one. *Noone.*"

"What?"

Noone. John No-one. She laughed when she got the joke. "Good joke, Lord Malcolm. I fell for that one, too."

"Regan—"

Without knowing what she was doing, Regan ended the call and the phone dropped onto the floor.

She closed her eyes and rested her head against the back of the chaise. There was no reason for Arthur to worry. She felt incredible...like she could fly if she wanted to. Still, it was lovely to hear Arthur so worried for her. He did care about her. He really did. Sweet lad. Her beautiful brat. If only she could love him, wouldn't that be...lovely? Too bad she couldn't. She'd sworn she'd never get married again, and Arthur had to get married. He have little brats of his own. He was the hare.

Heir, not *hare*. Regan giggled drunkenly to herself. This pomegranate wine was making her silly. When was the last time she giggled? Never?

Arthur wasn't a hare. *That* was a hare.

A brown hare, long-eared and white-footed loped past the fireplace and toward the garden terrace doors.

Regan rose from the chaise and followed it. How had a hare gotten into the penthouse? She was on the top storey.

It wanted out. She saw it sitting up on its hind legs at the doors, terribly polite of it. She opened the door and it hopped onto the terrace. Regan went after it.

The garden terrace wasn't there anymore. Or it was, but it had been transformed somehow into a forest. A dark night-time forest lit only by a waning moon.

Some part of her rational mind still functioned and warned her to stay away from the forest. There was danger in these woods. Yet, she couldn't deny herself the beauty that beckoned even if it was foolish to follow its call.

This is how she'd gotten herself entangled with Arthur

Godwick, she knew—her love of beauty, even dangerous beauty. And what was more dangerous than making love to the heir of the family she most despised in the world? Walking into an enchanted forest at night alone and unarmed, of course.

Two spreading yew trees, limbs twisted and gnarled, formed a gate at the edge of the wood. Siddal's *Haunted Wood*. A wind gust pushed the boughs apart just enough she could slip through them.

Ahead of her the brown hare paused in a shaft of silver moonlight, then fled into the woods.

The city sounds of London were muted inside the forest. No cars. No rumbling lorries. No sirens. No voices or laughter echoing from the streets below. She heard nothing but owls hooting, the sighing wind, the lonesome cry of a wolf.

There were no wolves in England. They'd all been slaughtered three hundred years ago.

A bird landed on a branch. She looked up. A raven.

"Gloom," she said with relief. "Come here, baby." She held out her arm.

"Leave my loneliness unbroken," Gloom said, and flew off. Regan could have wept.

"What do you want from me, Malcolm?" she whispered as she walked through the yew trees and into the impossible forest. The ground was soft under her feet, soft like the earth of a freshly dug grave. "What are you doing to me? If you want me to stop hating the Godwicks, fine...I already do. I won't hurt them, not even Charlie, though he probably deserves it."

It was all that made sense to her, that Lord Malcolm was trying to heal the breach between her and the Godwicks. That's why he'd been scaring her over and over again into Arthur's arms. Could he see into the future? Could he see that if she'd caused Charlie to be cut off from the family, he would spiral down into the gutter too far to be brought back, as Arthur feared?

"I'll return your portrait to the family," Regan said in a hushed tone. "If that's what you want, message received. The Godwicks can have your precious painting back. Charlie can work off his debt at the hotel."

Nothing happened. She'd hoped that if she promised to return the painting, she'd wake up as if from a nightmare. But no. Malcolm had more to show her, it seemed. More pretenses to abandon, more promises to make or break.

How was this real? Regan could smell the rot of dead trees emanating from the forest floor. She could feel leafy branches on her face, catching in her hair. As she passed a thorn tree, she lifted her fingers to a branch and pricked her finger on one of its wicked thorns.

The pain and blood should have woken her if this had been a dream. But, just as when she'd slayed Holofernes, she could not seem to wake herself.

As Regan walked past a towering ancient oak tree, she sensed a presence behind her. Footsteps following her. She froze and every nerve in her body screamed a warning and every hair on her arms stood on end. She would not look back, however. She would not let herself look.

She kept walking, kept moving forward, letting the light from the moon guide her path.

"Why am I here..." Regan muttered.

"You know why you're here," came a woman's voice behind her.

Regan inhaled sharply, but walked on. It was her own

voice that she'd heard. An echo of words never spoken, or something else?

"You live in a tower at the very top where no one can reach you," said the voice. "You think you're safe in your tower, but you aren't safe. You're only alone."

"Alone where no one can hurt me," Regan said, arguing with her own shadow self.

"You can hurt yourself. You've been hurting yourself for years. The Tower can't protect you. It never has. You know that. That's why you invited Arthur into your tower —to protect you. Who do you wish was here with you now, in this forest?"

Arthur. She wanted Arthur here with her.

"You want Arthur?" the voice taunted. "He's here. Let's find him. Follow me."

A whisper of white, like the hint of a mist, passed Regan and floated in front of her. Regan walked faster, chasing the mist until it brought her to a clearing in the trees. A fairy circle of stones ringed the clearing. In the center of the circle burned an enormous dancing bonfire.

From behind the bonfire, Arthur stepped into the clearing. He was naked and beguiling in the firelight. Her desire for him was immediate, and she tried to step over the circle of stones but couldn't. It wouldn't allow her inside to be with him.

Regan leaned against the trunk of an ancient tree, clung to the bark, and stared at Arthur, willing him to see her, to come to her.

She called his name but he seemingly couldn't hear her inside the stone circle.

Regan could only stare, worshipping him with her eyes, the long lean strong body she'd explored every inch of, the chest she'd slept on, the arms that had held her, the mouth that had kissed her lips and her clitoris, the hands that had given her more pleasure than she knew she deserved.

He must be waiting for her. Why else would he be naked? She was his lover, no one else. Yet there was someone else.

A woman came out from behind the bonfire. A beautiful young woman, she looked about twenty, no more. Ten years younger than Regan. She had rich dark hair that fell to her waist and vivid blue eyes, large full breasts and pert nipples, pink and tender.

Regan could only watch as the girl went to Arthur. He took her by the waist and pulled her close. They kissed, a deep passionate kiss, and Regan tried to call out to him, to remind him who he belonged to. *Her.* Not that girl in his arms.

The girl's eyes gleamed with such desire it looked more like greed than passion. Ravenously, she wrapped her arms around Arthur's neck to latch onto him as she opened her mouth, greedy for his kisses.

Regan watched, sick to her stomach, bile in her mouth, as the girl drew Arthur to the ground. She positioned him onto his back on the bare ground and took his cock into her hand, stroking it until it grew stiff. She rose up over him and put it into her body, sinking down onto it as Regan watched in impotent rage.

The girl rode him in a frenzy. Arthur didn't touch her, which could have comforted Regan but didn't. Vines growing from the ground had wrapped around his wrists. He was tied down. The girl's breasts bounced as she bobbed on top of him, her face a parody of pleasure. She cried out with her climax but it was an exaggerated cry, almost a scream, like she was playing a part and playing it poorly.

The vines broke and Arthur was able to free himself, but even as he stood up the girl turned and offered her body again to him. She bent over at the waist, her cunt wet and open, glistening in the firelight. With a thrust Arthur was inside her hole, rutting in a fresh frenzy, holding the girl by the hips with a bruising grip. Regan knew those should be her hips he held, her cunt he fucked.

The bonfire grew higher, formed the shape of a tall oval and reflected the vision of Arthur and the girl coupling madly.

All of this was hers, Regan knew, her nights with Arthur. Who was this young woman who dared take what didn't belong to her?

And now they were waltzing naked around the fire. And now he was pushing her to the ground where he mounted her and penetrated her ripe red vagina. And then he was out of her but she was on her back, her legs spread so wide it looked obscene. Arthur held a string of pearls in his hand and, one by one, pushed them into the girl's open waiting hole.

Even as Regan watched in horror, her body remembered that night. She remembered how shocked she'd been Arthur would do something so daring, so erotic. How smooth the little pearls were as he'd slid them through the opening of her vagina, how slick and cool. The strand was long and Arthur had been determined to fill her with every inch of them.

At first it had felt like nothing more than a ridged dildo inside of her, so much like the ones her husband had used on her, forcing her to have one powerful orgasm after another until she would weep for him to stop.

But it wasn't like that for long. The more Arthur had given her, the more she'd wanted. As the pearls filled her,

her cunt had begun to clench and contract, protesting the intrusion even though she'd wanted it. But then...gradually, her body had opened to take it all and as the pearls filled her beyond what she thought she could take, her vagina opened itself like an iris to receive every last one. She still felt them inside of her, touching every nerve, spreading her out, working their way into every secret cleft inside of her...

It had been the most erotic moment of her life, and when they'd seen the book and the painting—*Woman with a Pearl Necklace*—after, she'd felt such a horror at the thought that the most precious, private, erotic moment of her life had been witnessed by anyone other than Arthur.

Now she was being forced to watch as her lover did that to another woman, a younger woman, a woman he clearly wanted more than her. If he could betray Regan like this...

It wouldn't stop. Arthur kept pushing the pearls into the girl's open cunt. It had to stop. But as endless as the pearls were, so was the girl's capacity to take them. When the entire strand disappeared from view finally, she took Arthur's whole hand inside of her, all the way to the wrist and then the forearm. The girl's stomach swelled as if he'd impregnated her with those glistening white pearls, and Regan couldn't bear to watch anymore.

She tore herself away from the tree, fled the fire and the fairy circle and the sight of Arthur with that woman who was not her. As she fled, the white whisper of mist floated behind her, mocking her.

"How long until he leaves you for a girl who will love him?" she said. "How long will he allow you to take his love without giving any in return? How long...how long...how long...and what will you do when he's gone? Will you die?"

"I don't want to die," Regan called out.

"Then live," the voice said.

Regan nearly stumbled over another ring of fairy stones. She stopped at once, unable to cross them. Panting, heart in her throat, she stared into the ring and saw a woman standing at an easel. In the moonlight, Regan saw the woman was painting. At first she didn't recognize the woman with the chin-length brown hair and the glasses, wearing paint-spattered jeans and a man's shirt, the too-long sleeves rolled to her elbows. Inside the ring of stones, a shadow moved and out of the darkness stepped Arthur. He was dressed this time. He came up behind the woman at her easel and rested his chin on her shoulder.

Desperately Regan longed to be inside that circle of stones, but the magic kept her back.

"Painting again?" Arthur said.

"This is the secret to eternal life," the woman replied with Regan's voice. She smiled and leaned back against his chest.

"I knew you'd find it." He kissed her cheek and returned to the shadows. The woman smiled and Regan saw it was her own smile. This was her? The woman, the other Regan, put her paintbrush into a glass of muddy water and followed Arthur away and into the darkness.

Regan tried once more and found that now she could step over the stones and into the fairy circle. She had to see what the woman had been painting. If it revealed the secret of eternal life, she'd sell her soul to see it.

Slowly she went to the painting sitting on its easel, glowing in the moonlight. She walked around it and stood there, seeing but not understanding what she saw.

The painting was of her. Just her. Regan Ferry. Surely there had to be more to it than simply a portrait of herself.

It was supposed to tell her the secret of eternal life, not taunt her with her own bloody face.

Regan reached out and touched the wet canvas, angrily smearing the paint.

The portrait burst into flames and Regan screamed.

She ran through the woods, away from the ghosts and the things they showed her. She heard a howl of endless agony. The wolf again? No. This time the howl came from Regan. The cry was hers. The agony was hers.

"Regan," Arthur said. "Wake up. Wake up, Regan. Look at me."

HER EYES FLUTTERED OPEN. Regan was in her sitting room lying on the chaise. Her glass lay overturned on the rug, spilling red pomegranate wine like blood.

A profound relief rushed through her body. It felt nothing like waking from a nightmare. It felt more like she'd been drowning and someone had pulled her from the choking waters.

With a gasp she sat up. Arthur knelt at her side on the floor. She put her arms around him and pressed her forehead to his.

"Are you all right?" he asked. "What happened?"

She told him about the wine, the strange happy sleepy feeling that had come over her. The hare loping through the penthouse, the cry of a wolf, and Gloom reciting Poe. Finally the forest and the ghost and the vision in the fire.

"I would have rather seen myself burning in the fire," she said as she drank from the cup of water Arthur had brought her. Her hands shook, spilling water on herself. "I would rather have seen myself eaten by the flames than see you with another woman."

"So you don't want to love me, but you can't stand it if I love someone else?"

He asked the question very gently, so as not to hurt her.

It hurt her anyway.

Before she could make any protest, he said, "I'm sorry. Forget I said that. I'm not going to be with anyone but you."

"But you will someday," she said. "You have to be. I'm not going to marry you, have your children. And you're the hare."

"I'm the hare?"

She smiled tiredly. She'd never felt so fragile before. "The *heir.*"

"It's the twenty-first century, Regan. No one's going to force me to get married if I don't want to."

"Yes, but you want to, don't you? You want to get married?"

He didn't answer. He didn't have to.

"I saw something else in the woods," she said. "A woman who was me, but not me. She looked like me, except for the clothes and hair. She was painting a portrait of...me. And she said that was the secret of eternal life, whatever that means."

"It means this," Arthur said. He took her hand in his, gently unbuckled her watch band and stroked the faded ink embossed onto her wrist.

Art is Eternal.

"Yes," she said, "but you don't want to marry a painting, do you?"

She drank more water, felt like herself again, though

her head ached. "You said Malcolm only interferes for good, yes?" Regan asked. She needed to believe there was a light at the end of this dark, strange tunnel.

"For the good of our family."

"But I'm not part of your family."

"He's playing too rough," Arthur said. "I don't think we should do this anymore."

"Do we have a choice? He was at your townhouse, the Half Moon... God, what does he want from us?"

"I don't know, but if he doesn't stop tormenting you I'm throwing him on the fire."

He said that last part loudly, as if Malcolm were listening. Regan rather thought he was listening. Listening and laughing.

"He's in Hell, supposedly?" Regan said. "Wouldn't think he'd be afraid of fire."

Arthur ran his hand through her hair. "Are you all right?"

"I am now. Let's go upstairs."

"Are you sure? You can rest here and—"

"I want to be in bed with you. I want you to stay the night with me."

"Let's go back to the townhouse."

"Why? He was there, too, remember?"

They were playing Malcolm's game, and had been from their first night together. The game wouldn't end until someone won—Malcolm, most likely.

"I don't want to be afraid," she continued.

He took her by the hand and helped her to her feet. They went up to her bedroom and Regan switched on the bedside lamp. Weary and worn-out, she sat on the end of the bed and rested her head against the post.

Arthur stood by her side, facing the portrait of Lord Malcolm Godwick, thirteenth Earl of Godwick.

"One more day, old man," Arthur said to the painting. "You have until midnight tomorrow to tell us what you want, or I will throw your portrait in the Thames. Maybe you aren't afraid of fire, but I will make you afraid of me."

Nothing happened. She could only hope Lord Malcolm didn't call their bluff.

Regan thought about what she'd seen in the haunted wood, what the ghost had said to her, what she'd felt watching Arthur with that girl...

Something told her that Malcolm, for whatever reason, wanted her to care for Arthur. Why else would he have tortured her with visions of Arthur with another woman if he didn't want them together in some way?

"You have until midnight tomorrow," Regan said, "or I will send Arthur away, and I will never see him again."

Arthur looked at her in shock, his eyes wounded.

The fire in the gas fireplace kicked on, and the moment they both turned their heads to look, the portrait of Malcolm fell off the wall.

"He didn't like that," Regan said.

Arthur nodded. "Neither did I. You didn't actually mean that, did you?"

"No," she said. Thanks to her marriage, she knew how to lie and lie well. "Of course not."

11

MARS AND VENUS

Arthur stayed the night with her in the penthouse bedroom. He held her to his chest as she fell asleep, his body wrapped around hers, covering her like a shield.

Sleep didn't come easily for her, but it came more easily than usual in his arms. She might have slept the whole night through but for her phone ringing.

The first ring jarred her brutally from sleep. Regan sat up, hand to her head, looking around as if an alarm had gone off.

"Your phone," Arthur said, his voice drowsy.

She'd left her phone on the charger in the bathroom and ran to get it. The call was from Zoot. And the time was nearly three in the morning.

"Zoot? What's wrong?" she asked. Arthur was already sitting up in bed, waking up, ready to do what needed to be done. She sat beside him and put the call on speakerphone.

"Sorry to wake you, Boss, but the security blokes called. Alarm at Ferry Hill's gone off. They drove by, gave the place a twice-over and didn't see anything but some lights on that shouldn't be on—master bedroom, they said. They got their orders not to go in without permission."

"Those were Sir Jack's orders, not mine," Regan said. She sighed. "He'd rather his wife be murdered in her sleep than allow the riff-raff to step foot in his precious house."

"You want me to go and see what's what?"

She looked at Arthur who quietly mouthed, "Malcolm?"

Malcolm? Yes, maybe. He'd already shown he could cause trouble anywhere he wanted.

"No," Regan said. "We'll go."

"You and me?" Zoot said.

"Arthur and me. He's here."

"Ahh..."

"Stop ahh-ing."

"Ooh..."

"Zoot."

"Be safe. Probably just a rat running around, tripping the sensors, but you never know."

"Thank you. I'll see you in the morning."

She ended the call. Arthur was already out of bed and pulling on his clothes. "I can go alone, if you—"

"Don't," he said as he tugged his t-shirt down and grabbed his wallet. "Get dressed. I'll drive."

A sudden lump formed in her throat. She had trouble getting off the bed.

"What's wrong?" Arthur asked, brow furrowed in worry.

"I suppose I didn't realize you really meant it when you said you'd protect me."

He stood in front of her, cupped her chin in his hand. For a moment, she felt like the younger one, like a girl again, scared and shy, and he was the older one, the one in charge.

"I meant it," he said.

After that, she was able to get up and get dressed. She put on jeans, boots, and her favorite grey cashmere jumper. Arthur helped her into her black trench coat and in ten minutes they were in his car on their way to Ferry Hill.

Arthur drove a black Land Rover, which was exactly the sort of car she expected he'd drive—attractive but practical, sturdy and steady, high quality but not ostentatious. No flashy sports cars for him. And he drove it expertly and carefully like he was transporting precious cargo.

"You'd make a very good father," she said.

He glanced at her before putting his eyes back on the road. "I'd make a good teacher, doctor, and lawyer, too, according to the stupid aptitude tests they made us take in school, but I'm not going to be any of those either."

"Do you have any idea how young you are? No one regrets not becoming a lawyer. They do—"

"Everyone regrets becoming a lawyer. And I won't regret anything if we're together." He paused. "I hated being a child. I hated childish things. A life without children sounds more than fine to me, all right? End of discussion."

He reached over and squeezed her knee to show he wasn't cross with her. No need. She knew. She knew and she'd never felt so loved. If only she could let herself love him back.

They drove on through the night on roads dark and empty but for the occasional lorry. The last time she'd been out at three in the morning was the night Sir Jack died, and she'd driven alone from the hospital to The

Pearl, unable to stomach returning to Ferry Hill. It was supposed to be a temporary move. She hadn't been back to their house—*her* house, now—in seven months, she told Arthur.

"So this is sort of a homecoming," he said.

"It's not home," she said. "It was Sir Jack's home, never mine. Like I told you, I wasn't even allowed to move the saltshaker from one side of my plate to the other. The Pearl's the only place that ever felt like home to me. And even then it wasn't home so much as just...safe."

"Are you selling Ferry Hill?"

"That's the plan, as soon as I can make myself go in and clear out my personal things."

"I'll help you. Anything you need," Arthur said.

"If you're still around when all this is over, I'll let you."

"If?" He glanced left at her, just a split second before putting his eyes back on the road. All she'd needed was that split second to see the hurt and fear in his black eyes.

"Don't you feel like we're driving into a dragon's lair?" she said.

"A little," he said with a shrug. "But there's always treasure in dragon's lairs, right?"

"Always dragons, too."

They continued on in silence.

———

TOWERING English oak trees lined the winding drive of Ferry Hill. Arthur drove slowly through the tunnel of shadows and toward the house.

"There it is," she said, feeling stupid, as if he couldn't see the ten-thousand square-foot Tudor-revival manor looming in front of them, its exterior facade pale ivory and glowing under the spotlights in the front garden.

Arthur parked the car at the front steps. There were no other vehicles in sight. No sign that anybody was here but them...no sign except for the light still on in the master bedroom window. The housekeeper could have left it on, she told herself. Except that didn't explain the alarm...

Regan waited as Arthur got out. He came around and opened her door, helping her out though she didn't need the help.

"You're all right?" he asked as she stared up at the house—its steeply-pitched roof like a witch's hat, its white walls ghostly glowing, its timbering giving it the faintest impression of medieval prison bars...

"I swore I'd never set foot in this place after Sir Jack died."

"I can go in alone," he said. "You can stay in the car."

"No, I want to go with you."

"We'll go in together," he said, "but stick to me like glue. I mean it. If you have to use the toilet, I'm watching."

She laughed. "Good thing I went before we left."

She took a deep breath, steadied herself and started toward the enormous front double doors, so grand she could have ridden a horse through them and put on a circus in the entryway.

Inside, Regan took a breath, breathing in the scent so familiar. Sir Jack's cologne lingering in the air, sandalwood and orange bergamot, a scent she would forever associate with old men and older money.

The house was quiet, mostly dark. She disarmed the security system and turned the overhead lights on. She peered right into the music room where Sir Jack would play records on his father's ancient Victrola, the sound warped by age and time. She looked left into the sitting room where she'd spent a thousand interminable evenings entertaining the wives of Sir Jack's friends, women decades her senior.

Between the two rooms stood a large double staircase that curved to the west and east wings. The master bedroom was in the east wing, and that's where the security guards had said they'd seen a light on when they drove by.

"Upstairs," she said. "To the right. You don't have a gun with you, do you?"

He laughed. "I haven't been issued a sidearm yet, but I'm not sure what a gun would do against a ghost."

"I just wanted to shoot a few holes in the bed."

"Next time, I promise. I'll see if I can't get my hands on a grenade launcher."

Arthur smiled and she felt ready to start up the stairs. They went up together, Arthur first, Regan behind him—his order.

The bannister was polished and gleaming in the light of the brass wall sconces. She kept a housekeeper on the payroll to see that things were kept up, but Regan wouldn't have cared if she'd found the place covered in dust, ransacked with rats eating through the walls. No matter how well-tended the house, it was always damp, always cold and clammy, like Sir Jack's hands.

They reached the top of the stairs. Arthur walked a few feet alone into the shadowy hallway. His silhouette was strong, tall and confident. His strength gave her strength. She went to him and he turned to glare at her.

"You said to stick to you like glue," she reminded him.

"Which door's the bedroom?"

"End of the hall," she said.

Before they'd been married, she had hoped she and Sir Jack would have separate bedrooms like an old Victorian couple. In her fantasy, sex would happen once a month, if that, quickly and politely and with as little fuss or muss as possible. If only. Sir Jack had wanted her all the time, even when he couldn't perform sexually. He'd made her play the part of the devoted wife. Never a partner in his life, merely a luxury accessory.

"I chose this," she said softly, running her hand along the wall with disgust.

"You didn't choose this," Arthur said. "You chose safety and security and got fear and cruelty. It's called bait-and-switch. Treating you like property was his choice, not yours."

"My choice to stay. He never made me stop painting, you know. He told me to quit art school, but he never actually said I had to stop painting. It wasn't as if I didn't have plenty of free time. That wasn't him. That was me."

"You made a mistake," he said. "You more than paid the price for it."

"Yes, but—"

Arthur planted a hard, passionate kiss on her mouth, then pulled back and smiled.

"What was that?" she asked.

"That was me protecting you from saying something embarrassing like you deserved to be treated like shite by your husband."

She met his eyes, glared. "I'd almost forgotten what a brat you are, Brat."

He grinned wickedly. "That's why I reminded you."

They were at the door. Light streamed out from underneath it. No sounds inside. Arthur kissed her again briefly on the lips, then opened the door.

A large rectangular Tiffany lamp stood on the bedside table. It was on, but that seemed to be the only sign anyone had been in here. The bedroom was just as Regan remembered it. Dark wood wainscoting with hunter green wallpaper and a picture rail hung with the portraits of all Sir Jack's illustrious ancestors trapped inside their dusty frames. And the bed, of course, large and layered with luxurious sheets and a brown and cream counterpane. All very male. All very stuffy and stodgy.

One thing had changed, however.

"What's this?" Arthur asked as he stared at the painting hanging over the cold and empty stone fireplace. "Modern art? In *this* house?"

She recognized the painting at once. A painting of Mars, the Roman god of war and Venus, the Roman goddess of love. They lay twined together in a golden net that trapped them in a bed made of clouds.

The side of the bed belonging to Mars was midnight blue, heavy, manly, and the side of the bed Venus lay upon was pale pink and bright and light.

"I was inspired," Regan said, "by the famous painting *Mars and Venus* by Angélique Mongez. She was the first Frenchwoman to become a full-fledged history painter. Very groundbreaking considering it was the early nine-teenth century and women were only expected to paint family portraits if that. In her version of *Mars and Venus*, Mars is about to leave Venus to go off to war. He's got one foot on his war chariot while Venus sits with their son Cupid, trying to lure Mars back to her. His side of the painting looks like a hellscape. Hers looks like a magical spring morning. I loved that, dividing the canvas in half—his and hers. I stole that idea, put my own spin on it."

In her painting, Mars and Venus were floating in the sky—Mars in the night sky, Venus at dawn.

"You painted this?" Arthur asked. "This is one of yours?"

She nodded. "*Mars and Venus In Vulcan's Net*. I must have known... Venus was forced into marrying the ugly old Vulcan and then she—"

Regan couldn't even say the word "love" and despised herself for her cowardice.

She continued, "She saw the young soldier Mars and started an affair with him. Vulcan knew she was betraying him so he pretended to leave their home, and when Mars snuck in...he trapped them in bed together."

"It's incredible," he said. "Really incredible, Regan."

She warmed at his words, but quickly soured. "I didn't hang this painting here," she said.

Her blood was cold and she clung to Arthur's hand, but he didn't seem troubled at all.

"This must be it," Arthur said. "Lord Malcolm's trying to tell you to start painting again. Last night he gave you a vision of yourself painting again, and now this?"

"Why would he care if I painted or not? Or golfed or danced or started a bookshop?"

"Who knows what he knows that we don't know," Arthur said. "But even if he's not telling you that, I am. My parents own over a dozen art galleries. I've been to a thousand galleries in my lifetime, seen a million paintings. I know talent. You have it."

"*Had* it."

"It's still there. I know it is. God, this is so good. It's

stylized, like that Polish painter, I forgot her name, did those wild Art Deco portraits. Mum loves her work."

"Tamara de Lempicka?"

"That's her."

"She's one of my favorite artists. Big influence."

"If you don't want this, can I have it?"

He meant it. She could tell from the way he looked at her painting he genuinely admired it. It almost made her want to try painting again. Almost. But why bother? It would take years to relearn what she'd forgotten and she didn't have years. Still...Arthur made her want to try anyway.

She felt something stirring in her heart, something she couldn't ever remember feeling before there. Something terrifyingly tender, tenderly terrifying. And desire, too. Lust. Need.

"You can have it," she said, "if you make love to me right now."

He looked at her like she'd gone mad. "Here? In this bed?"

"Definitely here. And *definitely* this bed. I don't want to be afraid of ghosts anymore—Sir Jack or Lord Malcolm."

"Tell me what you want," Arthur said. "Anything you want."

She told him and his eyes widened.

"Are you sure?" he asked.

She was sure. Scared, but sure. He undressed her quickly, and then stripped himself. He pulled her to the bed and tossed the covers back. The sheets were white, pristine, changed weekly by the housekeeper even though they were never slept in.

There had been nights in her marriage she had wanted to tear the bed apart with her bare hands, cut the sheets with knives, set the mattress on fire and watch it burn. Now she wanted the bed to burn with pleasure, to be defiled with her wetness and Arthur's.

Arthur lifted her up and laid her on the bed. She waited, flat on her back as he looked through the bedside table drawers for what he needed. When he found it, he came back to her, laying on her, both of them naked as Adam and Eve in the Garden.

Even as beholden as she'd felt toward Sir Jack, she had stood her ground and refused him sexual acts she thought she couldn't bear. She had discovered with Arthur that she not only could bear them, but wanted them as long as it was with him.

Arthur turned her onto her stomach. She braced herself on her elbows, opened her thighs wide to offer all of herself to him. He had lubricant and used it to carefully fill that tightest hole with his fingers. Regan fought every self-protective instinct to pull away, to clench her muscles to force him out. He wanted her love, but she couldn't give him what she didn't have. She could give him her body, though—all of it, especially the parts of her she'd refused her husband.

Arthur opened her with one finger, the sensation was a welcome intrusion.

A second finger was uncomfortable, but the tension quickly passed. Soon she was breathing hard as he fucked her slowly and gently with his slick fingers. A third finger was almost too much, but she breathed through it and slowly opened up again.

The bed shifted as Arthur mounted her from behind, and she was certain she'd never wanted a man's cock in her more in her life. Here. In the bed her husband bought, in the bed where she'd sold herself night after night of their loveless marriage, she was being entered in the arse by a man who would have been her husband's worst nightmare—a man younger, fitter, more handsome. A future earl. A mere boy he'd have to address as "my lord."

The tip of Arthur's thick cock slid into her body easily, and Regan groaned as he entered her by inches.

The shaft of his cock was harder to take than his three fingers. He was so thick, so stiff...but also so gentle. He went slowly, easing his length into her with the slightest of thrusts. Regan spread herself wider, parting her knees and thighs. She arched her back and he moved in more, filling her to the point of pain, then retreating.

Slowly the orifice relaxed, gave way, made room for him. He applied more lubricant to her and himself and then it was easy going, almost, as he thrust in deeper. Regan moaned, mouth open against the bed. She closed her eyes tight and let herself feel every inch as he slowly speared her, every inch as he withdrew, every inch as he speared her again. Arthur lay himself over her, gathering her to him.

"Does it hurt?" he asked.

She answered in all honesty, "Nothing has ever hurt me less."

"Good," he said, his voice low and husky in her ear. He kissed the back of her neck, all the while fucking her with the slowest, deepest, most sensual thrusts she'd ever felt. But this was only half of what she'd asked from him, half of what she'd commanded him to do to her, and if Arthur was anything, he was obedient.

With his arms around her, he rolled them both, still joined, onto his back so that she lay on his chest, her knees up, her thighs wide. Arthur had found one of the many vibrators Sir Jack had used on her in the table drawer, and now he would use it on her.

Arthur turned it to a low setting. The moment the tip touched her clitoris, she flinched reflexively.

"I can stop," he said.

"Never stop."

His soft male laugh in her ear was utterly pornographic, a laugh that said yes, maybe she owned him body and soul, but it was him spearing both her holes so take that, my *lady*.

Her clitoris swelled as he ran the tip of the vibrator over it in little circles, swelled and ached, ached and throbbed. Inner muscles began to lightly tremor. She felt the sensations swirling in her lower belly as the deep nerves of her clitoris buzzed and quivered. With his long strong arm, Arthur held her against him, held her tight, as he pushed the vibrator into her vagina, pushed it past the resistance and into the slick passage. Her inner walls clenched the phallus but allowed it in, an inch, then two, then three, all the way to the aching and waiting core of her.

Regan could barely move with one cock in her arse and another in her cunt. She could only writhe in tiny tight circles as Arthur moved under her, with her, into her. She had never felt so full, so filled beyond what she could take and yet she was taking it and taking it and taking it.

Her orgasm built in record time and the pressure brought tears to her eyes. Her stomach muscles tightened painfully and her vagina poured wetness out of her and onto Arthur's muscular thighs and the white sheets.

From under her, Arthur ground his hips into her, working his cock deeper. She was beyond pain, sobbing almost, panting. He gripped her breast in his free hand

and held it tightly, clutching her to his chest as he used both her orifices for her pleasure and his.

Another hand, it seemed, grasped her by the wrists, spreading her arms to each side of the bed. Regan lifted her head—how could that be happening?—and saw a golden cord wrapped around her arms.

She was too shocked at first to react, especially with her body on the edge of orgasm. Another cord found her thigh, then her other thigh, prying her legs apart.

Arthur was able to say only, "What—" before another golden cord whisked from under the bed and wound around his mouth, gagging him.

In seconds, they were both tied down by powerful unseen forces, tied to the bed and to each other. Golden cords wrapped around their hips, locking them together, trapping Arthur's hand between her legs so that he couldn't pull the vibrator out of her.

Ecstasy and panic crashed into each other, spurring her to a climax stronger than she'd ever experienced before. Regan tried to fight against the orgasm, but twisting and thrashing against the cords only worked Arthur's cock and the vibrator in deeper. It seemed every muscle in her pelvis and back contracted at once, every nerve fired, and she arched against the ropes, suspended in place by the staggering force of her release, and she shut her eyes and cried out in ecstasy.

WHEN REGAN OPENED HER EYES, she saw a man slipping out of the shadows by the fireplace and advancing on them.

Sir Jack.

"No," Regan said in horror, "you're dead. I buried you."

It was him, without a doubt—her husband, dead and gone since May. A distinguished-looking man, silver hair receding, eyes glinting hard as diamonds. A king in his own mind long past his prime.

He shrugged. "You fuck this child to spite me as if I were in the room. So here I am." He lifted his hands and grinned, showing tobacco-stained teeth. "Let's get on with the show."

"This isn't real. Let us go."

She was terrified, humiliated to be caught like this, Arthur's cock trapped inside of her, the vibrator still plunged deep, against her womb, silently stoking her toward another climax.

"Look at you," Sir Jack said, his accent so proper, his tone a cold sneer of utter disdain. "Look at you in bed with a ripe young man and all you can think about is me... How could I possibly be dead? You keep me alive with your hate. How many times did you swear to yourself the second I was in the ground, you'd pick up your paintbrush and start your life all over? Off to Paris, to a studio with north-facing light, that you'd cut your hair like Coco Chanel and never put on another string of pearls ever again?"

The buzzing phallus inside her stimulated her g-spot and Arthur's fingers brushed her swollen clitoris. The tip of the vibrator pulsed against her cervix, and she contracted sharply around it, gasping, nearly coming again even as her dead and hateful husband watched and laughed.

"If you won't let me go, let Arthur go," she said. He was gagged and couldn't speak so she must speak for him.

"Let him go?" the apparition said. "He's fucking my wife."

"I'm not your wife anymore."

"No? Then why do you act as if we're still married, like my opinion still matters? He's offered you everything and you can't even love him. It must be because you still love me."

"I never loved you," she said and moaned. Tears trickled from her eyes. She was close to coming again, and she couldn't let it happen, not with him watching her, not with the cold dead eyes of all his ancestors glaring down at her from their frames like a Greek chorus of mockery.

"Shouldn't I kill him? The man fucking my wife in my own bed? Any good husband would."

"If you so much as touch a hair on his head," she spat at him, fighting the ropes, ready to tear him apart, "I will dig you up just to burn your corpse to ashes."

"Give me one reason why I shouldn't kill him. One, Reggie. Just one."

Reggie. He'd always called her that, like a term of endearment, a name she hated beyond words and he knew it.

He lifted a poker from the fireplace, its iron tip burning orange. "What is he to you but a whore you hired to spite me? Isn't that all he is? You don't care about him. You don't even want him. You only want to hurt me by having him. You certainly don't—"

"If you touch him I will kill myself and hunt you down in Hell. Even Satan will show you more mercy than I will."

"Because you love him? You can't love. You never could. You never could and you never will."

"I couldn't love you, but I can love him. I do love him, you bastard. I love him, and I *always* will."

And with those words, the cords broke like tender vines and disappeared into dust. The specter of Sir Jack vanished as Regan cried out, her very being shaken by an orgasm so powerful everything faded to black.

WHEN SHE CAME TO, she was lying on her back with Arthur staring down at her. Her body was limp, listless, almost lifeless even as her interior muscles continued to give little gasps and shivers.

She felt wetness, Arthur's semen dripping onto the bed. When had he come?

"Regan? Are you all right?" He stroked her face. "I think you came too hard. You passed out."

She sat up, held him by the shoulders. "Did you see him?"

"Lord Malcolm was here?"

She didn't answer at first. Of course it was Lord Malcolm. He'd made her see Sir Jack, made her think she was tied to Arthur, trapped against him. He'd forced her to realize that...

She loved him. She loved Arthur. She loved him and she'd said it out loud...except Arthur hadn't heard her conversation, hadn't seen Sir Jack.

Relief rushed through her so fast and hard she was dizzy again. She lay naked on the bed, wet and well-used. It humiliated her how glad she was Arthur hadn't heard her say she loved him. There was no chance they could stay together. Telling him she loved him would only make the inevitable end of them all the more agonizing.

"Yes," she said, lying to protect him. "Malcolm was here."

"What did he say?"

Regan touched Arthur's face. The face of the man she loved, the man she owned, and the man she couldn't keep.

"You were right," she said. "He wants me to paint again."

"Told you so," he said, smiling broadly. Arthur looked so terribly young with his raven-hair wild from the sex and his dark eyes gleaming like two priceless black pearls. "Let's find a twenty-four-hour art store. Those are a thing, right?"

"I think I can wait until morning. Until then...let's get out of here, please."

When she left Ferry Hill that night, she took only one thing with her—her painting of Mars and Venus.

12

A MOTHER AND CHILD

Dawn was gently breaking as they drove back into London. Silver shoots of morning light pierced the grey November clouds like arrows. Regan fell asleep on Arthur's shoulder and only woke up when he pulled into The Pearl's underground parking garage.

Arthur laughed softly at her. "Finally wake up?"

"Sorry," she said, sitting up straight. "I'm not used to getting up at three in the morning to visit haunted houses."

"Go up and get some sleep," he said. "I'll stop by later."

"You don't want to come up and sleep with me?"

"How much sleep do you think we'd actually get?"

She smiled tiredly. "Fair point. See you soon."

When she started to leave the car, Arthur stopped her by putting his hand gently on her arm. "Will you promise me something?"

"What is it?"

"Whatever he's doing...and for whatever reason, please don't let it..."

"Arthur..." She wanted to tell him everything would be

all right no matter what occurred, and that they would be together and happy until the end of time.

"I can't make that promise," she said. "You know I can't make you any promises about the future."

"I know." He nodded. "I know that."

Why must love be so impossibly difficult, she wondered? If she'd loved him less, she could have promised him more. When she looked at their future, all she saw was pain—his pain. He'd tire of her saying no to his marriage proposals. He'd resent her for not wanting to adopt children. He'd wonder why he wasted so many years on a woman doomed to an early death, when all that time he could have been finding love with a girl his own age who'd marry him in a heartbeat and give him a half-dozen bouncing Godwick babies.

The heartbreak was that Regan knew he'd marry her tonight, even knowing all of that. Proof he was absolutely mad, which meant she had to be the sane one.

"I can promise you right now," she said. "How's that?"

"I'll take what I can get."

She kissed him, then watched him drive off. How many more kisses were left to them—a thousand? A hundred? Ten?

Regan returned to the penthouse, doing her best to avoid the curious eyes of The Pearl's staff who must have been wondering why the boss was dragging herself across the lobby at the crack of dawn. She found her bed waiting for her. She undressed and crawled under the sheets, and fell into a deep and lonely sleep.

WHEN SHE WOKE UP, it was raining again. Regan heard the endless drumming of an autumn shower on her windows and walls. Her bed felt enormous and empty without Arthur. How had she gotten used to him being there so quickly? After Sir Jack died, she'd sworn she'd never sleep in the same bed with another man as long as she lived. Now, barely seven months later, she was clutching Arthur's pillow, searching out his scent.

Hunger finally drove her from bed. She ordered room service—Cuban coffee, lobster ravioli in brown butter sauce, salted caramel ice cream—and ate every bite. After a long, hot shower, she dressed in a grey wool skirt and matching jacket. She went downstairs to the sitting room, where she froze. Someone had changed the painting above the fireplace.

It was an original she'd picked up years ago at an auction—a haunting portrait by the American painter Elizabeth Nourse called *A Mother and Child*. Both the mother and the child wore somber expressions. Behind their heads were painted pale nimbuses like the icons of saints, though this mother was not the Virgin Mary, just an ordinary woman. The child wasn't Jesus, but a normal baby boy.

Zoot might have hung it, but she had never before changed the paintings out without Regan's permission or at her request.

Malcolm, then.

What did he mean by hanging a portrait of a mother and child in her home? Was he taunting her?

Regan took the painting down and might have thrown it into the fireplace if she hadn't been such a fan of Nourse's other work.

She carried it into her office and hid it behind the

desk, turning it to face the wall. She picked up the phone and called for Zoot.

"I have a painting I want taken to Sotheby's," Regan told her. "You can bring up a replacement, too. Anything. Today, please."

She hung up before Zoot could ask what the great bloody rush was over one single painting. Regan was in no mood to argue.

She stared at the back of the painting, which opened all her wounds at once. Why didn't she get to have a mother growing up? Why was her decision to have or not have children taken out of her hands by a set of bad genes? Why couldn't she let herself be selfish enough to marry Arthur anyway, knowing she'd leave him childless and widowed when she died?

"What do you want from me, Malcolm?" she asked through tears. "What are you trying to say? Why won't you just say it and leave me alone?"

"I'm trying to say...I'm very sorry, my darling girl. So very, very sorry."

Regan spun around, but there was no one there.

Except someone *had* been there. She had heard a man's voice—cultured, monied, but deeply contrite.

And where before there had been nothing but the rug on the floor...Regan spotted a single brass key.

Shaking, she picked it up. It was warm, like it had just come from a man's pocket.

"Regan?"

Arthur's voice, this time.

"I'm in my office," she called out to him.

The key was in her palm. Arthur came in and saw her holding it like a bird in her hand.

"He was here." Regan met his eyes. "Malcolm. I didn't

see him, but I heard him. When I turned around, this was on the rug."

Arthur gently extracted the key from her hand and examined it. "What did he say?"

"He said..." She blinked and tears ran down her face. "He said he was sorry. He called me his 'darling girl.'"

"Sorry for what? Torturing you?"

She had no answer.

Arthur closed his fingers around the key and took her into his arms, held her head against his shoulder. "What's wrong?" he said. "What is it?"

Between soft sobs, she told him about the Elizabeth Nourse painting, how it had cut her so deeply to see it. Arthur pulled her toward her desk chair, sat down, and set her into his lap.

"You know I want to be with you, don't you?" she said. "You know I would if I could."

"You can though," he whispered into her ear. His hand stroked her back and her hair.

"If I still hated you, maybe I could do that to you."

"But you don't hate me anymore?"

She raised her head. "No. I don't hate you at all."

He wiped her face gently with his hands. "What would it take to convince you it's all right to let yourself have a life with me?"

"A miracle," she said, then laughed pitifully at herself.

"A ghost just brought you a magic key. Isn't that enough of a miracle for you?"

"Depends on what the key's for."

"It's small," he said, holding up the key. "Not a door key then."

Regan took it from him. Yes, a very small brass key for a lockbox or a small safe. Or...

"The desk drawer," she said, meeting Arthur's eyes. She slid off his lap at once and kneeling, pushed the key into the lock of the drawer that had been shut up for years.

The key turned. "It worked," she breathed.

"Let me," Arthur said. "God knows what's in there."

She moved out of the way as he pulled the drawer all the way open. Peering past him, she saw ledger books, a bundle of letters, a small picture frame turned facedown.

He turned the frame over. It was a photograph, yellowed and aged, of a woman with a baby. The pose was remarkably like that of the painting leaning against her office wall. The faces were too grainy to make out clear features but there was something about the woman... something familiar.

Arthur squinted. "That's not my grandmother. Or my great-grandmother." He flipped it over and undid the clasps to remove the photo.

Regan took the ledger from the drawer. These were Lord Malcolm's accounts. What he owed his tailor. What he owed The Pearl. What he owed his art dealer, his mistresses, his whores.

"Hannah Howell," Arthur said.

Regan stopped perusing the ledger and looked up at him. "What about my mother?"

"The photo," he said, passing it to her. "Her name's on the back, but it's dated 1938."

Hannah Howell and Angus, Age 1. August 1938. Regan turned it back over and examined the faces. "It's not your great-grandmother," she said. "It's mine. My mother was named after her. And Angus was my grandfather..."

She'd seen something in the ledger, something that made no sense.

"H.H.," she said, reading a set of initials aloud. "Malcolm was paying her. A whole series of monthly payments, beginning in June 1937."

"Paying her? For what?"

Regan raised an eyebrow at him. "The obvious, obviously."

"Would he pay her directly? Or the hotel? Never paid for it before. How does it work?"

"Not like this," she said. The payments had begun when her great-grandmother was heavily pregnant with Angus. "Pay for play, not one payment a month. It's more like..."

Child maintenance payments.

Regan knew what she would find in the letters, and yet she read them one by one in order, passing them to Arthur when she was finished. First were the letters from Regan's great-grandmother Hannah. Then there were letters from Lord Malcolm's mother, the Dowager Countess of Godwick. Together, they told the story of a brief, torrid affair that ended as all brief, torrid affairs did. This one, however, had unintended consequences.

"Lord Malcolm was your great-grandfather," Arthur said finally, having reached the same conclusion she had, the conclusion she couldn't bring herself to say out loud. "Regan...we're second cousins."

She nodded slowly. "It seems we are."

"Good thing you don't hate us wicked Godwicks anymore," he said with a laugh. "You're one of us."

13

THE PRISONER

"My God," Regan said, closing her eyes. She leaned forward, head in her hands.

"Regan. Regan?" Arthur's voice pushed past her defenses. "You can't believe for one second that matters to me or anyone."

Of course it didn't matter. Not that. First cousins could marry in Europe and did. Even if they were brother and sister it wouldn't matter because she couldn't have children.

It would never be that. It was this:

"Your grandfather turned away his own niece."

"He did," Arthur said.

"His own niece. His own family. He must have known..."

"I'm certain he did." Arthur sat back on the floor. "How could he do that? What was he afraid of?"

"A legitimate claim on the family fortune?"

"Probably, yes. Especially since Malcolm gave your great-grandmother financial support for their son."

Regan stared at Arthur, still in shock. "If Malcolm can

do all this—move paintings, give people dreams and night-mares and throw keys at them...why didn't he try to save my mother?"

"Maybe he did try," Arthur said. "You don't know that he didn't. Good chance my grandfather just ignored all the signs and warnings. Now Malcolm's trying again."

"Too late now."

"Not for you. You said it would take a miracle to convince you to have a life with me. You got your miracle, didn't you?"

"Arthur..." She shook her head.

It wasn't that simple. It was never that simple.

A knock surprised them both. A knock and a door opening.

"Boss?"

It was Zoot. She didn't wait for an answer but marched straight into the office holding a wrapped painting.

"Boss? What're you two doing on the floor?"

"Oh, just going through some old papers," Regan said. She quickly stood up and gathered herself. Arthur went to the window that looked out onto the city.

"You wanted me to take something to the auction house, right?" Zoot asked.

"Yes, this one." Regan passed her the Nourse painting. "And you can hang the other painting over the fireplace."

"I'll do it," Arthur said. He took the wrapped painting into the sitting room, Zoot following.

"Regan?" Arthur's voice came from the other room. Something in his tone made her run to him straight away.

"What is it—" Then she saw.

"What's wrong, Boss?" Zoot asked. "You want something else? Thought Evelyn de Morgan was your girl crush."

She'd told Zoot to bring up another painting, any painting. The painting Arthur had unwrapped was by Evelyn de Morgan—indeed her favorite. And she knew this painting well. It was of a woman wearing a blue gown, adorned with a peacock feather, a net of pearls in her hair, and manacles on her wrists—one cuff made of iron, one made of gold.

The Prisoner.

"No," Regan said. "It's fine. You can go."

Zoot gave her a long look, and Arthur, too. Perhaps sensing the tension, she made no other comment and simply left with the Nourse painting.

They stood alone, side by side, she and Arthur, the painting slightly trembling in his hands.

"*The Prisoner?* What do you think it means?" Arthur said. "Am I supposed to chain you up? I wouldn't mind it. Regan?"

She stared at the painting without speaking.

Something stirred in her. She'd looked at this very painting a thousand times without feeling anything but admiration for the technique, the colors, the details on the woman's gown and hair.

Now Regan saw something else in the painting.

Herself.

"She has your eyes," Arthur said. "Pale grey. A little scared, a little trapped."

Regan was the prisoner, trapped by bands of iron and gold in a luxurious prison. Those links on the manacles on her wrist looked flimsy as paperclips. The woman in the painting had only to pull her hands apart and they would snap off. And once she did that, she would be free. She was already free. She just didn't know it yet.

Regan glanced around the penthouse of The Pearl, a

hotel girded with iron and steel and decorated with dazzling gilt and gold.

She turned to Arthur and kissed him. A soft kiss. A tender kiss. A goodbye kiss.

"Do me a favor," she said.

"Anything."

"When you start your tour of duty, don't get yourself killed, please."

He stared at her, eyes narrowed in confusion. "Wasn't planning to. Why?"

She smiled, but didn't answer. "I need to get to work," she said. "I'll...I'll see you later."

"Later tonight?"

"I have to do a few things first."

"Tomorrow?"

"Soon," she said. She touched his face and kissed him one more time. His handsome face, those eyes so dark there was no telling the pupil from the iris. Her lover. Her protector. Her family.

"Are you all right?" he asked.

"I will be."

He nodded. "I'll see you tomorrow then, or whenever you're ready."

He took his coat off the back of the chaise, went to the door. There he stopped and turned back.

"I know you can't make me any promises," he said, "but I can make you *this* promise. I will love you forever, and you can't stop me so don't bother trying. I'll love you and I'll wait for you, but if you run from me, I'll find you."

"Just...let me find myself first, can you?"

"Remember when you said I belong to you?"

"I remember," she said.

"I don't know if you meant it, but you have to know I

believed it. I'm always going to belong to you. No matter where you are, wherever you go, I'm always yours."

She smiled. "Mine."

"All right. What are you going to do?"

"What I should have done ten years ago."

"Don't be long," he said. "I love you."

He turned to go and Regan whispered to his back, "I love you, too, Brat."

The door closed behind him and she was alone. Alone again. She wanted him back so badly she almost ran after him. But she would only be leaving one gilded cage to put Arthur in another.

She went out onto the terrace and found Gloom waiting for his lunch. She fed him raw fish by hand and stroked the silky feathers along the back of his elegant head.

"I have to leave, baby," she said. "I have to fly away for a while, like you do. Someone will take care of you, I promise, but for now this is goodbye."

He raised his head. "Bye-bye, baby."

She laughed through tears and when Gloom flew away, she imagined he was taking her with him.

In a daze she returned to her office and picked up the phone.

"Yes, Boss," Zoot said when she answered.

"Would you mind feeding Gloom for me? I'll be...I'll be gone for a bit."

"Whatever you want, Boss. Where you going?"

"Paris."

"Paris? What's in Paris?"

"Art," Regan said. "Loads and loads and loads of art."

PART III

14

MORNING STAR AND EVENING STAR

Arthur was in Hell.

Two weeks had passed since he'd last seen Regan, and she wasn't answering his calls. He'd even gone by The Pearl twice to see if she was there. Zoot said she wasn't, and couldn't—or wouldn't—say where she'd gone.

All he could do was wait while Regan did whatever it was she needed to do. Wait and hope and trust that his dead great-grandfather wouldn't cross planes of existence to put them together just to let them fall apart.

December came and suddenly Christmas was everywhere Arthur looked. Outside the window of the Piccadilly townhouse, he spied greenery hanging from streetlamps, white lights on Christmas trees glowing through windows. His parents would be home in one week and they'd all convene at Wingthorn, now fully renovated.

Arthur tried to look forward to it, to his last Christmas with his family before he joined the army and left home for good. But he'd happily skip the whole season and all the gifts and parties if it meant knowing where Regan was, that she was safe and still wanted him. Every time it rained

—which was nearly every day now—he was plagued with sightings of Regan on the shining sidewalks, but it never was her under those black umbrellas.

These were the wistful thoughts in his head as he put the last of the decorations on the Christmas tree he'd bought for the townhouse. Rather than cheering him up, the decorating made him miss Regan more. Would they ever have the chance to do this together as a couple? To choose a tree for their home—just the thought of "their home" made his breath quicken—and decorate together, arguing over the placement of the nutcrackers and the fat little robins and the golden bells?

He knew her life might be cut short. No matter how many times he told himself that fact should scare him away, it never did. If anything, it only made him love her more, want her more.

God, if only she'd call or text. He'd take a single note or a message from Zoot delivered to his doorstep along with a few dozen insults. She could call him Lord Dogshit and the Rude Baron all she wanted if she also told him where Regan was hiding herself. Hiding herself to find herself.

The front door of the townhouse opened and slammed shut. He stood up straight, tiny ceramic robin in hand.

Nobody slammed the door of the eighteenth-century townhouse except for one person.

"In here, Charlie," Arthur called out. "Sitting room."

Charlie came in, looking better than the last time Arthur had seen him. Wide awake, not hungover, cloud lifted. He held up a large wrapped rectangle.

"Got old Thirteen back," he said.

In all the madness, Arthur had almost forgotten about Lord Malcolm's portrait. He set the robin on the coffee table and took the portrait from his brother, uncovered it. There he was, in all his smirking glory.

"You're out of the doghouse," Arthur said. "Congratulations. How did you get it?"

"Some weirdly hostile blonde who called me 'Lord Dogshit's brother' brought it by the flat where I was staying. She brought this one, too."

He passed Arthur another wrapped rectangle, about the same size.

Zoot knew where Arthur lived. She'd been by enough with Regan's notes to have her own room here. Was she taking the easy route by giving something to Charlie to give to him? Or was this Regan's doing, forcing Charlie and Arthur into the same room?

Arthur carefully removed the packing paper to reveal an original oil painting. An Evelyn de Morgan. He read the brass badge on the frame. *Phosphorus and Hesperus (Morning Star and Evening Star)*.

"What is it?" Charlie asked, peering past Arthur's shoulder.

"The two sons of Venus," Arthur explained, setting the painting on the mantel. "The Morning Star and the Evening Star. Brothers."

"That's what Mummy used to call us. Didn't have the heart to tell her the Morning Star and the Evening Star are just the same star."

"I think she knew," Arthur said.

"Can't remember the last time she called me her Evening Star," Charlie said almost wistfully. "I get nothing but *Charles* now."

"That's because it's a term of endearment, and you haven't been very endearing lately."

Charlie rolled his eyes. "God, not again. I'm leaving if you're going to start this up."

Arthur stared at him. Unbelievable.

"Didn't we used to be best mates? Or did I make all that up in my mind?"

"Yeah, and we used to be virgins, too. Then we grew up, all right. So grow up." Charlie turned to leave.

Arthur said his name, sharply, and Charlie spun on his heel to face him. "What now?" he demanded.

Arthur socked his brother in the face.

Good punch. All knuckle straight to the chin. Charlie fell back onto the sofa, dazed and gasping.

He cradled his face in his hands. "What the... Bastard, what was that for—"

"You fucked my girlfriend the day I broke up with her," Arthur said, shocked by how much cold rage came out in his voice.

"That's why you hit me? That was over two years ago!"

"Yes, and I'm still waiting for an apology."

"You're mad."

"No, I'm furious. You know she called you just to wind me up," Arthur said. "You know that, yes? Or do I need to show you the screenshots of her text messages to me mocking you? She sent me a pic of you two in bed together, you sleeping like a baby next to her while she was texting me about how easy you were."

Charlie moved his mouth, adjusted his jaw. It wasn't broken. Not that Arthur would have felt too badly if it had been.

"No," Charlie said. "You don't have to tell me or show me. I knew."

"You knew? Then why did you sleep with her?"

His brother gave a sad self-deprecating laugh. "Why?

Because of you. Because you get absolutely everything all the time and forever and ever. You get the title and the houses and the respect, and I get sod all and jack nothing."

Arthur sat down hard on the coffee table, across from Charlie. He tried to meet his brother's eyes, but Charlie wouldn't look at him.

"I know I'm a fuck-up," Charlie said. "Why not? No one expects me to be anything else. Dear Mummy and Daddy already have their perfect daughter and their perfect son. I might as well not even exist. Why should I bother?"

Charlie touched his jaw and winced again. It was starting to swell.

"Stay," Arthur said. "If you're not here when I come back from the kitchen, I will find you and break your nose."

"I'll be here." Charlie's voice was small and defeated. Arthur wanted to hug the stupid boy but knew Charlie wouldn't allow that. With a sigh he left the sitting room and went into the kitchen to put ice in a tea towel. Regan had been right. Charlie had slept with Wendy on purpose, out of spite, hurt pride, and self-pity. As much as Arthur wanted to punch his brother again—how many people would kill to be in his shoes with his family's money and power and the Godwick surname?—he also wanted to shake him until he realized that none of the titles and inheritances meant anything. Arthur would have traded his titles to the first person he saw walking down the street if it meant Regan would call him and tell him where she was.

And with that thought, he knew what he could do to help Charlie.

He returned to the sitting room and gave Charlie the

ice. The swelling wasn't bad, but the bruise would be nasty.

"I need to tell you something very important," Arthur said, standing in front of Charlie. "So pay attention."

Charlie met his eyes.

"I'm going to marry Regan Ferry," Arthur said.

Charlie laughed. When Arthur didn't smile, he stopped laughing. "You're joking."

"No."

"She's richer than we are. What's she want with you?"

"You'll have to ask her that. But it doesn't matter. I'm marrying her as soon as I can."

"This is fast, Art. Like...you've known her a month."

"Our own mother and father were married one day after meeting. One. Twenty-five years later, and they still can't keep their hands off each other."

"Don't remind me."

"Sorry. Anyway, for reasons you don't need to know or understand, we won't be having children," Arthur said. "Therefore, I'll be naming you my heir. The Godwick line will continue through you and your children whether I die tomorrow or sixty years from now."

The silence in the room was so deep and long Arthur could hear Christmas music being played by the Hyde Park buskers.

"God, you're serious," Charlie said. He sat up straight, the first time Arthur had seen him sitting in anything other than an angry slouch in two years.

"I couldn't be more serious."

"What if, you know, you two change your mind?"

"We won't. And as my heir you can't go on like this. You'll either be the seventeenth Earl of Godwick or the father of the seventeenth Earl of Godwick. Your gap year is officially over, starting today. I don't care where you go to university but you're going. If not university, then Sandhurst. I'll let you decide, but you are not going to spend another day wasting your life when you're the heir to a massive estate and a title that will need protecting and managing. The drinking has to stop. Spending money that's not yours has to stop. And your friends are not friends, they're hangers-on who will drop you the second they realize they can't squeeze another penny out of you. Do you understand me?"

Shockingly, Charlie nodded. He even looked almost contrite and even...possibly...maybe...a little bit proud.

"Have you told Dad any of this?" Charlie said.

"No, but I will at Christmas."

"But what if..." Charlie sat up even straighter. "What if you two don't end up getting married after all?"

"Then we're still in the same boat. Because it's her or no one, and I'll still need an heir." Arthur smiled at him. "Someone's got to be Lord Dogshit the Seventeenth."

"Right," Charlie said. "I'll talk to Dad about what he thinks I should do—university or Sandhurst. Although I'd thought about maybe...LSE?"

"LSE" was the London School of Economics. This was the first Arthur had heard of his brother having any interest in business or the economy. What else did he not know about Charlie?

"LSE would be brilliant," Arthur said. "The family's basically run as a business, after all. While I'm away with my unit, I'll want you at the board meetings of the Godwick trust, too. One of us needs to be there, taking notes and learning the ins and outs. Will you do that?"

"Of course," he said. "Yes, absolutely." There was life in

Charlie's eyes again, a determination to live up to the enormous responsibility he'd been given.

Arthur felt a lump in his throat. He wanted Regan with him more than ever, so he could tell her about Charlie, that he was already a changed man, growing up before his very eyes.

"Good," Arthur said. "Now, do you want to help me with the tree?"

"I thought I might take old Thirteen's portrait back to the house before anyone notices it's gone."

His chin was turning blue already. Arthur said, "You stay here and keep the ice on your face. I'll take it home. We'll have supper when I get back. You can get Indian takeaway if you like."

"Only if I can have it Indian-spicy."

"You've been my heir for three minutes, and you're already trying to bump me off?"

"Just payback for the busted face."

"You were prettier than me anyway," Arthur said. "Now we're equal."

"Right," he said. "Equal."

Arthur picked up the paintings. Charlie was already on his phone, but Arthur was relieved to see he was pulling up the webpage for the London School of Economics.

He loaded the paintings into his Landy. The drive home was about an hour, and he spent every minute of it dreaming of a future with Regan that might or might not happen. It had to happen, though. Didn't it? Lord Malcolm had brought them together once. Maybe he could do it again?

The sun was setting as he drove through the imposing gates of Wingthorn, their ancestral home. He carried the paintings to the front door, put in the house code. The doors popped open for him. He stepped into the entryway, which smelled of fresh paint and plaster. New stair bannister. The ancient ceilings didn't look quite so ancient anymore. A fine face-lift all around.

As he passed his mother's morning room, Arthur noticed one thing had changed quite dramatically. The room which had been rose-red for a century or more was now white. He stepped inside and switched on the lights. The old red damask wallpaper was gone, replaced now with white wallpaper covered in scrolling green rose vines.

The wallpaper Regan had seen in her dream. It had to be.

He walked to the white fireplace mantel and gazed up at his mother's portrait. His mother's name was Mona Lisa, and so in her portrait she was dressed as the *Mona Lisa*—same hair, same outfit. A quirky portrait for a countess. Then again, his parents were rather notoriously eccentric.

The very first Countess of Godwick had hung her own portrait in this room, and this is where all the countesses' portraits would hang until the end of the line. In the dream Regan had described, the one with Lord Malcolm, she had seen her future. One day she would be the next Countess of Godwick.

And even if she hadn't seen that future, Arthur could see it, and it was more beautiful than any work of art in Heaven or on Earth.

15

PORTRAIT OF AN ARTIST

The feeling came on softly, like the way the morning warms slowly in late May. First she'd been almost chilly as the night air lingered, comfortable, then warm, warmer, finally almost hot as the sun climbed into the sky. Happiness. Regan was happy. Happy with her work today. Happy with the soft northern light permeating her Montmartre studio. Happy to be alive.

She wiped sweat from her brow and took a long drink of mineral water and ate a handful of blueberries. After ten years without painting, she'd nearly forgotten how physically taxing the work could be. Standing for hours lifting a brush heavy with paint. Her back ached and so did her feet. Not even sore feet and a little back pain, however, could dent her happiness. Not now that she was painting again and free.

And she saw the proof of her freedom every day in the mirror. She'd cut her hair off into a chin-length bob. It was Sir Jack who'd wanted her hair long, more "feminine" supposedly—but in her mind, simply impractical for a painter. Now she just tucked her hair behind her ears every morning, pulled on jeans and a paint-stained t-shirt and went straight to work. And no more contact lenses, only glasses, which she pushed up on her head when doing fine detail work, put on her face again when she was making her broad strokes. Short hair. Glasses. A wrist tattoo, no watch, and torn jeans. Regan felt seventeen again with her whole life ahead of her, even if it wasn't a long life, she thought, maybe...it might be a happy one.

She made a few final touches to her painting and stood back, arms crossed, brush dangling from her right hand, heedlessly dripping paint on the floor.

She tilted her head left, then right, then took another step back. Was it done, really? Finally? Should she deepen the shading? Should she change the background color from grey to blue?

"It's perfect."

Regan jumped and spun around.

Arthur stood in the doorway of her studio.

She could only stare at him a moment, standing before her like an apparition. He'd changed, too, since she'd last seen him in early December. Almost six months had passed, and he already looked years older. Shorter hair, too. Taller? No, but he had on his army boots, which gave him more height. His camo fatigues were rolled up to his elbows, showing off his tanned and muscular forearms. He looked bigger, older, more powerful. He looked like a man who could protect her from any and everything.

"What are you doing here?" she asked.

"I'm on leave," he said. "One week."

"How did you find me?"

"You had Zoot send you your things."

"She wouldn't give you my address."

"No," he said, smiling, "but she would *sell* it to me for five grand."

Regan laughed, shook her head. "I'm going to fire that girl. She swore to me—"

"Everyone has a price, yes?"

She sighed.

"Don't pretend you didn't want me to find you," he said. "You put the name 'M. Regan Le Fay' on your mailbox downstairs."

"You caught that joke, did you?" Morgan Le Fay was King Arthur's half-sister, his enemy and his lover.

"I'm the smart one in the family, remember?" He grinned and her blood temperature shot up to a steady boil. She'd been happy here in Montmartre, painting, living alone, being herself. Happy and lonely, which she never knew could go so well together until she'd started using her loneliness in her art.

"I'm a Godwick, too," she said. "You're not the smart one in the family anymore."

"May I come in?" He was standing right on the threshold. She'd kept the door cracked for better ventilation. He hadn't broken in, not really. He probably would have if it had come to that, she thought.

"Yes, you may come in."

The urge to run into his arms and kiss him was nearly overwhelming but she held back. She'd left to heal, to escape the prison she'd made for herself. She'd also left to break whatever spell she'd cast over Arthur, so that he'd see they shouldn't be together for more reasons than she could count. Six months had passed. That should have done it. He should have been long over her by now.

Well, she should have been over him, too, and yet here

she was, heart stampeding through her chest like a horse that had escapes its pasture.

He came to her and stood before her.

"You cut your hair," he said.

"Like it?"

"Love it. It's you."

"You cut your hair, too."

"Had to. Like it?"

"Hmm...not bad. I liked it better longer."

He laughed. "It'll grow back when I get out."

"So...are you in Paris for your leave? Taking a holiday?"

"Honeymoon."

"Brat." It wasn't easy to sound annoyed while one's heart was dancing, but she managed to do it. "Did I or did I not order you to never ask me to marry you?"

"You did say I couldn't ask you to marry me. I'm not asking, though. I'm telling you—we're getting married. Never give a Godwick a loophole."

"Or any other hole, so I hear," she said.

Ignoring her, he said, "I've made Charlie my heir. I've already told him. It's as official as these things can be."

She stared at him. He meant it. She could tell he meant it. His voice was serious, his eyes earnest.

"You did?" Her voice came out strangely hoarse. She cleared her throat. "That's not...you can't offer that to someone, then take it back."

"I won't take it back. Best thing I've ever done. It's changed his life," Arthur said. "You were right about him feeling worthless since he was the 'spare.' Soon as I made him my heir, it was like he grew up almost overnight. He's started at the London School of Economics for Lent Term. He's already planning changes to make the Godwick trust an 'international philanthropic arts foundation.' Whatever that is."

"I'm happy for him," she said. "He's not a bad kid. Just...lost. Very glad he found himself."

"Thanks to you."

"Thanks to me berating you."

"I needed it," he said. "And I even liked it. But you liked it, too."

She shook her head. She had to put a stop to this. "Arthur, you know we can't get married. You're being ridiculous."

He didn't seem to hear her. "That..." he said, pointing at her easel, "is going to look perfect hanging in our home —right over the fireplace. And eventually in the morning room at Wingthorn."

Regan was too shy with her art to employ a model, so she'd done what artists had been doing since the mirror was invented and had painted a self-portrait. A simple portrait of a woman painting herself, but if anyone looked closely, they'd see it was full of symbols. On the side table in her painting lay a strand of pearls, a wrist-watch, her plait, all discarded. She called it *A Portrait of an Artist*.

"'I paint flowers,'" she said, "'so they will not die.'" She smiled at him. "Frida Kahlo said that."

"You're not going to die. I won't let you. Eventually, yes —when you're a hundred and seventy-three. Not a day before."

"You are living in a dream world," she said.

"Yes, and you're going to live in it with me. Ready?"

"You want children, don't you?"

"No," he said, "I want you."

"Don't you want someone you can grow old with?"

"You're wasting time. I'm in the army. I could get my head blown off tomorrow, you know."

"I'll make a terrible wife for you. Look at me. I'm covered in paint, look a mess, never want to wear high heels again..."

He reached past her and picked up the bowl of blueberries she'd been snacking on that morning and put it into her hands. Then he dropped to his knees and looked up at her, waiting.

She felt like Eve in the Garden, about to feed the forbidden fruit to Adam and about to make the whole world fall.

Ah, who was she kidding? She wasn't Eve and he wasn't Adam. She wasn't Morgan Le Fay and he wasn't King Arthur. But she *was* Regan Ferry and he *was* the man she loved.

She popped a blueberry into his mouth.

He swallowed it and smiled. The next thing she knew she was on her back with her pants round her ankles and his cock was out and pressing hard against her stomach. She reached down and grasped the thick shaft, stroked it and held it firmly.

"You belong to me," she said into his ear.

"Only you."

She wanted him beyond words. Her blood rushed through her veins, and her cunt throbbed in anticipation of being entered. He pushed up her shirt, yanked down the cups of her bra to bare her breasts. He sucked them until they were hard and tender. She moaned as he lifted her and thrust into her, impaling her. Regan gave a cry, shameless, for all the world to hear. His cock split her and filled her. She'd never been so wet, so slick and open so that it felt like he pounded right into the deepest core of her. Her moans were loud and anguished. He grunted in her ear with his rough thrusts, an animal sound. He held her hard against his chest and the fabric of his shirt abraded her nipples. Regan wrapped her arms around his shoulders and held him. And when her climax came and shattered her, she was too broken to stop herself from crying out his name, from crying out that she loved him.

He gasped at her words and came inside her with thrust after thrust until he was empty, until she was full again.

After that final, savage orgasm, they stayed bound together, her legs around his hips, his arms around her back.

"I always wanted to make love in Paris," she said.

He lifted his head and looked down at her. "You love me?"

"Of course I do, Brat," she said as if it were as obvious as two plus two. She left the tangle of his arms reluctantly, stood up and pulled herself together. "Why do you think I left you? I wanted you to be happy more than I wanted me to be happy."

"Guess what? There's a way we can *both* be happy..."

Before she knew it, he was standing on his feet, and she was thrown over his shoulder.

"Would you rather get married in Cyprus or Gibraltar?" he asked. "Both are good for eloping."

"Put me down, Brat."

"Is this painting acrylic?"

"What?" She glanced at her painting—it even looked good upside-down. "Yes. Why?"

"Just making sure it's dry. We're taking it."

She was laughing so hard it hurt, which made it very

difficult to properly yell at him as he plucked the painting off the easel and carried it and her to the door.

"Cyprus or Gibraltar?" he said. "I'm leaning toward Gibraltar, but Lia's in Cyprus right now. Want to meet my sister?"

Regan was going to throttle the man blue when he finally put her down. She tried punching him on the back, but it was like throwing cotton balls against a brick wall. While attempting to make a dent in him, she glimpsed the tattoo on her wrist, no longer covered by her watch because she no longer wore a watch.

He was going to regret this. Maybe. Or not. What did she know? What was it that Evelyn de Morgan's daughter was famous for saying about her parents? *All artists are fools?* Maybe she was right.

"Gibraltar," Regan said, catching her breath.

"Brilliant. We can spend a few days in Spain, too, if you like. You can meet Lia at Christmas."

At that he put her on her feet and kissed her. But it wasn't a long kiss. That would come later.

First she had to pack a bag, find her passport, change her clothes. She did it all in record time, and soon they were in a taxi on their way to Charles de Gaulle Airport. She did convince him to leave the painting behind to dry thoroughly, but only after promising she would ship it to Wingthorn after their honeymoon. Her last wedding had taken months to plan and this one was rushed, hurried— mad, mad, mad, but that was as it should be.

Art might be eternal, but life was short.

They didn't have a moment to lose.

16

THE PEARL

There was no art in Hell.

That's why it was Hell.

Hell is a place of destruction while art is the act of creation. Destruction and creation repel each other and so when Malcolm knew he could bear Hell no longer, he did the only thing he could do to free himself.

He created an artist.

For decades he'd kept an eye on his "children." When he'd discovered his illegitimate great-granddaughter had taken a wrong path and gotten married instead of pursuing her art career, well, he realized he could kill a whole brace of birds with one stone. All he had to do was set her on the right course again, turn her back into the artist she was meant to be. The moment Regan signed her name to the first canvas she'd finished painting in ten years, Malcolm had been spat out of Hell like Jonah from the belly of the whale.

He'd found a perfect match for Arthur, got Charlie back into the family's good graces, and reunited the two halves of the Godwick family, divided just long enough that there would be no negative consequences to bringing them back together again. As for their future together... Malcolm had reason for hope.

Hell was, quite frankly, hellish. The devil's favorite torment was showing the damned all the agony their loved ones are and would suffer in the future, including their deaths, if they were early or painful. That's how he knew Regan would make it, because although Old Scratch had shown Malcolm visions of an arduous cancer battle— Arthur at her side the entire time—Satan had not shown him a vision of her tragic too-soon death. That meant she'd recover. She'd live and love and make art for a very long time.

So. Praise the Lord and pass the pretty girls, Malcolm Godwick was a free man again. Well, a free man with some stipulations. He wasn't whisked away into Heaven. No, he'd been sent back to Earth, given a second chance. He was even allowed to choose where he could start his second life.

Really, he thought as he glanced around The Pearl's smoking lounge, it didn't look much different from his day —a hundred years ago. Same dark paneling. Same old chairs and sofa. Same musty, dusty leather-bound books on the shelves no one could be sodded to read. A new painting was hanging in the lounge, however. Must have been a purchase by Regan, the future Countess of Godwick. The painter was the magnificent Lilla Cabot Perry, and the painting was of an elegant young woman in fine dress, holding a single pearl between her finger and thumb. Appropriately, it was called *The Pearl*.

Malcolm sat down with *The Times* and a cigar. Nice to see that politicians were still as daft and corrupt as they'd ever been, that the papers still printed the same rot and gossip they always had. The women, however, were even more beautiful now than they'd been in his day. The vote had been very good for them. Wonder if he could convince a young lady today to give him her vote of confidence. Now, in fact, would be a good time.

He closed his paper and tossed it aside. Snuffed out his cigar and left the smoking lounge.

Immediately, he saw a girl walking toward the lifts, blonde with big blue eyes. Her red coat suited her nicely, but would suit his bedroom floor even more nicely.

At the lifts, he caught up with her. "Pardon me, miss," he said, "but do you work here?"

"I work for the boss, Lady Ferry," she said.

"Oh, but you don't..." he lowered his voice, "*work* here."

She looked him up and down. Ah, he adored these modern girls who weren't afraid to treat a man like a piece of meat.

"Dunno," she said. "Maybe I do work here. Do you have the cock of a horse and the body of a soldier?"

Liberated women. Legal prostitution. Reliable contraception. Lord Malcolm Godwick was going to love the twenty-first century.

"Yes," he said.

"Eat cunt on command?"

"No, but I will if you ask nicely. Twice if you beg."

"You like spanking?"

"That would be the understatement of the century, my dear."

That comment arched one lovely blond eyebrow. He always did enjoy a bit of rough before lunch.

"All right, so I suppose I do work here then."

"I'm called Malcolm. And you are?"

"Zoot," she said. "Well, that's just a nickname. It's really Greta."

"Ah, you do belong here then. Did you know the name Greta means 'pearl'?"

"Does it? Never knew that." She smiled broadly. "Not a pearl of great price, promise you that. I'm very reasonable."

"I like you more and more every second," he said.

"You want to see my room? I have a pet raven."

"I'd rather see your clitoris."

She blinked, then grinned. "You can see that, too."

They stepped into the lift. The doors closed slowly and for a brief moment they surrounded Lord Malcolm Godwick so that he appeared to be standing inside a gilt portrait frame, a wicked smile on his wicked face, with lovely Greta, a pearl of not-so-great price at his side.

The whole world was his oyster.

THE END.

ACKNOWLEDGMENTS

It may take only one madly determined and stir-crazy author to write a book, but it takes a village to edit one. Thank you from the bottom of my heart (and the heart of my bottom) to Jenn LeBlanc, Bethany Hensel, and Kira Gold for their eagle eyes and brilliant brains. *The Pearl* is a much better book thanks to them. Thank you to my handsome genius of a husband, Andrew Shaffer, for the beautiful cover and all the many hours of work he puts into every 8th Circle Press title. Thank you to my readers for embracing the Godwicks series. They do so love to be embraced, those naughty Godwicks. Among other things.

ABOUT THE AUTHOR

Tiffany Reisz is the *USA Today* bestselling author of the Romance Writers of America RITA®-winning Original Sinners series from Harlequin's Mira Books.

Her erotic fantasy *The Red*—the first entry in the Godwicks series, self-published under the banner 8th Circle Press—was named an NPR Best Book of the Year and a Goodreads Best Romance of the Month.

Tiffany lives in Kentucky with her husband, author Andrew Shaffer, and two cats. The cats are not writers.

Subscribe to the Tiffany Reisz email newsletter and receive a free copy of Something Nice, *a standalone ebook novella set in Reisz's Original Sinners universe:*

www.tiffanyreisz.com/mailing-list

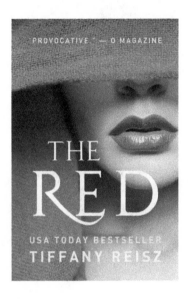

Mona Lisa St. James made a deathbed promise that she would do anything to save her mother's art gallery. Just as she realizes she has no choice but to sell it, a mysterious man offers to save The Red...but only if she agrees to submit to him for the period of one year.

"Deliciously deviant.... Akin to Anne Rice's 'Beauty' series." — *Library Journal* **(Starred Review)**

eBook, Paperback, Library Hardcover, and Audio from 8th Circle Press and Tantor Audio

MEET ARTHUR'S SISTER, LIA GODWICK

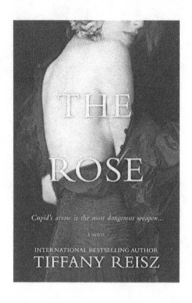

On the day of Lia Godwick's university graduation party, she receives a beautiful wine cup, a rare artifact known as the Rose *kylix*. It was used in the temple ceremonies of Eros, Greek god of erotic love, and has the power to bring the most intimate sexual fantasies to life...

"Intense, lengthy sex scenes, set in lush and creative imaginings of the mythological world, elevate this erotic novel above more prosaic fare."
— *Publishers Weekly* **(Starred Review)**

THE GODWICKS RETURN IN...

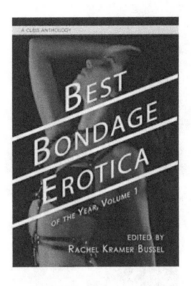

Erotica maven and award-winning editor Rachel Kramer Bussel has compiled the most scintillating bondage stories into one amazing collection, *Best Bondage Erotica of the Year, Volume 1*. Featuring "The Beguiling of Merlin," a stand-alone Godwicks short story!

"Tiffany Reisz's [short story] 'The Beguiling of Merlin' leaves a lasting impression with its sexy, creative premise." — *Publishers Weekly*

eBook, Paperback, and Audiobook from Cleis Press

CPSIA information can be obtained
at www.ICGtesting.com
Printed in the USA
LVHW110921021220
673036LV00025B/3090